THE CIRCLE OF GOLD

THE
CIRCLE
OF
GOLD

THE BOOK OF TIME III

GUILLAUME PRÉVOST

Translated by
WILLIAM RODARMOR

ARTHUR A. LEVINE BOOKS
An Imprint of Scholastic Inc.

Library of Congress Cataloging-in-Publication Data

Prévost, Guillaume.
[Cercle d'or. English]
The circle of gold: the Book of Time III / by Guillaume Prevost; translated by
William Rodarmor. — 1st ed.
p. cm.
Summary: Sam journeys through time to save the lives of his father, his friend
Alicia, and ultimately his late mother.
ISBN 0-439-88377-6 (hardcover : alk. paper)
I. Rodarmor, William. II. Title.
PZ7.P9246Ci 2009
[Fic] — dc22
2009012208

ISBN-13: 978-0-439-88377-1
ISBN-10: 0-439-88377-6

10 9 8 7 6 5 4 3 2 1   09 10 11 12 13

Printed in the U.S.A.   23

First edition, September 2009

CONTENTS

THE CIRCLE OF GOLD

The Story So Far

On his fourteenth birthday, Sam Faulkner visits his father's antique bookstore on Barenboim Street in the Canadian town of Sainte-Mary. His father, Allan, has been missing for ten days — part of a pattern of increasingly odd behavior since Sam's mother's death three years earlier. In the basement of the bookstore, Sam discovers a hidden room containing an odd-looking stone statue engraved with a sun and six rays, as well as a few old coins with holes in them. A book lies near the stone statue, every one of its spreads describing "Crimes and Punishments During the Reign of Vlad Tepes." When Sam casually puts one of the coins on the statue's sun, he is suddenly whisked away . . .

. . . to a grass-covered island, where he meets a group of monks who wear robes and live in medieval conditions. After the monastery is attacked by Vikings, Sam realizes the truth: He went back in Time! He makes his way back to the stone and finds another coin to put on the sun. This one takes him to France in the middle of World War I. Eventually he jumps again to Egypt in the age of the pharaohs, where he meets Ahmosis, the son of the great priest and time traveler Setni.

Ahmosis helps Sam return to his own time, where he discusses his situation with his cousin Lily and attends a dinner with his grandparents; Lily's mother, Sam's aunt Evelyn; and Aunt Evelyn's boyfriend, the overbearing Rudolf. He learns that his father was an archeological intern in Egypt many years earlier — working on a dig at Setni's tomb, in fact — where he seems to have learned about the stone statue and time traveling. Sam and Lily theorize that the book with identical pages is a Book of Time, which shows the last place and time to which someone traveled. But that means that Allan Faulkner went to see Vlad Tepes — a fifteenth-century Romanian lord better known as Dracula.

Sam acquires another coin from his neighbor Max and goes back into Time to try to reach his father. He travels first to Bruges, Belgium, where he encounters an alchemist named Klugg. A book in Klugg's workshop shows the stone statue and many other esoteric markings and languages, along with a message in Latin. When Sam returns to his own time, Lily helps him translate the message, which strongly implies that if a time traveler can gather seven coins with holes in them and use them on the statue, he can travel anywhere in Time he chooses. At a judo tournament, Sam sees Alicia Todds, a friend from whom he became estranged after his mother's death. He realizes that he has long been in love with her. Inspired by the encounter, he defeats two opponents to win the tournament. Afterward, Lily shows him a picture taken in the dungeons of Bran Castle, the home of Vlad Tepes: Someone has scrawled "HELP ME SAM" on the wall.

The writer can be no one but Allan.

In order to get enough coins to travel directly to Bran Castle, Sam decides to break into the Barenboim coin collection at the local museum. (The collection is named for Garry Barenboim, the original owner of the old house where Faulkner's Antique Books is located.) The theft is foiled, however, by another robber who is after the same coins. In the course of their fight, Sam notices a strange design — like a pair of horns surrounding a sun — tattooed on the man's shoulder. He manages to escape the thief and the museum, but he doesn't get any coins.

Nonetheless, he is still determined to try to reach his father, so he goes back into Time. This trip takes him to ancient Greece, where he is accused of helping to steal a precious object called the Navel of the World. He is cleared of the crime and returns to the present, but he begins to suspect that his father is the real thief, stealing antiquities to ease financial pressures on the bookstore. He learns that a company called Arkeos recently sold the Navel of the World at auction for more than ten million dollars; moreover, the Arkeos logo is the same as the symbol tattooed on the thief at the museum (whom Sam begins to call "the Arkeos man"). He also discovers a notebook with a curious code in his father's handwriting, including the line "Meriweserre = O."

In a conversation with Alicia, Sam explains the circumstances that caused him to withdraw from her in the first place: His mother died in a car crash, on her way to see Sam at the hospital while he was having his appendix removed, and guilt over her death made him feel that he shouldn't allow himself any pleasure, including friendship with Alicia. However, feelings may be awakening on both sides. . . .

When Sam next time travels, Lily accidentally comes with him. They end up in prehistory, where they barely escape from a huge bear and a bloodthirsty tribe. They then travel to Pompeii in 79 A.D., right before the volcano Vesuvius erupts. Fleeing to Chicago in 1932, they run into some gangsters but also meet their grandfather, who is, at that time, a six-year-old boy. At all of these places, they notice the Arkeos logo drawn near the stone statue. Sam forms a theory that the tattoo on the Arkeos man's shoulder allows him to travel among these locations at will.

In order to return to their own time, Lily and Sam take the train back to Sainte-Mary. On the way, they meet the fabled Setni, Ahmosis's father. Setni tells them about the Golden Circle, a gold bracelet that will enable a traveler to go directly to a date of his or her choosing, using a coin from that time. Setni gives Sam a special capsule that will shoot him straight to Bran Castle to meet his father. Setni also hints that Sam has a special destiny, perhaps linked to Setni's own vocation as a master of Time. Sam and Lily return to the present, where they explain the circumstances to their grandparents, and Sam researches Bran Castle to prepare for his trip to rescue his father.

Finally Sam sets off for fifteenth-century Wallachia, Vlad Tepes's domain. He finds his father in the dungeons of Bran Castle, seriously ill and half mad from the terrible conditions and the lack of food. But Allan refuses to leave until Sam retrieves a copy of the Golden Circle — also known as the Meriweserre bracelet — from its vault in the highest tower of the castle. Sam confronts Vlad Tepes in the tower and steals the bracelet, then races to get his father and take him to the stone statue. As they prepare to travel back to their own time, Allan tells Sam that he wasn't time traveling to gather antiquities and make money. Rather, he wanted the Meriweserre bracelet for one reason: to go back in time and save Sam's mother from her fatal car accident.

The present volume begins a few days later.

CHAPTER ONE

Room 313

"You've got to hang on, Dad," Sam whispered. "Can you hear me? You've got to hang on."

Allan Faulkner lay motionless on the hospital bed, eyes closed. An oxygen mask covered his mouth and nose, sustaining his labored breathing, while a battery of machines blinked and beeped around him. Now that the nurses had cut his hair and beard, Allan looked frighteningly thin. His six months of captivity in the dungeons of Vlad Tepes — better known as Dracula — had made him a fragile shadow of his former self.

Sam held his father's hand. The greenish fluorescent light above the bed cast a sepulchral light over them, and the room reeked of disinfectant. In the three days since he and Sam escaped from Bran Castle, Allan hadn't regained consciousness.

"The doctors say there's no point in talking to you, Dad, but I don't think that's true. You can understand me, can't you? Can you recognize my voice?"

No reaction. His father's hand was as cold as ice.

"I don't know when the nurse is coming back," he continued, "so I guess I should say this quickly. I'm not mad at you. I thought a lot about what you told me, what you hoped to do with the Golden Circle and why you never said anything about the stone statue. I think you did the right thing. If I didn't have to figure out all this time-travel stuff for myself, or if I hadn't had all the experiences in Time that I've had, I'd never have had the strength to save you. You had the right idea from the very beginning. Though you could have made it a *little* easier," he added with the ghost of a smile.

Sam glanced at the screen that displayed his father's pulse and blood pressure. Aside from its regular beeping, it didn't show the slightest twitch of activity.

"I also want to say I'm sorry for something. In the weeks you were missing, I started thinking you were using the statue to steal ancient books for the bookstore. I knew you were having business problems, and we have this mortgage. . . . I couldn't see why you hid all this from me, or why you just left us without a word. I'm sorry. I shouldn't have doubted you."

Beep! Beep! Was it a coincidence, or had Allan's pulse quickened slightly? It wasn't much of an increase, just from sixty-one to sixty-four beats a minute. But maybe he was reacting to what Sam said. . . .

"You can hear me, can't you?" he said, squeezing Allan's hand. "It's me, Sam. You've got to fight! You've got to wake up!" He paused. "I was so scared; you have no idea. When we got back from Bran, I thought you were dead. You weren't moving, you didn't seem to be breathing and . . ."

Sam's voice choked with emotion. Leaning over his father's

motionless body in the bookstore basement had been one of the worst moments of his life.

"Grandpa and Grandma were wonderful," Sam continued. "When I phoned them and said you were back but you were really messed up, they didn't ask any questions, they just came right away with the ambulance. I'd already told them about the stone statue and Vlad Tepes and all, so they knew you wouldn't be in great shape when you got back. Anyway, they stood by me, and they kept their mouths shut. Which really shows how much you matter to them, doesn't it? To me too, you know."

Sixty-six beats a minute, read the bluish figures. Two points higher. It couldn't just be a coincidence. This was Sam's chance to tell Allan something important. Something that might bring him out of the coma and give him the will to live. Something Sam had been mulling over for the last three days.

"I'm going to do what you asked me, Dad, and go into the past to save Mom. I don't know where or how I'm going to find the right coin to bring me back to the day of the crash, but with the Meriweserre bracelet, I'll manage." He spoke slowly, praying with all his heart that his father could hear him: "I swear I'll save her, Dad. For both of us."

Beep! Beep! The pixels on the screen began to dance: Sixty-eight . . . Seventy-two . . . Seventy-six beats a minute! And it continued: Eighty-two . . . Eighty-six! Sam was thrilled. He was right! His father hadn't sunk into a terminal coma. Somewhere, his spirit was still alive and flickering. Sam had no clue how to travel exactly three years into the past; he knew the idea of saving his mother was both crazy and terrifying. But if it would restore his father's will to live, it would be worth it.

Eighty-eight . . . Ninety — Allan seemed to be agreeing.

"Well, well," exclaimed the nurse as she entered the room. "Seems to be some activity here!"

Sam turned to her, beside himself with excitement. "I . . . I feel he's getting better, ma'am. I was talking to him and his heart started beating faster and faster, as if he could hear me. That's a good sign, isn't it? You think maybe he'll wake up?"

The nurse, a young blond woman whose badge identified her as Isobel, gave him an almost maternal smile. The state of the patient in Room 313 had affected all the nurses on the floor. They knew Sam had lost his mother a few years earlier, at the exact time that he was undergoing an appendectomy in that very hospital, and they hoped he wouldn't lose his father too. It was as if fate was pursuing the family.

The bluish figures were beginning to go down now: Eighty-seven . . . Eighty-five . . . Eighty-three . . . Allan might not be strong enough to come out of the coma yet, but he now had a powerful reason to do so. They just had to give him time. *I won't give up on you, Dad,* Sam thought.

Isobel gently touched him on the shoulder. "I imagine this must be very hard for you," she said. "You'll have to be brave, whatever happens. If you ever feel like talking, come see me at the nurses' station. Meanwhile, there are two people out in the hallway who'd like to see your father. I told them to wait, because I have to get him ready for a scan, but they can come in and say hello afterward."

Sam nodded and gave a last look at his dad's only personal possession in the room — a little round watch with a white dial that Allan was very fond of. His pulse was now back below seventy.

Sam left the room, wondering who could be paying Allan a visit, since the rest of the family wasn't due until the afternoon. When he recognized the two people standing near the soda machine, he exclaimed with delight: "Mrs. Todds! Alicia!" It was the best surprise he could have had.

Her arms spread wide, Helena Todds ran over to him. "Sammy, darling, we came as soon as we could. What bad luck!"

She hugged Sam tight, overwhelming him with her floral lemon perfume. Behind her, Alicia stood motionless, clearly having mixed feelings. Her loose blond hair made a halo of light around her beautiful face. Sam blinked at the sight. They had barely spoken for three years — the result of Sam's guilt and grief over his mother's death, his feeling that he didn't deserve any pleasure from his old life. But they had been talking a little bit more recently, and Sam could feel their former friendship reviving. Maybe this was why she looked so unsure of her feelings today, probably torn between some remnant of affection for Sam — he could hardly hope for more — and resentment of him. When her mother finished hugging Sam, Alicia simply gave him a little nod, keeping her distance. Sam responded the same way.

"So how is he doing?" asked Helena Todds.

"He's still in the coma," Sam answered with a sigh, "but I'm sure he's going to get better soon."

"Of course he's going to get better," said Helena firmly. "Allan is tough." She paused. "I didn't want to bother your grandmother about this, but what exactly happened to him?"

Sam looked down slightly. He hated lying, especially to the Todds family, who had taken him in a few days earlier when he needed to stay away from home. But except for his grandparents and his cousin Lily, nobody could know about the stone statue, not even Alicia. So he'd had to invent an official story that people would find plausible — even the police, who were naturally curious about the events at Faulkner's Antique Books.

"Dad was attacked by a bunch of robbers," he began. "We thought he'd gone down to the United States to buy old books, but actually he was kidnapped and held somewhere. The evening I left your house, I got a call that was forwarded from his cell phone. A man's voice just said, 'He's at the bookstore.' I called my grandparents right away, and we found Dad lying on the doorstep, half conscious. He mumbled something about a rare book and kidnappers, then passed out. That's when we took him to the hospital."

Sam stopped talking and put on a candid expression that apparently fooled Helena Todds.

"A kidnapping! What did they expect, a ransom?"

"The police think Dad may have acquired some valuable books. There was another robbery at the bookstore a few days ago," he added. On that point, at least, Sam was telling the truth.

"My God, what kind of the world are we living in? One of our neighbors was robbed the day before yesterday — Miss Maggie Pye, remember her? Someone broke into her place at dinnertime and made her give him the contents of her jewelry box. The poor old woman; she was sure he was going to kill her!"

"She should stop parading around in her pearl necklaces and those great big rings," Alicia broke in irritably. "She's blind as a bat — maybe that's why she always dresses like a Christmas tree!"

"Alicia, please! What if that burglar is still in the neighborhood? And she is a friend, after all!"

"Yeah, right! Maggie Pye is an old cow. Remember the time she caught me and Jerry kissing in the street? She roused the whole neighborhood! I'd be glad if this makes her shut up once and for all."

Helena Todds made a gesture of exasperation, but for his part, Sam thought that if Miss Pye had separated Alicia from her creepy boyfriend, Jerry Paxton, she had been right to butt in. Luckily the nurse stuck her head out the door just then.

"You can come in now, but one person at a time, and no more than five minutes."

"Go ahead, Mom," Alicia urged her. "I'll go later."

Helena entered Room 313, and Alicia walked over to Sam, frowning.

"My mother may have swallowed that story, Sam, but not me. Even when we were little, I could always tell when you were lying to me. I guess it's because we grew up together. At least we still have that." She shook her head in a way that hurt Sam more than all the reproaches in the world. "I don't know what really happened with your dad," she continued, "but I don't believe this stuff about a kidnapping and a phone call. It's like that research you were doing about Dracula the other day, with the weird puzzles on all those sheets of paper. You didn't want to tell me about it, but I figured you were hiding something from me — something serious. What's going on, Sam?"

Sam tried to meet her eyes, which were so blue you could drown in them. How could he tell her the secret when his father's life depended on his keeping it? And how could he lie to her again when he couldn't stand lying to her in the first place?

"Forgive me, Alicia," he whispered, his throat tight. "If there's one person in the world I want to tell everything to, it's you — really. But for now, I just can't. Not as long as my father's sick. Afterward, you'll be the first to know, I swear."

She sighed. "You're really hard to figure out," she said, looking disappointed. "You're the one who came to see me, remember? But every time I take a step toward you, you run away like you're afraid. What am I supposed to make of that?"

For just an instant, Time seemed to pause in its course, and it was as if they were a few years younger, as if they could see in each other's faces all the things that had made them inseparable. The connection they felt from the very first day Alicia moved to Bel View, the fits of laughter they'd shared, their endless conversations, the pranks they'd pulled, and so much more. It was the measure of the depth of what divided them today.

They might have stood there much longer, silently bringing up the ghosts of the past, but Alicia's mother came out of Room 313.

"He looks as if he's just fallen asleep, doesn't he?" she said with forced cheerfulness. "A little like Sleeping Beauty. I'm . . . I'm sure he'll wake up eventually!"

CHAPTER TWO

The Arkeos Man Returns

Allan's condition showed no improvement over the next two days. Sam had hoped that their "conversation" would trigger some further spark of life in him, but he had to face facts: If his father had gotten his message — and Sam refused to believe that he hadn't — it would take much more to bring him out of his coma, like somehow giving him his beloved Elisa back. Yet each time Sam thought about that, it made his head spin. Besides the difficulty of traveling back exactly three years into the past, there was the wrenching matter of Sam's own feelings. Could he stand to see his mother alive again without falling apart? Would he be able to convince her to come to his present with the help of the stone statue? And what would happen then? Would she agree to stay with them, or would she want to return to her own existence?

Not to mention the terrible transgression that saving Elisa from death represented. During Sam's only meeting with Setni, the guardian of the Thoth stones and the wisest of time travelers, the high priest had warned him: "A series of infinite catastrophes could follow if someone decided to change the unfolding of the world." Then he'd added, "That is why there must always be someone to guard the stones. And I am convinced that you, Samuel Faulkner, would be worthy of fulfilling that function." The venerable Setni saw Sam as an incorruptible defender of Time just as he was getting ready to change its course!

If only Sam could talk to somebody! But his grandparents were so worried about Allan's health, it would be cruel to alarm them with news of more time traveling. And his beloved cousin Lily, who'd shared so much with him during these last weeks, had been shipped off to a summer camp hundreds of miles away. Sam kept her up to date by e-mail, but it wasn't always easy for her to answer. He would have to make his decisions alone.

On the morning of the sixth day after his return from Bran Castle, Sam was still asleep when his bedroom door flew open.

"Sam, wake up!"

Someone rushed over in the darkness and started shaking him.

"Sam!"

"Mpff?"

"You've got to get dressed," said the intruder, snapping on the bedside lamp. "Quick!"

Shading his eyes, his brain still sluggish, Sam recognized the man: Rudolf, his aunt Evelyn's boyfriend. This couldn't be good. Rudolf and Evelyn had eased off their constant criticism of Sam since his father reappeared, but he still didn't like one of them rousting him from his bed.

"What's going on?" he grumbled.

"It's Helena Todds," answered Rudolf. "She's downstairs."

Sam glanced at his radio alarm clock: 7:05 a.m.

"Helena Todds? Now?"

Rudolf looked annoyed. "She'll explain it herself. Your aunt and I had just driven up from the States when she rang the doorbell. You better come downstairs."

Sam jumped out of bed, feeling a stab of anxiety. Why in the world would Mrs. Todds be there so early in the morning? He slipped on some clothes and tumbled down the stairs. Helena was slumped on the living room sofa, sobbing into a handkerchief. Evelyn sat next to her, clearly trying to comfort her. "Mrs. Todds?" stammered Sam.

She looked up at him, her eyes red and her hair uncombed.

"Have you seen her, Sammy?"

"Seen who?"

"Alicia. She didn't come home last night. She was supposed to go to the movies yesterday evening and . . . She didn't call me, or her father, or anybody. Usually she phones when she's going to somebody's house, but here . . . We called her cell dozens of times, we called all the hospitals. She's nowhere to be found."

Sam felt his leg begin to twitch. He didn't like the sound of this at all.

"When did she disappear?" he asked.

"Around six last night," answered Helena, sniffling. "She had a date with Jerry to get something to eat and then go to a movie."

"Jerry Paxton? Did you ask him?"

"Of course! Apparently they had a fight yesterday, but when we let him know she was missing, the poor boy was just as upset as we were. He went around to all the movie theaters just

11

in case, and he called a couple of times with no results. It's as if Alicia just vanished! Between your father's kidnapping and Maggie Pye's robbery, I'm terribly worried!"

"Did you call the police?"

"We phoned around midnight and told them Alicia had disappeared. They said she might have run away, and that we'd know better in the morning. But running away doesn't make any sense. She would have taken her money and a change of clothes, wouldn't she?"

"And you thought she might be here?" asked Sam.

"I don't know! I couldn't stand staying at home, so I left Alicia's dad by the phone and drove around in case I ran into her. When I found myself in your neighborhood, I thought maybe she'd told you something."

The face she turned to Sam was so eager that he was angry at himself for being in the dark.

"I'm really sorry, but she didn't tell me a thing."

"Not even a hint? Someone she wanted to meet? Some place she wanted to go?"

Sam quickly ran through what he remembered of their last conversations, but nothing occurred to him. Besides, Alicia was perfectly able to go wherever she wanted without having to hide. And running away wasn't like her.

"I really can't think of anything."

"What about a message?" she asked desperately. "Could she have left a message on your cell phone?"

"I'll go check," he said.

He ran up to his bedroom, feeling as if he was coming down with a bad flu and his whole body had turned to mush. He grabbed his phone, which he had plugged into the charger the night before. The message inbox was empty, of course. Why would Alicia bother calling him? She had her parents, she had Jerry. Unless . . . Just in case, he turned on his computer and checked his e-mail. A single message had arrived during the night, with an intriguing return address: *guesswho@arkeos.biz*. Arkeos was a business that specialized in selling ancient objects. As for Guesswho . . .

Feverishly, Sam clicked on the e-mail. It was a long message, topped by a design he immediately recognized: the sign of Hathor, daughter of the Egyptian god Re, showing a long pair of horns with a solar disk between them. Sam had often seen the sign — which was also the Arkeos logo — during his recent time travels. He'd even glimpsed it on the shoulder of the figure he called "the Arkeos man," a mysterious hooded man he had fought over a batch of coins in the Sainte-Mary Museum. The Arkeos man was a time traveler too, and he had gone after Sam's father, ransacked the Faulkner bookstore, even tried to kill Sam and Lily when they were still in the past. A message from him now couldn't be good news.

Dear Sam:

I never expected to be writing you. Life is full of surprises sometimes. You don't know me yet, but I've been watching you for a while. You don't lack courage, I must say, or cleverness — though not exactly intelligence, more like cunning and resourcefulness. A bit like your father. The poor man always lacked ambition, you know. He could never understand what he had in his hands, what he could have done if he'd been less of a coward, what we could've done.

But enough chitchat, Sam. I'm writing because I have two pieces of news for you, one good and one bad. Which would you like to start with?

First, I have to confess something. It's true that in the last few weeks, I've tried to get rid of you. At the museum, for example, I was on the point of strangling you. Or later, I stole your Book of Time and tore out some pages to keep you from returning to the present. . . . That wasn't exactly fair play, I know. But you were becoming a nuisance, sticking your nose into things that didn't concern you. Luckily for you, you managed to pull through. And you've really had some luck; amazing luck, I should say!

As a result, I've had to reconsider my strategy. Since you're so lucky, I figure we may as well take advantage of it. Yes, you read that correctly — we — the two of us! Instead of fighting, let's work hand in hand as partners, the way Allan and I could have if he'd been a little less stubborn. I promise not to cause you the slightest harm, and you agree to do me a few favors. Together, I swear we can become masters of Time. Isn't that good news?

Astonished, Sam stopped reading for a moment. Was this a joke? But if it was, how could the writer know all those details? No, it must be the Arkeos man. The message seemed to confirm Sam's theory that the Arkeos man had been his father's fellow archeological intern in Egypt in 1980, when Allan first discovered the magic of the Thoth stones and the possibility of time travel. As for this proposal of teaming up with him, it was insane. He had done everything he could to kill Sam. He was delighted by Allan's fate, he was looting archaeological treasures, he . . .

But Sam's curiosity was stronger than his indignation, and he continued reading.

I imagine you must be wondering, hesitating. You're think-ing about your father, about everything he's endured up to now, and you're not convinced. Am I wrong? Well, so be it. Here's the bad news.

You and I have something else in common: Each of us has some-thing that the other wants. I need the Meriweserre bracelet and a few other items I want you to get for me. (I'll tell you about those later.) I suppose I don't need to spell things out for you with the bracelet. I know your father was at Bran Castle, I know why he went there, and I know what you brought back. I need it, and that's not negotiable. And in exchange . . .

Before I tell you, let me go back in Time a little bit — that's something you're used to, right? I thought you two looked very sweet at the hospital the other day. I was coming up the service stairs and you were standing near the coffee machine. You were looking at each other so intensely, you couldn't think of anything to say. You seemed so tentative at that moment, so awkward, I didn't want to disturb you. But it gave me an idea: What better thing to trade with you than Alicia?

Sam swore and slammed his hand down on the desk. The Arkeos man had kidnapped Alicia!

You've got good taste; she's a very pretty girl. It would be too bad if something more happened to her. You can't tell the Todds family about this, of course; that's part of the deal. But you'll be pleased to

15

know Alicia didn't suspect a thing when she came to our meeting, because she thought she was going to meet you! Life is full of surprises.

Sam heard footsteps on the landing and just had time to close the e-mail before Rudolf entered the bedroom, followed by Aunt Evelyn and Helena Todds.

"Well?" he asked. "We heard you shout. Was there a message on your phone?"

"No," mumbled Sam. "Alicia didn't call me."

"You look white as a sheet," said Mrs. Todds.

It took Sam an effort not to break down and tell them everything he knew about the Arkeos man and the Meriweserre bracelet. Maybe they would support him, or at least free him from the terrible burden he was under. But aside from the fact that none of the three would believe him, Alicia's life might depend on his keeping quiet.

"I'm just a little shaken up, that's all," he said apologetically. "I — I really like Alicia, and —"

"She likes you too," said Helena Todds, who came over to pat his hand. "It's no accident that her relationship with Jerry got strained after you came to see her. It must have stirred some things up."

Sam bent his head. He was thinking that if it hadn't been for him, Alicia wouldn't have been kidnapped.

Helena continued with great weariness, "Maybe Alicia just wanted some time to herself without having to check in with anybody. She'll show up later this morning, flash a big smile, and apologize for making us worry." She glanced at her watch. "I have to get home. . . . Please say hello to your grandparents for me, Sammy. I hope I haven't woken them up. I promise to call as soon as I know anything."

With a heavy heart, Sam watched her leave, ushered out by Rudolf and Aunt Evelyn. He wasn't able to give Mrs. Todds the least word of hope or encouragement. Everything was his fault.

Once alone again — and prepared for the worst — Sam brought the Arkeos man's e-mail back onscreen.

Now that we both know where we stand, let's get down to brass tacks. When I left Alicia, she was terrified. On the edge of a breakdown, even. She couldn't understand what was going on, she was crying. She is in the middle of a war zone, after all, soldiers everywhere, lots of people wounded and dead. It's no place and no time for a young woman to be wandering around, if you ask me.

The best thing would be to settle this business as quickly as possible. And if you obey my orders and hold your tongue, everything will be finished by this evening. You will see an Internet link at the bottom of the page. Just click it to let me know that you agree to our collaboration. You'll then get new instructions. But don't wait too long. The clock is ticking.

Best regards,
Your new partner

For a moment, Sam sat stunned in front of his computer. "He sent her back in Time!" he said under his breath. *"He sent her back in Time!"*

And so, with no other way to save Alicia, he clicked on the string of blue letters and numbers at the end of the message.

CHAPTER THREE

Mission Impossible

Sam spent the next three hours anxiously pacing his room, racing to the computer every few minutes to see if "arkeos.biz" had e-mailed him. He clicked the Internet link again and again, hoping to get some sort of reaction, but from the infinite depths of the Web, nobody answered. What was the Arkeos man waiting for? For Alicia to go out of her mind? Or worse, to be killed?

To pass the time, Sam decided to ready the items that he would need to reach her. First was the Meriweserre bracelet, which he'd wrapped in a handkerchief and hid under a pile of clothes. Each time he picked it up, he felt the same mix of surprise and fascination. In daylight, you would've thought the bracelet was just a bracelet — elegant enough, but not that unusual. It had a small hook closure, a few delicate notches along the perimeter, and a finely etched solar disk on its face. But when strung with six coins, or "disks of Re," it would send a time traveler directly to the time he or she hoped to reach — the time of the seventh coin, which had to be placed directly on the sun carved in the center of the stone. The problem was that Sam only had three coins. The one with the black snake had allowed him to travel to Dracula's time; Sam had found it on the floor next to the stone statue when he returned to the present. A second, newer coin bore inscriptions in Arabic, and his third coin looked like a blue plastic poker chip. All three had holes in their centers. Would they be enough for him to go to where Alicia was? He greatly doubted it.

Sam took the Book of Time very carefully from the back of his closet. Ever since the Arkeos man had ripped out some of its pages, its venerable red cover had looked worn and shabby, as if losing part of itself had affected the entire book. Its contents hadn't changed in the last six days, however. Each spread still displayed an identical article titled "Crimes and Punishment During the Reign of Vlad Tepes," which meant that nobody had used the stone statue under his father's bookstore since their return from Tepes's castle. That meant that if the Arkeos man had carried Alicia back in time, he had to have used a different stone statue.

Toward eleven a.m., as Sam was checking his e-mail for the hundredth time, his grandmother called to him from downstairs.

"Sammy! There's a package for you."

"I'm coming, Grandma! I'm just finishing something."

A package, he suddenly thought. Of course, it would be a package!

He flew down the stairs, nearly bowling over his grandmother, whose drawn face and stooped posture reflected her anxiety over Allan's health. She was holding a thick envelope from an express delivery company.

"Your grandfather was mowing the lawn when the messenger

arrived," she explained, holding up the package. "Are you all right? You look strange."

"I'm fine," said Sam. "I'm just worried about Alicia, that's all."

"Alicia's a big girl; she can take care of herself. I'm sure she'll be home by this evening!"

"I'm sure too," Sam agreed. "This messenger, what did he look like?"

Grandma opened her eyes in surprise.

"What a funny question! Like a messenger, I suppose! Why? Is there a problem with the package?"

Sam took the envelope and kissed her on the cheek.

"Not at all, Grandma. Just curious."

"We're going to see your father later," she called after him as he raced up the stairs. "You haven't forgotten, have you?"

Sam didn't answer. Back in his room, he locked the door and examined the envelope from every angle. It seemed perfectly normal, with all the usual stamps, but there was no return address. In the Sender box, an odd name was written in capital letters: ZIB SERAKO. Sam saw that reordering the letters produced ARKEOS.BIZ. *Very clever,* he thought. But there wasn't any useful information about the place or the date of shipment. Too bad Grandpa let the messenger get away.

Sam cut the flap and emptied the envelope onto his bed. Some folded sheets of paper and a small cloth purse with three metal coins fell clinking onto his duvet. The first coin was shiny gold and might have seemed new if its irregular shape hadn't betrayed its great antiquity. It had a hole in the middle and bore an inscription: *Candor illaesus.* Was that Latin? On its other side you could make out a kind of sun with rays shooting into the central hole. Another sun!

The second coin, a copper one, seemed less valuable. It was green with age and bore some raised letters that looked like Chinese characters. It did have a distinction, though: Its central hole was square. Would it still work with the stone statue in spite of this oddity, or did the Arkeos man anticipate that Sam would use it some other way? The third coin was covered with a sort of grayish substance and, except for its hole, had no distinctive markings.

Sam then turned to the two sheets of paper. One showed an old engraving of a fortified city on a river, with a jumble of houses and monuments. The other was a letter printed from a computer.

Dear Sam,

You haven't wasted any time. That's perfect. I had everything ready, so all I had to do was confirm the shipping order for this package. As you see, we already make a good team!

Just between us, you must really be in love with Alicia to have reacted so fast. I could tell you a little something about the danger of feelings and where they will lead you, but you're clearly still full of illusions and determined to save your girlfriend at any cost. All the better for me! So here are my instructions:

In the purse, you will find the three coins you need for your mission. Use the Meriweserre bracelet to travel to China with the copper coin, then to Rome with the gold coin. You can return to the present with the gray coin, whose main virtue is that it will bring you back immediately.

I am enclosing a contemporaneous map of Rome, on which I've written some numbers in magic marker. Number 1 is the stone statue's location. Number 2 is the special library where I want you to retrieve a treatise that interests me — your father isn't the only one who collects old books! The Treatise has a blue cover with the number 13 stamped on it. At the time in question, it was stored somewhere in the library, inside a cabinet decorated with a sun. It will be up to you to find that cabinet.

Once you have retrieved the Treatise, go to the place on the map marked number 3. Show the gold coin and ask to see Captain Diavilo — remember that name — on behalf of Arkeos. Give him the book and the Meriweserre bracelet. In exchange, he should free Alicia. I say "should" because things are unstable there and unless you act quickly, there's no guarantee she will still be alive.

In case you're tempted to head directly to Rome without making the stop in China, be aware that you will seriously hurt your chances of saving Alicia. Only the detour to China will reveal the way to the Treatise — and no Treatise, no Alicia. It won't be an easy voyage, Sam. Indeed, I don't know of anyone who has come back from it, which is why I am letting you go in my place! In the interests of all three of us, be extremely careful.

After that, we will be even, I promise.

Sam read and reread the letter until he'd practically memorized it, trying to guess at the Arkeos man's real intentions. He was apparently asking for just two things in exchange for freeing Alicia: the Meriweserre bracelet, of course, but also a treatise of some sort. Sam's dictionary defined a treatise as a book containing "a systematic written account of or argument on some subject." Was the Arkeos man interested in the systematic knowledge, or just the money he'd make from selling the book?

For the time being, the *Treatise* was hidden somewhere in Rome in the Middle Ages, by the look of the engraving on the second sheet. The Arkeos man had taken Alicia there without stealing the book himself, so he must lack some crucial information needed to succeed — information Sam could get only by using the Chinese coin. So on that topic at least, he must be telling the truth, and Sam had no choice but to go to China.

But how much credence could Sam give the rest of the letter? If he was able to bring the *Treatise* to Diavilo, for example, how could Sam be sure he would free Alicia? He might have very different orders, like to kill both of them. Why not? In a time of trouble and war, two victims more or less . . . And even if Sam and Alicia managed to come home via the gray coin, how could they be sure the Arkeos man would leave them in peace afterward?

The only sure rule was: Don't trust the Arkeos man.

One major obstacle remained: coins. Counting the three that the Arkeos man had just sent him, Sam still only had six, and as far as he knew, he would need seven to use the Meriweserre bracelet. And without that, saving Alicia was an impossible mission.

"Sammy?" Grandma called from downstairs. "It's time to go to the hospital, dear. Are you ready?"

Sam stuffed everything back in the envelope, slipped it under his bedcovers, and came downstairs. The entire family was standing by the door. "I'm really sorry," Sam began, "but I'd rather stay home. If the Todds family calls about Alicia, I want to be here."

"Your staying here won't bring her back," objected Aunt Evelyn. "You would do just as well being with your father."

"Besides, if anyone wants to reach you, you've got a cell phone," added Rudolf. "Or your grandmother's, anyway. Just go get it."

"Cell phones aren't allowed in the hospital rooms," said Sam stubbornly. "I'm staying here."

The conversation was about to turn nasty when Grandpa stepped in. "Seems to me Sammy's already spent most of the last three days at the hospital. He has the right to a little peace and quiet, doesn't he? Give him a break!"

"What a pity," said Evelyn. "When we could all be together at Allan's bedside for once . . ."

"Tell Dad I love him, and that I'll come see him soon," Sam said firmly. "And especially tell him not to get discouraged."

Grandma blew him a kiss, Grandpa winked, and Rudolf and Evelyn spun on their respective heels and strode off. Sam waited until Rudolf's big 4x4 rounded the corner of the street, then rushed upstairs to get his supplies. Every second counted.

Sam turned the bolt on the front door of Faulkner's Antique Books, crossed through the reading room, and went up to his father's bedroom. He tried not to notice Allan's personal things — his bathrobe hanging on the rack, his favorite pen on the night table — and chose one of the white linen outfits that let him time travel in comfort.

He then went down to the basement, where his father had built a secret room to hide the stone statue. Sam slipped under the hanging tapestry, turned on the light, and carefully shut the door. From his judo bag, he took out the Arkeos man's envelope and the Golden Circle. He then put on his "time trav-eler" shirt and pants. But as he was changing, Sam felt an unusual wave of heat fill his chest. The spike of fever was accompanied by a strange, very distant, very slow pulse that seemed to match the beating of his heart. It wasn't painful, or even unpleasant. It just made him feel as if he wasn't quite alone, as if someone or something alive had curled itself around him.

Sam turned to the darkest corner of the storeroom, where the Thoth stone stood in the shadows. Its rounded top seemed to vibrate with the same dull pounding that echoed inside him. *Boom . . . boom . . .* The same diffuse rhythm, the same slow-ness. *Boom . . . boom . . .* As if his body was linked to the stone; as if it could feel his heartbeat!

Sam pulled out the Meriweserre bracelet. In the darkness it cast a beautiful halo of light, like the ones around saints' heads in religious paintings. Maybe the presence of the bracelet explained the new and powerful connection with the stone that Sam was feeling — a connection he hoped would bring him luck.

Sam slipped the engraving of Rome into the cavity at the base of the stone, the one that served to transport objects. He then unhooked the bracelet and strung the six coins onto it like keys on a key ring. He was missing a coin, so he would just have to wander the paths of Time until he found one more. Then he could go straight to China as instructed. Of course, this was assuming the bracelet would work without all seven coins; but Sam couldn't know that until he tried it.

Once the bracelet was ready, he set it against the sun carved into the stone and tried to fit the coins into the six slits radi-ating from the solar disk. Sam had feared that this might be tricky, but each coin seemed to pop obediently into place as soon as it was brought near a slit. No doubt about it: The Egyptian gods who created the statue had been pretty practical.

"Now what?" he wondered aloud.

He laid his hand on the stone's smooth top. A piercing buzz arose from somewhere, and the basement floor seemed to start trembling. Then it was as if a flow of lava burst from the center of the earth to envelop him in a burning sheath. Sam opened his mouth to scream, but he was already gone.

CHAPTER FOUR

Going Back

Slumped on the floor, Sam felt as if he'd swallowed a spinning centrifuge and then spat it up again. His skin, flesh, and bones burned, and his stomach was turning cartwheels. Sam gave himself a few moments' rest to catch his breath and clear his head. He was in complete darkness except for the ring of warm light cast by the Meriweserre bracelet. It lay on the dusty floor — it must have fallen off the stone — with the six coins still strung on it. So Setni was right: The bracelet allowed you to time travel without losing any coins. Why the magic had worked with six of them instead of seven remained to be seen.

Sam got to his knees, then struggled to his feet. As he reached for the bracelet, he noticed that the twin pulses in his chest hadn't fully subsided. In addition to his rapid heartbeat, he could feel the other, much slower pounding deep within him. He lifted the bracelet up to light the darkness.

"No way!" he exclaimed.

In front of him, a golden sarcophagus rested on a stone block whose base displayed a carved sun with six long slanting rays, the cavity gaping underneath. This version of the stone statue was familiar, because Sam had encountered it during one of his very first voyages. He was back in Egypt, in Setni's tomb!

Sam took the map of Rome from the cavity and stepped back a little, using the bracelet for light. No doubt about it, he was in the high priest of Amon's final resting place. Gleaming with gold leaf, the walls displayed the same sacred scenes featuring Setni's favorite god, ibis-headed Thoth, the patron of magicians and the juggler of hours and seasons. The funerary furnishings were the same too: a little wooden boat to carry the dead man to the other world; chairs for his comfort after the journey; a spear to protect him; statuettes of animals to keep him company; jars of food to feed him in the afterlife; and other necessities.

But one thing was different. The last time Sam was here, the only way to get out of the funerary chamber was to climb a knotted rope dangling from an opening in the ceiling. That opening had been sealed up. On the other hand, there was now a big hole in the back wall.

Sam walked through the hole to find a narrow, rubble-strewn tunnel leading away into the darkness. A pick and shovel stood against one wall, and a blue plastic bag lay on the floor. When Sam opened it, he was overwhelmed by the disgusting stench of rotten meat. He had no idea what the bag was doing there, but he was sure of one thing: If it was plastic, it didn't date from antiquity! Sam unstrung the coins from the bracelet and spread them on his palm. He set the gray one aside — some of its coral-like crust had broken off when the bracelet fell — and carefully examined the coin with Arabic writing. It was the very first one he had ever held, having picked it up a few weeks earlier when he found the secret room in his father's basement and started his time travels. Now he understood what the coin was. Allan must have brought it back from Thebes after working on the excavation of Setni's tomb some twenty years earlier. This seemed especially plausible since, according to articles Sam had read, the high priest's funerary chamber was undisturbed when the archaeologists reached it. The tunnel in the wall must have been dug by Allan's archaeological expedition. So his father might be somewhere outside the tomb right now, twenty years younger!

If Sam's hunch was right, it meant that the stone statue hadn't sent him to Egypt by accident. It had "chosen" his destination among the six coins strung on the Golden Circle. Six coins meant six possible destinations — an early version of Russian roulette! If Sam left right away, he had one chance in six of reaching China immediately and getting the information he needed to save Alicia. But he also had five chances of being sent somewhere else.

Still, Allan couldn't be far away. If Sam could talk to him, maybe he could supply one more coin with a hole in it, which would take Sam straight to China. Maybe he could even convince his father not to get involved with the stone statue in the first place, preventing the series of events that led to his hospitalization and Alicia's kidnapping. A few minutes' detour could avoid so many problems!

Sam put the coins in his pocket and squeezed into the passageway. It wasn't wide enough to remove any objects from the tomb, which probably explained why everything was undisturbed. He made his way along the rock walls for a dozen yards until he brushed a knotted rope hanging down in the darkness. Grabbing it, he easily climbed to the top of a kind of well that opened onto a wider hallway. By the light of the bracelet, Sam followed the hallway and climbed several flights of steps while admiring the stars painted on the huge domed ceiling and the lively scenes of daily life on the walls.

When he reached a crude wooden door at the top of the last stairway, he held his breath: The way out was right in front of him. He lifted the latch and peeked outside. It was nighttime, which explained why the tomb was empty. He slipped quietly outside, pricking up his ears. A full, reddish moon floated in the sky, and the air felt deliciously warm. On the left, a path led steeply down about fifty yards to a camp on a ridge surrounded by a barbed wire fence. Beyond the fence, the slope steepened again, and the eroded mountainside fell away to the broad plain of the Nile, which looked like a dark ribbon in the distance.

Sam observed the little tent city for a moment, weighing his chances of reaching it undetected. Nearly everybody seemed to be asleep; a light was on in only one tent. Sam knew his father was a light sleeper, so if one of the treasure hunters below was awake in the middle of the night, it was likely to be him.

Sam skirted the rocky cliff, trying not to bruise his bare feet. But just as he was about to head down the path, he noticed a light moving in the camp. He stuffed the Meriweserre bracelet under his shirt and froze. It was a lantern or flashlight held by a man in a long white robe with a sort of dark bag at his side. . . . No, not a bag: a dog. The camp had a night watchman with a dog!

Sam was tempted to turn around, but reasoned that the man's job must be to keep people from breaking into the camp, not to chase those who were already inside. He waited until the guard turned his back, then raced down the path, realizing once again how much softer the soles of his feet were than the stones of the world. He slipped in the steepest section, but caught himself on one of the stakes that lined the path.

Sam cautiously continued his descent, reaching the first tent without further incident. He saw the night watchman coming his way, so he ducked into the canvas shelter, using the Meriweserre bracelet to light his way. Crates, tools, and food — it was a supply tent. He huddled against a pallet of tin cans and held his breath. As he did, he noticed that the slow pulse in his chest had diminished. Maybe he was too far from the Thoth stone.

After half a minute, he heard the guard slowly shuffling along, accompanied by the scratching of the dog's claws. The animal stopped level with the tent and growled quietly. Sam's hands joined in silent prayer.

"What's the matter, Sultan?" said an old man's voice. "You had your dinner, you can wait until tomorrow. It's time for my cigarette."

The dog continued to growl, but Sam heard a kind of scraping sound, as if the animal was being dragged along by its leash, and the watchmen moved off. Sam counted to fifty before daring to move. Using the bracelet's light to keep from bumping into things, he noticed a long, dark-gray coat, a plate of date pits, and a piece of pita bread on top of some crates. A bowl of gnawed bones stood on the ground nearby.

Sam picked up the scratchy coat. It had a hood and was the ideal color to cover Sam's white outfit, making him invisible in the darkness. He put it on and slipped out of his hiding place, crossing the camp to the illuminated tent without any trouble. The tent's light was now joined by background music: a lively guitar tune jamming at low volume. That was another good sign, because Allan Faulkner loved rock 'n' roll.

Sam parted the canvas flap and mosquito netting and saw a chalkboard with a map — Setni's tomb, probably — and some scrawled notes. He raised the flap farther, and realized that the tent was both bedroom and office and that its occupant wasn't exactly a tidy housekeeper. Crumpled balls of paper littered a brightly colored Oriental rug, shorts and T-shirts lay piled on a folding chair, and a couple of statuettes had been tossed on a camp bed. Books and magazines were casually stacked on what Sam could see of a desk, along with a big cassette player and some empty liquor bottles. Leaning in farther, Sam saw a man sleeping slumped on the desk, one arm over his head.

Crouching down, Sam noiselessly entered the tent. Even at low volume, the guitar and drums gave him good sonic cover. The song sounded like a rock standard his father liked, but in an exotic cover with incomprehensible lyrics. On his hands and knees, he circled the chalkboard and stopped in front of an open trunk at the foot of the desk.

It contained old, tattered books, including an open photo album with a series of Polaroid pictures. They all showed a Victorian house with faded green shutters surrounded by a high fence. Half a dozen dogs were roaming the yard, and two of the snapshots showed slavering jaws angrily snapping at the wires. Aside from the color of the shutters and the fact that it looked like a kennel for crazed dogs, there was absolutely no doubt that it was a picture of the Faulkner's Antique Books building, taken twenty or thirty years earlier.

Intrigued, Sam turned the pages of the album. Every picture showed Barenboim Street in Sainte-Mary: old postcards, black-and-white snapshots, and a dozen color prints. Even before he moved to Canada, Allan seemed to have assembled a complete album on his future bookstore!

The last notes of the song died away and Sam cast an anxious look toward the desk. Even if the unknown man was his father, he wouldn't like waking up to find someone rummaging through his things. When the next tune started, Sam put the album down and crawled closer to the chair. The man was wearing a blue shirt, faded yellow pants, and a white scarf around his neck. In the shadows, Sam still couldn't make out his face.

He made his way around the chair and came face-to-face with a pistol hanging from the man's belt. This wasn't just an archeological dig, it was a high-security zone! He stood up slowly.

And frowned: The man slumped on the desk wasn't his father. He was older, in his fifties at least, with three days' growth of beard and grayish skin. His open mouth was drooling onto a sheaf of pages covered with fine writing. But in the middle of the jumble on the desk, Sam spotted something interesting: Propped against a pencil jar stood a book with a blue cloth cover and a big number 13 stamped in gilt. It looked exactly like the *Treatise* the Arkeos man had sent him to recover!

Sam hadn't found his father, but he may have stumbled on a way to bring Alicia home sooner than expected. He reached slowly over the chair for the book, but just as he was about to grab it, the wide sleeve of his coat brushed the sleeping man's cheek. The man snorted noisily and shook his head, then opened his eyes. At the sight of Sam, his sleepy expression immediately became a snarl of rage. He lunged for his pistol.

CHAPTER FIVE

The Archeologist

Sam was faster. He grabbed the pistol and pointed it at the man.

"Hands up! Don't move or I'll shoot!"

Sam shouted this in a melodious language that rolled easily off his tongue, even though it bore no relation to his native English. Arabic, probably. Thanks to the magic of the Thoth stone, the words came to him naturally, the way they always did when he changed places and times. In any case, it worked: The man raised his hands, looking at Sam with a mix of surprise and indignation.

"You're the bugger who's been sneaking into the camp at night, aren't you?" the man asked with a slight accent. "And stealing coins from the tomb?"

Sam almost said no, but then he remembered that if his father had used the stone statue, he would have had to take some coins to make it work. The chance to give him an alibi was too good to pass up.

"That's right."

"And now you're after the rest, is that it?"

"Among other things," Sam answered evasively.

"Among other things," the man groaned. "You're not going to hurt me, are you?" With his chin, he gestured to a matchbox on the desk. "The only coin I have left is in there. Take it if you like. I won't tell anyone, I promise. But don't shoot me, all right?"

The man was sweating, and a few strands of sun-bleached hair lay across his waxen forehead. He was clearly in bad health and didn't deserve to be frightened any more. On the other hand, he probably knew a lot about the coins and the *Treatise*. It was a great opportunity to find out what he was doing here.

"I need some information," said Sam. "Who are you?"

"Who am I?" asked the man in astonishment. "You're holding me up in my own tent and you don't know who I am?"

"I'm the one with the gun," answered Sam, using a line from his favorite cop show. "I ask the questions."

"Very well. I am Daniel Chamberlain, and I am in charge of this excavation."

Chamberlain — of course! The archaeologist who had hired Allan and another intern to work on the dig. Sam hadn't imagined him as a sick, frightened alcoholic — or connected him with Sainte-Mary.

"There's an open photo album in that trunk," Sam continued. "The pictures are all of the same house. I want to know why."

Chamberlain gaped at him as if this was the oddest question anyone could ask. But curiously, it almost seemed to relieve him, as if he'd expected worse.

"It's my great-grandfather's house," he said with a hint of a smile. "An extraordinary man. The street in the pictures bears his name. He was rather a star over there."

Now it was Sam's turn to be astonished. Barenboim, the man who a century earlier had used the stone statue in the basement of the future Faulkner's Antique Books! So Chamberlain was one of his descendants. . . . Allan must have heard about Sainte-Mary from him!

Sam nodded slowly. If he played his cards right, he might be able to turn the situation to his advantage.

"So you're Garry Barenboim's great-grandson."

"Great Scott, how can you know that?" Chamberlain gasped. "It's unbelievable! You're so young!"

"Don't let my age fool you," said Sam enigmatically. "It's enough that I know that fact and many other things. If you don't want trouble, you better not tell me any lies."

The archaeologist couldn't have looked more surprised if one of his mummies had sneezed under its wrappings.

"In that case . . . Well, yes, Garry Barenboim was my great-grandfather," he stammered.

"Why an album with all those photos?"

"Let's just say that I've been trying to get the house back for some time. It was sold years ago, after my ancestor's death. A kind of madwoman lives there now with a mob of dogs. She refuses to sell, and there's no way to make her see reason."

"Why do you want to buy the house back?"

"I think Garry Barenboim left a treasure behind, and it's hidden in his house. I'm not sure, but I think it's something valuable. A way to know history better," he added with a glint of covetousness in his eyes. "A thing that would make me the most famous archaeologist in the world! That's a good reason, isn't it? The problem is that in order to get my hands on it, I must be able to search the place at leisure."

He was speaking with more confidence now. "I've told you the truth. Are you satisfied? Can I put my hands down? I'm getting tired."

Sam nodded, and Chamberlain lowered his hands to his lap. Obviously, a stone statue would be tremendously useful to an archaeologist! But that didn't explain what the *Treatise* was doing on the man's desk. "How did you figure such a treasure existed?"

"My great-grandfather left some letters and notebooks. They were gathering dust in my parents' attic until I found them when I was about ten. They talked about ancient civilizations, strange objects, mythic places. About the tomb of the high priest Setni too, somewhere in these hills. That's why I became an archaeologist. But I suppose you know all that as well."

Chamberlain rubbed his shoulder, as if keeping his hands in the air had been unbearable.

"In the beginning, I didn't understand much about them, the papers were so confusing. But the more I studied them, the more I realized that they weren't just fantasies. My great-grandfather pierced humanity's greatest mystery: He was able to travel through Time!"

Defiantly, Chamberlain watched for Sam's reaction. When he saw none, he started to chuckle.

"You should have reacted, my boy. Called me mad, or a joker. No one can hear such a statement and say nothing. Do you know what I think? I think I'm asleep and dreaming. I went a bit heavy on the whiskey and painkillers this evening, and I must've collapsed on my desk. You're in my dream. You're the incarnation of my conscience — my guilty conscience!"

He was getting excited, and his left eyelid began to twitch. But whatever his mental state, Chamberlain was perfectly capable of alerting the camp. Sam would have to get out of there soon, but first he needed the *Treatise*.

"That blue book over there with the number thirteen — give it to me," he ordered.

The archaeologist handed it over with a broad smile.

"The *Treatise*, of course!" he said. "Isn't that the source of all our hopes and all our troubles?"

Sam propped the book against his chest and peered at it. Although dog-eared and dirty, it didn't look especially old. The gilt 13 was certainly of a style that suggested the Middle East, but the book's glossy paper was modern.

"It's a copy, is that it?" asked Sam.

"Yes, it's a copy!" said Chamberlain with a bitter laugh. "That's exactly the problem!"

Sam blinked at this news. If it wasn't the original, there was no point in bringing it to Captain Diavilo for him to free Alicia. Back to square one!

He opened the book at random to a pen-and-ink drawing of an Easter Island statue with a stone statue at its base and a sketch of a sun that was missing two of its rays. The next page had a grotesque image of a bat with the head of a child. Written in black ink underneath was "Accursed cave of the Al-Mehdi wadi, an hour's walk northeast of Isfahan." A few pages later was a recipe that called for such unusual ingredients as arsenic, camphor, and sulfurated mercury. An alchemical preparation? Notes were scribbled next to it in red, but Sam couldn't decipher them.

He turned another couple of pages. These drawings and pictures . . . he had seen this book before! In Bruges, when he'd snuck into the alchemist's laboratory! He soon located the formula that first hinted at the power of the Meriweserre bracelet and its sister, the Golden Circle: "He who gathers the seven coins will be the master of the sun. If he can make the six rays shine, its heart will be the key to time. He will then know the immortal heat."

"*The Treatise on the Thirteen Virtues of Magic,*" Sam murmured. "Klugg the alchemist's book."

"There you go — Klugg!" said Chamberlain triumphantly. "It all comes back to him! So tell me, if you really are my unconscious, do you have a solution to our problem?"

"Our problem?"

"The pages at the end, you know, the ones that are missing!"

Without lowering the pistol, Sam managed to flip to the end of the book, where several pages were missing.

"Who removed them?" he asked.

"They were torn from the original during the invasion of Rome. This copy is an exact duplicate of what was left."

"Rome? Really? When was this invasion?" Sam asked, trying to hide his excitement.

"You're trying to test me, is that it? I may have gone overboard with the liquor and the drugs, but I haven't lost my memory. The sack of Rome in 1527. Charles the Fifth's troops overran the city, burning churches, wreaking havoc. I know all that by heart! That's when the *Treatise* was damaged and those crucial pages disappeared!"

Rome, 1527, the invasion . . . Sam slipped the book of spells under his arm and fumbled in his pocket for the coins. He picked out the one the Arkeos man had sent him and stuck it under Chamberlain's nose.

"This one's from that time, isn't it?"

The archaeologist squinted, then read aloud: "*Candor illaesus*, 'Unblemished brightness.' It's the motto of Clement the Seventh, who was pope when Rome was sacked. This coin is from those years, no question. It's part of the cache we found in Setni's tomb — the coins that were stolen. Are you trying to tell me that I have to catch the coin thief, is that it? I'm trying to. The camp is guarded and — "

Sam cut him off. "Forget about the thief. Instead, tell me what you think was on the missing pages."

"You know as well as I do," said Chamberlain. "Those pages held the secret of secrets, the one I've been pursuing for the last ten years — how to become immortal! Garry Barenboim refers to it in his correspondence. He claims to have heard about a ring of eternity that will give its owner infinite life without age or illness of any kind. That's what I need!"

So it's this "Eternity Ring" again, thought Sam. When he had confronted Vlad Tepes in the highest tower of Bran Castle, Tepes too had talked about trying to find a magical stone ring that granted eternal life. Could it be something more than a mere legend?

"What else have you learned about this Eternity Ring?"

"Nothing very specific, alas. The only letter where Garry Barenboim refers to it is so brief! But elsewhere in his papers he talks about two golden rings that you must bring together to open the gates of eternity. Which proves he was making progress in his search!"

"What's the connection with *The Treatise on the Thirteen Virtues of Magic?*"

"My great-grandfather made these discoveries by studying Klugg's notes in the *Treatise*. He was convinced that the missing pages would lead him to what he was looking for. But he was never able to find them, and now it's up to me to pick up the torch. I need that ring!" he said anxiously. "I'm ill, you see. Seriously ill. I only have a few months to live, or at most a few years. So if you can help me, even in a dream . . ."

He seized Sam's wrist pleadingly, knocking several of his coins to the ground.

Sam jumped back without lowering his weapon. "Don't move!"

But Chamberlain had already rushed to pick up the pierced coins.

"Unbelievable!" cried the archaeologist. "This one is just like the one in the *Treatise*." He was holding out the old coin with the Chinese characters. "Don't you recognize it? Look, just beyond where the pages were torn out!"

Sam opened the *Treatise* again, while keeping an eye on his prisoner. At the very end of the book was a sketch of a building with a pagoda roof under a forested mountainside. The sun in the sky was a perfect replica of the Chinese coin with its square hole in the middle. Some words were written in red at the bottom of the page, but Sam couldn't read them.

"That was the last place Klugg had to go, according to his notes. The tomb of Qin Shi Huang, the first emperor of China!

Qin too spent his whole life searching for the secret of immortality. Do you think that's where I should look for the ring?"

"It's possible," said Sam cautiously.

The archaeologist looked ecstatic as he examined the coin. "That's why I've had this dream. The information was all there, somewhere in my brain, but I wasn't able to pull it together. Qin's tomb was discovered just ten years ago! They uncovered huge pits with thousands of life-size terra-cotta soldiers, a whole army created to watch over the emperor's eternal rest. According to some texts, the tomb itself is under a huge burial mound, a bit like the hill in the *Treatise*. It's said that Qin built an exact underground replica of his kingdom, with palaces, houses, rivers — and fiendishly clever traps to defend them! That must be where the ring is hidden. That's where I have to go!"

"If there are traps, is the place dangerous?" asked Sam, who guessed that this was where the Arkeos man was sending him.

"Qin died in 210 before the Christian era, and his mausoleum has been untouched for more than two thousand years. Who knows what it might be hiding? The Chinese authorities have decided not to touch it. They're going to let future generations search it with more advanced techniques. But if I can get to the dig, I'm sure I'll be able to —"

Just then the tape in the cassette player ended with a click, cutting off the archaeologist's speculation as well. During the long silence that followed, Chamberlain's eyes darted between his music player and the young man who had appeared out of nowhere. He was starting to look doubtful.

"You . . ."

"Give me the coins back," demanded Sam, who sensed that the tables were turning.

"I'm not dreaming, am I?"

"This gun's totally real. The coins, please. I'm in a hurry."

Chamberlain obeyed, looking upset. "What about my dream, and Emperor Qin, and the ring?" he moaned.

"I have no idea," admitted Sam. "But if you do exactly as I say, I promise you'll soon be free to go see for yourself. Anyway, I'm leaving you the *Treatise*." He surmised that the Arkeos man wanted the complete book with all the pages intact, not this imperfect modern copy.

Defeated, the archaeologist stared at the ground. The flame animating him earlier seemed to have been abruptly snuffed out, leaving only a poor old man slumped in his chair, overcome with disappointment.

While keeping the gun on him, Sam came around the table and took a belt from the pile of clothes on the chair. "Put your hands behind you, close together," he commanded.

Chamberlain did as he was told. "So you're the thief, are you? Can you at least tell me what those coins are for?"

"I'm working for someone," answered Sam, thinking of the Arkeos man. "A man with the sign of Hathor on his shoulder. If you don't want him paying you a visit, nothing better happen to me tonight."

"Hathor, Re's daughter," muttered the archaeologist. "The two-faced goddess. She can punish people severely, but she can also reward them. Do you think I'll be rewarded someday?"

Sam finished tying the man's wrists to the chair rails. He'd just remembered: A few years after being criticized for his sloppy management of the Thebes excavation, the unfortunate Chamberlain had died of cancer.

"I think if your punishment is especially unfair, you can hope for an especially big reward," Sam said to comfort him. "And now I'm sorry, but I have to gag you. Before I do, one more question: Where is Faulkner's tent?"

"Faulkner's tent? What's the —"

"There's something there I have to get. Where is it?"

"It's the third one on the left as you go toward the fence. Are you going to put him through the same ordeal as me?"

Sam didn't answer. He took the white scarf Chamberlain wore around his neck, put it over the man's mouth, and tied it. "It should only take a few minutes," he said reassuringly. "You'll be freed soon."

Just in case, he turned over the tape in the cassette player and hit the PLAY button. As the first notes sounded, he took the matchbox near the pencil jar and removed the metal disk inside. It was an ordinary yellow coin, but it had the right kind of hole in the center. He pocketed it, slipped the pistol in his belt, and left the tent without turning around. Time to talk to his father.

CHAPTER SIX

Deductions

Sam breathed in the night air with relief. He wasn't very proud of the way he had silenced Chamberlain, but between the archaeologist's discomfort and the failure of his mission, he figured he had chosen the lesser evil. After making sure that the night watchman wasn't around, he followed the fence to the third tent. It was less imposing than the excavation leader's tent, and logically enough, was dark. How would his father react when Sam woke him up with a hair-raising story of traveling to the past and changing the future? He'd better get his explanation ready.

Sam put his ear to the canvas wall, but could hear only vague camp noises, crickets chirping, and the distant meow of a wandering cat. Allan must be deeply asleep.

Sam carefully slid the zipper down and stuck his head inside. There wasn't a sound, not even breathing. Taking out the Meriweserre bracelet, he shone its warm light into the darkness. From what he could see, Sam decided that Allan had no right to criticize his son's messy room ever again. Dirty dishes were stacked on a folding table with open tin cans and a half-finished bottle of soda, along with some sliced bread, crumpled newspapers, a deck of cards, and plastic poker chips.

The sleeping area was behind the kitchen space, and it looked more like a sidewalk vendor's display than a retreat for peace and quiet. A pile of casually folded clothes lay between two empty cots with wadded-up sleeping bags. A guitar leaned against a backpack; a hookah stood in the middle of a brass tray with a teapot and glasses; books and hiking boots spilled out of an open suitcase; a pair of towels and T-shirts hung on a cord strung from the central tent pole. Allan and his tent mate must share the same love of mess — and of midnight rambles, apparently, because the tent was empty.

The second intern, thought Sam. That phrase reminded him of his theory that the intern was also the Arkeos man. If he searched through the intern's things, he might find his real name. Sam spotted a backpack near the rear of the tent and went to investigate.

Something in a front pocket gave him a jolt: a round watch with a white dial and green numbers. It was Allan's watch, one he'd seen his father wearing ever since he was little. At this very instant, it lay on the night table in Room 313, patiently marking time early in the twenty-first century. *How ironic,* Sam thought, that this object was what connected him to his father beyond the paths of time!

"I'll be a little late, Dad," he said quietly. "I'm going as fast as I can, you know. I have to help Alicia."

Shaken by his find, Sam stood up quickly, forgetting the clothesline stretched above him. A towel brushed his face and he jumped back into the hookah, which toppled onto the brass tray with a resounding crash.

Sam felt his hair stand on end. Nothing happened for a couple of seconds, then a hoarse barking erupted outside, followed by a cry of command: "No, Sultan! Come back!" The night watchman's dog had heard him!

"Sultan, here!"

The stupid dog must've gotten loose, thought Sam, his legs shaking. *He's going to screw everything up!* He considered running from the tent, but it was too late. Instead he dropped onto the nearest cot and pulled the coat around him, leaving only a tiny slit to see out.

"Not in there, Sultan!" said the night watchman, whose lantern was casting rings of light on the tent walls. "Not inside!"

But Sultan didn't heed him. The dog was already raising the tent flap with its muzzle and growling. Suddenly aware of the pistol butt against his stomach, Sam slowly pulled out the gun. The growling had risen to an awful gurgling, with the dog's lips curled and teeth bared. Trembling with eagerness, ears flattened, the dog took two steps closer. Sam could almost smell its stale breath.

"Sultan, here!" called the watchman outside. "Come here right now!"

Sam raised the gun, put his finger on the trigger, and closed his eyes. He planned to shoot at the dog the moment it rushed him.

But then for some reason, it seemed to hesitate. The fearsome growling dropped a tone, and the dog sniffed eagerly at the coat, yelping happily. Sam felt a warm, slimy tongue mopping his brow. The coat belonged to the watchman, Sam realized. It recognized the smell of its master!

"Here, Sultan!" the watchman ordered.

The animal sneezed twice, as if the mix of human scents had thrown him off, and trotted out the tent door.

"Sultan, what were you doing?" hissed the guard. "Do you want to wake everybody up?"

Sam wiped his forehead, which was wet with saliva. The dog's affection was as sticky as it was unpredictable.

He lay motionless on the cot until the watchman's footsteps faded away. Everything had happened quickly, but it was a minor miracle the whole camp hadn't woken up. Sam needed to get out of there as soon as possible. He returned Allan's watch to the backpack and slipped outside. This time at least, Sam had avoided the worst.

CHAPTER SEVEN

"He who Gathers the Seven Coins . . ."

His mind racing, Sam hurried along the fence to the path up to Setni's tomb. He hadn't managed to talk to his father, but his stopover in Egypt certainly hadn't been a waste of time. He had picked up a coin with a hole, bringing his total to seven, and he had learned some vital things about the Arkeos man — in particular, just why he would want to retrieve *The Treatise on the Thirteen Virtues of Magic* and the Meriweserre bracelet. Like Vlad Tepes before him, he must believe firmly in the existence of the Eternity Ring, and to get it, he needed the pages ripped from the *Treatise*. The best way to get them would be to return to the past, to just before the book was vandalized, which was why the Arkeos man was sending Sam to Rome in the middle of Charles V's invasion.

Finding the ring depended on having both the Meriweserre bracelet and the original Golden Circle, which Setni had told him about. According to legend, the first Golden Circle had been crafted by the god Thoth and given to the great magician Imhotep. Later, the Hyksos invaded from the east, conquered Egypt, and made their own copy of the Circle. That copy, which was known as the Meriweserre bracelet, had been taken to the Middle East. Vlad Tepes stole the bracelet from the sultan of Turkey and brought it to Bran Castle, where Sam had acquired it while rescuing his father. As for the original Golden Circle, Sam knew the high priest Setni had kept it on his person and used it to travel. But what had happened to it when Setni finally died?

Stepping through the door to the tomb, Sam felt the stone's slow pounding revive in him, now accompanied by a kind of murmur that seemed to be rising from the depths of the earth. He stopped to listen. The murmuring wasn't coming from the stone; it was the sound of a conversation taking place somewhere inside the tomb.

"Dad?" he asked excitedly.

He raced along the stairs and the hallways, lighting his way with the bracelet. As he went deeper into the tomb, it became clear that what had sounded like a conversation was actually an argument punctuated with shouts and dull thuds. When he reached the well with the knotted rope, Sam realized that the words were spoken in a language he didn't know. But while he didn't understand them, the voices were clearly lifted in anger. Two men were yelling at each other — and one of them sounded like Allan!

Dropping from the rope end, Sam hurried along the tunnel that the archaeologists had dug to reach the sarcophagus. In the distance, he could make out a bright yellowish light and flickering shapes like shadow puppets. Emerging into the funerary chamber, Sam blinked in the glare of a lantern reflected in the gleaming walls. As his eyes adjusted to the brightness, he saw two men wrestling on the ground, wearing white time-traveler clothes. The man underneath was getting the worst of it. The one on top was shouting something and trying to strangle him.

"Mmm ganna keel yuu!"

Sam could only see him from the back, but he immediately recognized the Arkeos man's strangling technique, the effectiveness of which he'd personally experienced at the Sainte-Mary Museum. When Sam stepped aside to see the victim's face, he felt as if a lightning bolt had hit his heart: The man struggling for breath was Allan! A younger, slender Allan, with long black hair. He looked like a frightened boy being tormented by a bully in the school yard, except that this wasn't a schoolboy fight — it was murder.

Pulling the pistol from his belt, Sam ran over, raised his arm high, and blindly brought the butt down as hard as he could. The man on top groaned and slumped forward. Sam shoved him aside and, in a daze, leaned over his father to help him up.

The young man looked as if he was just past adolescence, but his eyes were sunken and his skin was the color of parchment, as if something was eating at him. *He must be sick,* thought Sam. Grandpa had said that when Allan came back from his Thebes internship, he'd caught a nasty virus and lost twenty pounds. It was a kind of warning that there was nothing to be gained by traveling through Time, a warning he should have heeded.

Looking dazed and exhausted, Allan gratefully let his future son pull him to his feet. "Tanks," he croaked. "Wizzout yuu, Ahn woood nt meke eet."

Sam nodded stupidly; he couldn't understand a word Allan said. He and his father were obviously speaking two different languages. Of course, that made sense; when Sam landed in Egypt, the stone statue gave him the gift of Arabic, the local language, but his father was speaking English! That's why Sam couldn't make sense of what he said; he no longer spoke his mother tongue. His conversation with Chamberlain had fooled him, because the archaeologist spoke fluent Arabic, and Allan didn't.

"Wazza motter?"

Sam grabbed his father's arm and pulled him over to the part of the sarcophagus with the stone statue.

"Don't ever touch this again," he said, pronouncing each word distinctly in Arabic. "Understand? Never!"

Allan frowned at his vehemence. "Me not understand," he said in heavily accented Arabic.

"Don't touch the stone, you understand? The stone is dangerous!" Sam yelled.

Suddenly suspicious, Allan pulled his hand away and took a step back. "Me not understand. Me leave! You leave!" he added, pointing at the tunnel.

"Wait," begged Sam in Arabic, enraged at not being able to make himself understood. "You have to promise me! It's very important! The stone statue brings nothing but trouble. It's cursed, do you understand? Cursed!"

Just then, the intern on the ground moaned. Allan seemed to make up his mind. He picked up his street clothes from behind a large jar and walked shakily toward the exit. Turning around, he looked at his partner lying on the ground. He hesitated a moment, then knelt and slipped something from the man's pocket — something Sam couldn't see. Allan pocketed it, then picked up the bag of rotten meat and waved it at Sam.

"Dog eat! Me leave!" Allan said with a thin smile, and stepped into the tunnel.

Sam was tempted to run after him, but there wasn't much more he could do. The watchman was still outside and Chamberlain could raise the alarm at any minute. And the other intern still lay on the ground.

The other intern . . . The Arkeos man.

At the thought, Sam felt a kind of poison spreading through his veins. Everything was that man's fault, and there he lay, unconscious, at Sam's mercy. He leaned over the man and shoved up his right sleeve. There was no tattoo on his shoulder. That didn't mean anything, of course. The mark of Hathor could have been tattooed much later. As for his identity . . .

Sam crouched down to turn the man over. He was tall and muscular, and weighed a ton. It took several tries before he was able to shift him. Finally the man rolled to his back.

"No, not him!"

Sam jerked back in dismay, and the man's head bumped to the ground.

"Not him," he gasped again.

The mysterious intern was none other than Rudolf — Aunt Evelyn's boyfriend! Rudolf, who'd practically set up camp in his grandparents' house in the last few weeks! Rudolf, who'd arranged everything from the very beginning, and played innocent while preaching to everybody else!

Almost without realizing it, Sam's grip on the pistol tightened. It would be so easy. Just a tiny pressure on the trigger, and no more Arkeos man, no death threats, no Alicia kidnapping. . . .

Sam considered it for an instant, but the weapon in his hand felt heavy and cold. It was one thing to knock somebody out, but quite another to shoot him, especially when he was lying unconscious. Even your worst enemy.

Sam got to his feet and hid the pistol as best he could in a corner with the funerary objects. In the short term at least, no one would find it.

He then came back and examined Rudolf more carefully. He looked barely twenty, just like Allan. But the Rudolf Sam knew in his present was in his fifties, a full decade older than his father. That was one of the main reasons Sam had never suspected him: He thought Allan and the Thebes intern were the same age, not ten years apart. How could they be the same age in the past, but ten years apart in the future?

Then Sam remembered something Setni had said — that he looked older than he was because he had spent a long time on the paths of Time. Sam himself had noticed that he seemed to have grown taller and stronger since he started "traveling" — as if he'd gotten older. Did using the stone statue cause premature aging? If so, that was another reason it was better to remain in your own time.

Rudolf's arm moved, and his lids fluttered. He was definitely coming to.

Sam stepped over the body and headed for the sarcophagus. In the lantern light, the room seemed different — bigger, higher; still beautifully decorated, but laid out differently. On Sam's previous trip, hadn't the stone statue faced the other way, toward the back of the tomb, not toward the tall figure of Thoth holding out a crown? But that was before Setni's burial, and by the light of a flickering torch — maybe more construction had been done. Besides, Sam had just emerged from Ramses's palace then and was encountering Egyptian funerary rites for the first time. He probably wasn't thinking very clearly.

He knelt in front of the limestone plinth bearing the coffin, stuffed the map of Rome in the transport cavity, and took out the bracelet. This was the moment of truth. If Klugg the alchemist's guess was right, he should be able to choose his destination and travel directly there: *He who gathers the seven coins will be the master of the sun. . . .*

He strung six coins onto the Meriweserre bracelet and set it on the carved sun. As before, each of the coins spontaneously snapped into its correct slit. Sam could feel his pulse accelerate, and the stone's slow pounding in his chest strengthened. He fingered the Chinese coin uncertainly and finally stuck it in the center of the bracelet, right on the sun.

At first, nothing happened, but after a few seconds sparks shot from the slits to merge into a shining bubble of energy. The bracelet looked like a miniature sun burning the stone. Meanwhile, the pounding inside him grew more powerful. *If he can make the six rays shine, its heart will be the key to time. . . .*

Fascinated, Sam stared at the brilliant bubble floating at the foot of the sarcophagus, then poked it with his finger. He pierced it, but it didn't burst; his skin merely prickled and then went slightly numb. He pushed farther and felt as if his fingers were sinking almost into the stone. He looked around the room to make sure that he wasn't the victim of an illusion, but nothing around him seemed to have moved. Actually, something had. Rudolf was now leaning up on one elbow and staring openmouthed at the phenomenon.

Sam pulled his fingers out of the incandescent bubble and quickly put his hand on top of the stone. Instantly, his entire body was shaken by a long, burning spasm, and every molecule of his body seemed to vaporize.

CHAPTER EIGHT

The Palace Under the Hill

Darkness once again.

When Sam came to, he was lying on his side, on hard, cold ground in a place that smelled of earth or mud. Shifting onto all fours, Sam reviewed the various parts of his body: He didn't hurt anywhere, and he didn't even feel nauseous — amazing, considering the violence with which he had been shot down the paths of Time. The takeoff was still as painful as ever, but maybe the link between the bracelet and the seven coins made the landing less painful.

Speaking of the Meriweserre bracelet, Sam wondered why it wasn't shining more brightly. When he felt around for it, he touched mud walls, and realized that he was in some sort of dead end. The stone statue was set into the back wall, and the Meriweserre bracelet was on the sun, where it belonged. Sam lifted it off, all six coins still attached, and retrieved the Chinese coin from the sun and the map of Rome from the transport cavity. He put everything in his pockets.

Bumping his head on the ceiling when he straightened up told Sam he must be in a sort of tunnel. Twenty yards farther in, he glimpsed a thin shaft of light outlining a round door. Opening it revealed a vast, shadowy space dominated by a tall building with a pagoda roof and an elaborate portico. The house under the hill, just like the drawing in *The Treatise on the Thirteen Virtues of Magic*! He had reached Qin's mausoleum!

Sam was about to walk over to the pagoda's entrance when he remembered Chamberlain's warning: The tomb complex was full of traps. He stepped through the door very cautiously, and took his time studying what he could see. The pagoda was two stories high, with roofs with curving corners, and surrounded by a series of terraces bounded by stone walls. Overhead, a celestial dome glittered with stars, but a careful look revealed they were too close and too numerous to be a real night sky. If Sam was indeed in a space underground, maybe they were precious stones that reflected the light, or some sort of phosphorescent substance.

A garden, most of it in shadow, stretched in front of the palace. A few feet below Sam, a pathway of square black slabs snaked through a bed of mosses and stones. Twisted dwarf trees lined the mossy bed, and evenly spaced stone niches housed statues of small plump figures.

Sam walked the three steps down from his perch. He was a mere forty yards from the palace — an easy stroll. But when he stepped on the nearest stone slab, he felt it sink under his foot. On a sudden hunch, he leaped backward just as something hissed through the air. An arrow grazed his arm and slammed into the mud wall with a sickening squelch just a foot from his shoulder.

Sam strained to see into the darkness to the left where the shot had come from, and gradually made out a line of human shapes: archers, or maybe crossbowmen. There were at least fifty of them in two rows, half kneeling, the other half standing up, all impassively waiting for him to take another step. Sam looked hopefully to his right, but the welcoming committee there was no friendlier: The same number of soldiers, also arrayed in two ranks and ready to shoot him if he moved forward.

What are they doing here, wondered Sam. *How did they know I was coming? And why aren't they shooting? It's a hundred to one!*

After many long seconds of anxiety, the immobility and silence began to seem suspicious. No orders were shouted, no armor clanged, no breathing could be heard. Hadn't Chamberlain mentioned terra-cotta warriors that defended Qin's tomb? *Of course!* Sam realized. These weren't flesh-and-blood soldiers, but statues! Automatons that loosed their shafts when someone came close, and . . .

Sam looked at the pathway again, carefully this time. The shiny black slabs were decorated with scarlet Chinese characters. Pushing a slab down must trigger an archer's shot through some underground mechanism. So maybe by stepping around them . . .

Without moving his feet, Sam pulled the arrow out of the wall behind him. It had a hardwood shaft and a razor-sharp bronze point. Bending over, he used the arrow to probe the gray moss that stretched like an ashy carpet on either side of the path. He had only poked the moss a few times when something slammed shut on the arrow, shattering it. The welcoming committee had thoughtfully included mantraps as well!

There's got to be a solution, Sam thought to try to encourage himself; *there has to be.* He again looked at the palace, which now seemed inaccessible, the shadowy garden with its hidden traps, the statues he could dimly make out, and finally the pathway of stone slabs. The stepping-stones were lined up two by two, each bearing a single scarlet character. At first Sam had thought this was decoration, but he now realized that if he concentrated a little he could understand their meaning:

ℙ = "moon," 冂 = "man," 川 = "fire," 朩 = "tree," 山 = "mountain." The simultaneous translation magic was still working!

But the characters seemed to recur at random along the path; if the series as a whole held some sort of meaning, it escaped him.

Then Sam remembered the last page of the *Treatise*. Instead of a sun, the artist had drawn a coin with a square hole above Qin's burial tomb. And the characters on that coin . . .

Feverishly Sam rummaged in his pockets for the Chinese coin that had brought him here. It was an exact duplicate of the one in the *Treatise*, stamped on both sides with the same two characters: 冂 and 山, "man" and "mountain" — two of the characters on the path. "The man in the mountain." Wasn't that exactly Sam's situation right now? Was it a kind of clue that would allow the visitor to cross the garden?

He again looked at the slabs below him. The left-hand one he had first stepped on bore the moon character, but the one on the right had the mountain one. Was that the place to start?

Very cautiously, Sam touched his toes to the slab marked

"mountain," ready to leap backward. The slab didn't budge. He shifted his weight onto the square and brought his other foot up. No archer fired his deadly arrow. The next pair of slabs displayed the characters for "fire" and "man." He chose "man," again with no reaction by the guards. So far, so good.

He continued in this fashion, carefully alternating "mountain" and "man," sometimes jumping over one or even two pairs of slabs, but always managing to land on at least one of the safe squares. It was no harder than playing hopscotch! Reaching the portico safe and sound, Sam pushed open the heavy bronze doors and stepped into the inner palace courtyard, where a putrid smell filled the air. The sight in front of him made his heart sink.

"Not again," he said under his breath.

Now three terra-cotta crossbowmen were facing him, ready to fire their bolts. They were about his height, with strikingly realistic expressions: fierce gazes, grim faces, jet-black mustaches, coppery skin, and carefully braided hair. They held their weapons braced against metal breastplates, the bowstrings taut. The path in front of them split into three branches, each marked by a series of slabs where the same pairs of characters were repeated: 冂 木 to the left, 川 屮 in the middle, and 冂 屮 to the right. It was a more complicated variation of the earlier challenge, and Sam had to choose wisely if he didn't want to be skewered.

He let himself be guided by the pattern of the characters, guessing at their meanings in combination. The first one, 冂 木, combined "man" and "tree" to express the idea of "rest." In the middle, the characters for "fire" and "mountain" naturally meant "volcano." To the right, "man" and "mountain" were the two characters that had brought him luck so far. A man living in the security of the mountain, separate from everyone else — wasn't that like an Immortal? And an Immortal was exactly what Emperor Qin wanted to become!

Without hesitation, Sam took the Immortal path. He stepped on one slab, two slabs, three — none moved underfoot, and the trio of crossbowmen remained motionless. Sam circled the statues about a dozen yards away, then stopped dead, holding his nose: On the ground lay an emaciated, almost skeletal cadaver, an arrow in the man's back. He had collapsed here, a few yards from the palace, a hand stretched toward a door forever out of reach.

Sam was about to detour around the unfortunate man when he noticed a large ring on one of the shriveled fingers. It was a silver signet ring with a crenellated tower design that Sam had seen before, in Bruges in the fifteenth century. It belonged to Klugg the alchemist, who was wearing it the day he caught Sam rummaging in his secret laboratory. So this lifeless body was Klugg! He had almost reached Qin's tomb, never imagining that it would also be his own.

Sam was taken aback. He had never liked the alchemist, but he was shaken to think that he had ended his days here, mortally wounded, far from his own time and his loved ones. Was that all these "voyages" amounted to, fruitless quests leading to certain death? And to gain what, in the end?

Sam stood up, murmuring a few words in his former enemy's memory. There was nothing else he could do except take the lesson to heart and redouble his vigilance. He cautiously crossed the last yards to the palace entrance. It was framed by two huge lamps with long, spiral wicks in five-foot-tall white vases half full of fish oil — enough to light up the place for quite a while.

Holding his breath, Sam crossed the threshold into the building. A vestibule decorated with a green and a yellow dragon led to what looked like an antechamber. Red hangings covered the walls, and low benches ran all around the room.

He entered the next room to find two terra-cotta wrestlers in loincloths facing each other, muscles tensed, in a large circle of yellow sand. A third figure stood next to the circle with his finger raised, as if to start or stop the fight. The bare white exercise room ended in a wooden staircase up to an illuminated terrace that overlooked the courtyard and garden. "Okay, guys," Sam said aloud, since he was starting to find the silence oppressive. "The traps and the wrestlers are great, but how do I get out of here?"

A careful examination of the terrace revealed nothing that looked like a stone statue. Sam crossed a little gangplank that led to a small red and white house. It was practically empty, dominated by a single statue at least six feet tall that was quite different from the others. The man it represented was in the fullness of his strength, with long black hair and beard, his face and gaze marked by unmistakable majesty. Unlike the crossbowmen, he was dressed in real clothes: a glittering yellow coat with wide sleeves buttoned over a silky green apron embroidered with a maze of floral designs. The statue was topped by an amazing headpiece from which little curtains of tiny pearls dangled, partly hiding the man's face — clearly, the height of fashion in 210 B.C. He wore a silver sword at his side and held his right hand out in a forceful gesture, as if imposing his will on the entire world. This was Emperor Qin, of course.

The walls around him were a funereal black, brightened only by a series of white banners with bold red inscriptions: *Han has been vanquished, Zhao has been vanquished, Yan has been vanquished, Wei has been vanquished,* and so on. Sam counted a half dozen of these banners, which probably commemorated the conqueror's most brilliant victories. At the foot of each one, an identical gray stele read, "The August First Emperor Qin Shi Huang did this." One thing was for sure: The guy wasn't given to modesty.

Sam took the stairs on the far side of the house down to the lower floor, and opened a bronze door to the area behind the palace.

"Unbelievable!" Sam gasped.

Under the starry black sky, a kind of magical park lay before him: a series of cleverly linked islands joined by quaint bridges across a silvery river. Each island was lit up by large lantern vases, and was populated by trees and statues, with a tall pagoda-roofed temple in the center. On this strange lake's far shore, the celestial dome curved down to a jumble of huge boulders, as if an earthquake had cut off any retreat toward the world of the living.

Sam took the moss- and pebble-lined path to the shore and dipped his finger in the shiny liquid. When he pulled it out, it was covered with a silvery, almost metallic substance — a lake of mercury! He crossed the bridge to the first island, which was guarded by two terra-cotta soldiers, their arms crossed and swords sheathed. A life-size bronze chariot pulled by four white horses looked as if it had just brought the emperor for his evening walk. A group of musicians awaited him a few steps away, followed by several servants, some of them bent double, others holding out cloths, baskets filled with fruit, and goblets of wine. The path then split, one to the right toward an island where motionless animals grazed, the other toward the elegant structure with the pagoda roof.

Sam took the path over the bridge and entered the tower, which had fretwork screens and two stone dragons defending its lower steps. It contained a single room with a huge white bed screened by four curtains of pearls. A real human body lay in state upon the bed; it must be Emperor Qin himself. Filled with respectful fear, Sam kept his distance. The old man was dressed in a multicolored silk funeral gown and lay very straight, with a long black cane at his side. The pearl curtain made it hard to distinguish his features, but Qin's cheekbones and forehead looked emaciated, as if his face had gradually dried out. Or had the body been embalmed in some way to make it still look alive? Except for some bronze seats against the walls, the room's only decoration was a white banner with a calligraphic inscription: "I ruled the empire with three armies: soldiers to conquer, workers to build, civil servants to administer." Three pairs of objects hanging above the banner illustrated his motto: a crossed arrow and sword, a hammer and chisel, and a brush and bamboo scroll.

Feeling ill at ease, Sam tiptoed out of the room. He preferred the company of the statues. He continued his exploration on the other shore. A darker area waited at the base of the mass of boulders. . . . Was that the way out?

When Sam stepped onto the sandy beach, he began to feel the twin pulses in his chest strengthening. *There must be another stone statue nearby!* A round door set in the wall of boulders led to a very simple grotto cut into the rock. And right in the middle of it . . .

For a moment, Sam stood stock-still, torn by contradictory feelings. A stone was there, and it was the right one, he was sure; he could feel the pulse beating hard within him. But the stone had neither sun nor cavity. It was completely smooth — and completely unusable!

Sam ran his hands all over the featureless rock, trying to understand the situation. The stone was alive; every molecule in his body told him so. But where was he supposed to put the Golden Circle and the coins? The stone was still raw, as if nobody had yet . . .

The legend of Imhotep, he suddenly thought. Setni had said that Thoth gave Imhotep the gift of creating stones. Moreover, Setni had added that under certain circumstances, an experienced traveler could carve his own: "Someone who travels the paths of Time feels the urge to carve the sun of Re at least once. If he chooses the place with care, and especially if his intentions are pure, the spell can work and the stone comes alive."

So this was the ultimate challenge facing Sam in Qin's tomb: to create his own stone statue!

"But I don't know how to do that," he moaned aloud. "I don't have any tools. I need something to carve with. You know, like a mallet or something."

Tools, he thought. Wait a minute — he knew where he'd

seen some! Without wasting a second, he sprinted back to Qin's mausoleum. Reaching up over the banner, he grabbed the hammer and chisel from the wall. He was about to leave the room when a rattling behind him froze his blood.

"Wait!" called a voice from beyond the grave.

CHAPTER NINE

Qin Shi Huang

Sam turned around in slow motion, as if all his joints had suddenly seized up. He couldn't believe what he was seeing. Emperor Qin had sat up and was pushing the curtain of pearls aside with a trembling hand. *A zombie!* thought Sam. *The man's a zombie!* He wanted to flee, but the old man spoke again.

"You and I have some talking to do. Come closer so I can see you."

Robot-like, Sam obeyed, unable to resist a will that seemed forged in the depths of time. Qin's features were those of a man burdened by the years. His hair and beard were still a handsome gray, but his face was just skin and bones, and the pupils of his eyes were almost white.

"You are very young," Qin grumbled, tying the pearl curtain out of the way. "He did not warn me."

"He?" whispered Sam.

"Yes. He promised that someone would come, but he could not predict when, and certainly not who. In any case, he did not think it would be a boy."

Qin's vocal cords seemed to be fraying with every word. How long had it been since he last spoke?

"You aren't . . . ?" Sam stammered. "I mean, when I first came by, you looked . . ."

Qin gave what may have been a burst of laughter, but it sounded like the creaking of a rusty hinge.

"Dead, do you mean? I am, in some ways, at least to those who buried me. How long ago was that? A hundred years? Two hundred? Three? I no longer remember. But if it makes you feel any better, I will be dead again soon. That is the order of things."

"I don't understand," admitted Sam.

"First, fetch me some water," Qin ordered by way of reply. "I am thirsty. Then I will explain. Go on," he repeated, seeing that Sam hadn't moved. "There is a well just behind us. My tomb was dug above the Three Springs, which have the clearest water in Xi'an province. You can leave your instruments here; I do not intend to steal them."

Sam put the hammer and chisel on one of the chairs and did as he was instructed. The well was a few yards away, equipped with a crank that raised and lowered a little ceramic bucket. Sam worked the chain first one way then the other, and sniffed the water he drew: It was clear and fresh. He thirstily took a swallow, then poured the rest into one of the porcelain jugs by the well. Back inside the temple, he held the water out to the emperor, who was now sitting on the edge of his bed. Qin took the jug without thanking him and made an alarming gurgle as he drained it. He swallowed the last drop and smacked his lips loudly.

"Ah!" he exclaimed in a clearer voice. "Drinking is what I

miss the most." He pointed a reproachful finger at Sam. "Know that you should always bow when you serve the emperor. Just because you come from some barbarian backwater does not mean you can forget your manners. And stop looking at me so stupidly. I have not spent my time waiting for a young fool with the eyes of a stunned flounder. Now sit down and do not interrupt me. I may look old and worn, but this arm of mine once vanquished my wartime enemies, and it can still give you a good beating."

Qin raised the long black cane, which was decorated with golden threads, and Sam diplomatically pretended to submit. He sat in one of the chairs, under the satisfied old man's milky gaze.

"All right, that is better," Qin said. "To start with, you should know some things about me. Open your ears, because you will be the last person to hear them and I do not want them to be lost. Judging by your rudeness, you probably cannot appreciate the signal honor of being in the presence of the illustrious Qin Shi Huang, the first emperor of China."

He paused to enjoy his title, and Sam mimed an expression of boundless admiration.

"As this inscription on the wall proclaims, I am the one Heaven selected to create the most powerful and enduring kingdom in the world. To do so, I gave it a stable currency, clear laws, a new kind of writing, and simple units for counting and weighing. I also had thousands of roads and canals built and erected a great wall to protect them, the likes of which had never been seen. In short, I made this country capable of defying time."

He nodded in a self-satisfied way.

"By the way, does China still exist in your time?"

"Sure it does!" said Sam.

"Is it the first among nations?"

Sam had to watch his step here. "Well, in some ways, yes."

"There you go! And all thanks to me! Do you realize the incredible favor I am showing by receiving you?"

"Incredible is the word for it," said Sam, pouring it on.

"Good, good," said Qin happily. "Your mind is beginning to open. But you must understand that I could not undertake such a task without forcing men and destiny a little. I have not always been understood," he said, clasping his shaky hands. "I had to fight a great deal of reluctance and opposition. Some stood against me and I had to punish them."

How many wars and how many victims? wondered Sam, whose eyes had been opened by his journeys through the centuries.

"As I extended my domination across the world," said Qin with a sigh, "I was led to make mistakes, some of them serious."

Silence fell, and Sam would have sworn that the emperor's pale gaze had become moist.

"It was no longer enough for me to extend my empire over peoples, you see. I wanted to extend it for eternity. Not just to rule over my fellows, but also over their children, their children's children, and all the generations to come. I decided to become immortal."

He briefly looked away, as if the admission pained him. Then, in an intimate tone, he asked, "Have you heard of Mount Penglai, young man?"

Sam shook his head.

"It is located on a distant island in the eastern seas. According to the ancients, it is the seat of immortality. Alas, every expedition I sent there failed or disappeared. Only one returned, with a sage who called himself Master Lu. He claimed to have climbed Mount Penglai and learned its secrets. As proof, he taught me a kind of meditation that allows the initiate to attain a state of bliss in which he floats free of present time. To enter this state, you must listen to the flow of Time within you and slow your heartbeat until the two are synchronized. If you are able to do that, you can slow the passing of seconds and minutes to the point of abstracting yourself from the normal course of your life. I was in that state of bliss when you found me earlier — a slumber of the soul in which the sleeper is only slightly affected by the aging of his body."

Qin frowned at the empty water jug, cleared his throat, and went on.

"Within a few weeks, Master Lu managed to gain my trust, unfortunately. He said that the state of bliss he taught me was only the first step on the path to eternity, but that if I scrupulously followed his advice, I would soon attain what I desired. Better yet, I might be able to learn the art of traveling between time periods. But to do that, he said I first had to go on a pilgrimage to the sacred mountains, so that Heaven might purify my soul and make me fit to receive this gift. Blinded by my lust for power, I was weak enough to believe him, and I set out.

"When I returned to my capital after long months of wandering along the fringes of the empire, I found that Master Lu had used my absence to accumulate power and riches. Still blinded by my dream of eternal life, I chose to ignore this." Qin sighed deeply. "Worse still, one day the scholars of the court presented themselves to express their suspicions about Master Lu and his true intentions. I not only refused to listen to them, I flew into a blind rage. They were demanding nothing less than the exile of the man who would make me immortal! Encouraged by that miserable snake Lu, I chose to punish them in exemplary fashion. Despite their supplications, despite the tears of their wives and the cries of their children, four hundred and sixty of them were executed to appease my anger. Buried alive," he sighed again. "On my order, and by my will."

Qin put his head in his hands and rubbed his temples.

"Their screams still haunt me. Strange, is it not? I, who for so many years remained unmoved by the deaths of my enemies, on that day lost both the ability to sleep and my hunger for immortality. Perhaps my stay in the sacred mountain had made me better than I was, after all. Who can tell?"

He removed his hands from his face, seeking an approval that Sam would have found hard to give.

"At first I was tempted to take revenge on the corrupt sage Lu, the man I considered to be the cause of everything," he continued. "But that was just another way of hiding my face. I was the only person responsible for the massacre, and sacrificing Master Lu would simply be making somebody else pay for my crime. So I merely banished him from the empire, forbidding him to come within ten thousand paces of my borders. As for myself, what sentence did I deserve but death? And who could be the executioner, unless it was I myself? I had to kill myself to erase my misdeeds.

"On the eve of the day I had chosen to end it all, I came to meditate one last time in this tomb. Its construction had just been finished after eighteen years of demanding labor. But where I hoped to be alone, I had an unexpected encounter. A small, dark-skinned man with a shaved head appeared out of nowhere. I drew my sword, thinking it was the ghost of one of the scholars I had executed, but he used some sort of magic trick to disarm me. Then he forced me to listen to him."

A small, dark-skinned man with a shaved head, thought Sam. *Who could it be but Setni, the high priest of Amon?*

"The man explained that he came from another world and that he knew how to travel at will along the course of Time. He knew what had happened here and offered me the chance to redeem myself. I could have called for my guards, but I immediately knew this man was telling the truth. If he could travel to the past, I asked him, why did he not instead suggest that I not execute the scholars? But he claimed that what was done was done, and that wanting to change the course of fate often led to a series of even greater catastrophes."

"I know him," Sam exclaimed aloud. "He's the guardian of the stone statues — a good man of great wisdom. He helped me too, just when I needed it most."

"The guardian of the stone statues," repeated the emperor. "Yes, that fits. It involved those strange stones. While I was away, Master Lu had carved one with an unusual sun in the part of the grounds defended by my crossbowmen. He had started a second one in the grotto nearby, but I banished him before he could finish it. I suggested to the little man that I destroy them, since Master Lu used them, but he replied that destroying such sculptures was a sacrilege. He said he had a better idea, which would both preserve the statues and give meaning to my remorse."

Qin Shi Huang rose to his feet with a groan. He took a few shaky steps over to one of the vase lights and inspected its contents.

"Just as I thought! The oil is almost gone but there is still plenty of wick. If I had the energy I would refill them all so they would burn for days and days. I have done it often enough up to now."

He turned to Sam. "So this is what I promised your guardian of the stones. I faked my death, arranged my funeral, and have been waiting here for someone to free me. I have used meditation and the state of bliss to extend my stay as long as possible. I wake up from time to time, eat from the food stores, refill the oil for the lights, drink water from the Three Springs, and wander in the garden — all the while waiting for my visitor to come."

"And your visitor is me?" croaked Sam.

The emperor leaned both hands on the cane in front of him.

"That is what I have to establish, my young friend. The little man insisted that I deliver a message to the person who reached me. Not give him anything in writing, but speak to him directly, to be sure this precious information did not fall into the wrong hands. Anyone can read a piece of writing or calligraphy, including someone with evil intentions. My role is to make sure that the person I deliver this message to is worthy of it. Your guardian of the stones figured that someone like me, having lived what I have lived, with my excesses and my faults but also my desire to repent, would be able to separate the wheat from the chaff."

For the first time since the beginning of their talk, Qin Shi Huang's face brightened a little.

"Aside from your deplorable manners and your obvious lack of worldliness, I doubt that you have evil designs. I am even impressed that someone as young as you could have avoided the traps my builders designed. That in itself is a sign of nobility!"

"What's . . . what's the message?" asked Sam.

Qin stared at him intently.

"First I must be sure that you have the necessary qualities, my boy. Give me your hands."

The emperor laid his cane across a chair and seized both of Sam's wrists.

"Close your eyes."

Sam obeyed as the bony fingers felt his wrists, as if looking for his pulse.

"They are both there," murmured the emperor. "Just as it should be. You can feel them, can you not?"

But aside from the old man's parchment-like skin, Sam couldn't feel anything at all.

"I don't know. What am I supposed to —"

"Concentrate instead of arguing. Can you not hear it, inside your chest? There is your heartbeat, of course, but there is something else. Another beat, another pulse, but much slower. I can perceive it just by touching you. It is strong and power-ful; so much the better. It is the rhythm of Time. Most people are completely unaware of it, but it flows through us as it flows through all things. If you wish to leave here you must learn to master it. Slow yourself in order to master yourself, and master it. Only then will it become your ally."

He released Sam's hands. Sam opened his eyes to see Qin Shi Huang looking almost friendly.

"The sap of Time flows powerfully in you, young man. I believe you are worthy of receiving the message. It is just a single sentence, and you must not ask me what it means, because I do not know. But your guardian of the stones felt it was of the greatest importance, able to tip the world toward good or toward evil. I have stayed alive until now so it could reach you."

"What's the sentence?" urged Sam.

"The little man said: 'Two suns cannot shine at the same time.'"

Sam wasn't sure he'd heard right. "'Two suns can't shine at the same time'? That's it?"

"Word for word."

"Nothing else?" Sam was baffled. "It doesn't make any sense!"

"There you go with your bad manners again," scolded Qin. "Do you trust this guardian of the stones, yes or no?"

"Of course, but —"

"Then you must not doubt him but rather yourself. Perhaps you are not yet worthy of the trust that others show you!"

"Trust? I'm not here for that. I've got a friend — she's waiting for me —"

The emperor shrugged his shoulders wearily and went to sit on the bed.

"That is enough, my boy. You must go. I have told you what you needed to know; I have spoken of the rhythm of Time. My debt is paid. None of this concerns me anymore. I also have a woman friend waiting for me, and I am very late for our meeting."

He stretched out with a sigh, as if every bone in his body hurt.

"Make good use of what you have learned, and be especially careful not to reveal it to anyone. As for me . . ."

Without paying Sam any further heed, Qin carefully positioned himself on the bed.

"She has been waiting for so long, it would not be proper to make her languish anymore, would it?"

He smoothed his hair and beard, as if he wanted to look his best for his ultimate rendezvous. He then stretched his arms along his body, slowing his breathing until it was barely audible.

"I only hope that it happens quickly," he murmured as he closed his eyes.

Sam stood helplessly, unsure of what to do. Should he intervene? Shake Qin and urge him to live? But by what right, and for what purpose?

In the end he decided that it was best to respect the old man's last wishes: to leave him in peace, face-to-face with eternity.

CHAPTER TEN

In Praise of Slowness

With Qin's words still ringing in his ears, Sam raced across the bridges to the far shore next to the boulders, opened the grotto door, and stood facing Master Lu's smooth stone. What did the sage have in mind by carving two Thoth stones in almost the same place? Did it have some connection to Setni's secret phrase, "Two suns cannot shine at the same time," and if so, what was it?

That the high priest of Amon had traveled here added to Sam's feeling of strangeness. The emperor said that even Setni didn't know the identity of the person who would visit the tomb. So was this curious formula really destined for *him*?

He hefted the hammer, trying to remember his experience in Egypt many centuries earlier. Peneb, the head of the workers decorating Setni's tomb, had managed to create perfect shapes and faces, his tools dancing over the rock. It looked easy then — maybe it would be easy now!

Sam set the Meriweserre bracelet against the stone so as to estimate the respective positions of the sun, its rays, and the transport cavity. He could easily have drawn them with paper and pencil. But with a hammer and chisel . . . Picking up his tools, Sam cautiously chipped at the upper part of the block to outline the solar disk. But what his efforts produced was neither very clear nor very round. Chips flew in every direction, but instead of a circle, his rough sun looked more like a flat tire studded with nails. It was not a good beginning.

He then decided to work on the transport cavity, which would require less skill and allow him to refine his technique. But there again the results were less than ideal. His hammer blows either barely dented the surface or skated off every which way in long ugly scratches, without producing the desired depth. But Sam *had* to find a way to do this; his and Alicia's lives depended on it!

He thought about trying to retrace his steps and returning to the stone statue by which he'd arrived, but given the booby traps he'd already encountered, that hardly seemed wise. To stem a rising wave of panic, Sam closed his eyes and breathed deeply. He could strongly feel the pulse from the stone, and was positive it could take him wherever he wanted. He just had to manage to carve it.

The stone's pulse — what had Qin told him about that? To escape from here, he had to master the rhythm of Time flowing through him, by slowing himself. *But how do you slow yourself down?* Sam wondered dubiously.

Standing in the shadowy grotto, he tried to concentrate. Perhaps he could slow himself by controlling his pulse. Every time he went to sleep, his heartbeat slowed, his body relaxed — a little like his comatose father, whose pulse was so weak. Or like Qin Shi Huang himself, who entered the state of bliss that delayed his aging so effectively. *Yes,* thought Sam. *First slow my heartbeat in order to "slow" myself.*

He began by driving all random thoughts from his mind, focusing only on the rhythm in his chest. As he concentrated, he gradually began to feel as if he were somehow entering himself, getting closer to his heart. With an extra effort, he was almost able to follow the flow of blood through his two ventricles. The right one sent the precious fluid to pick up oxygen from his lungs; the left one sent it to the rest of his organs. The auricles filled and emptied, the valves opened and closed, the movement of life itself pulsed within him. And right behind it beat that other pulse, calmer, more serene, that he absolutely had to match.

Sam felt filled with well-being, experiencing the kind of bliss he previously knew only when falling asleep. Yet he was absolutely lucid, all of his senses alert and focused on making the two rhythms within him beat as one. Quietly and obediently, his heartbeat began to slow, as if it had been prepared for this forever. Its rate fell to the rhythm of Time, matching it and merging with it.

Sam opened his eyes. Around him, the grotto had changed — or rather, the way he was seeing it had changed. Everything looked luminous, awash in a kind of soft, greenish fog. There was something unusual about Sam's gestures as well: Each one set off tiny, distinct vibrations in the air that expanded in concentric circles like ripples in water. Slowing his heartbeat certainly had odd effects on the way he perceived the world!

The stone, especially, now appeared to him in a new light.

Just by looking at it, Sam could discern the exact shape of the sun and its rays, as if they were hidden within the rock, just waiting to be freed. The stone held everything he needed for his journey; he just had to be able to see it.

Sam picked up the hammer and chisel with new confidence. Suddenly everything seemed so simple! He started tapping at the rock to liberate the sun he glimpsed within it. A perfect circle gradually emerged, surrounded by six skillfully drawn slits. With an ever-firmer hand, he effortlessly carved the lower part of the block, each of his blows precisely excavating the transport cavity. Like Imhotep and Setni before him, Sam too was mastering the art of carving a stone statue!

The task completed, he set down his tools, unable to say whether it had taken him an hour or a minute. He was still adrift in another temporal dimension, where the landmarks were no longer the same. He closed his eyes to allow his heartbeat to return to its normal rate. As it did, he felt a dry crack in the air, like a giant rubber band snapping. He'd heard that noise before, he realized — the day he met Setni, in the Sainte-Mary house in 1932. A gang of punks squatting in the house had rushed the old priest, but when he raised his cane, Time had miraculously seemed to slow down. His attackers froze in their tracks as he dispatched them one after another. After routing his assailants, Setni had released his hold on Time, and it began to flow again with that same whip-crack sound. In slowing Time around him, had Sam just duplicated Setni's exploit?

He opened his eyes, looking for a clue that would confirm his hunch, but the grotto looked just the way it had before.

Nothing had changed except for the stone statue, which now displayed a magnificent carved sun and cavity. Sam had managed to sculpt his own exit!

He pulled the map of Rome from his pocket, stuffed it into the cavity, and looked at Pope Clement VII's coin. Alicia had already been waiting for him for much too long.

CHAPTER 11

Blanketed in Fog

When Sam opened his eyes, he felt as if he'd been wrapped in a damp, white blanket: All-encompassing fog had replaced the darkness under the hill. He gratefully filled his lungs with fresh air. It was so much more pleasant than the stillness in Qin's tomb!

He stood up, dusted himself off, and gazed at the impressive wall above him. According to the map of Rome, the stone statue stood at the foot of the city's ramparts. That seemed about right, especially when Sam noticed some graffiti on the wall a few feet above the ground: a pair of long horns with a sun in the middle. It was a Hathor sign, the emblem the Arkeos man used to time travel — that *Rudolf* used to time travel, Sam remembered; but it was easier to think of his enemy by the older, less personal name. Searching the weeds below the Hathor mark, Sam soon found a suspicious-looking mound of earth. A little digging uncovered the stone statue, which the Arkeos man had covered with dirt. Sam retrieved the Meriweserre bracelet, which was dirty but intact, as well as the Clement VII coin and the map of Rome. He unfolded the latter in hopes of getting his bearings in spite of the fog.

The engraving showed a black-and-white view of Rome from some high hill. The artist didn't have much of a grasp of perspective, because the houses huddled like frightened chicks around outsized monuments. Three numbers were written on the map in Magic Marker. The number 1, which represented the stone statue, was indeed at the foot of Rome's western fortifications. But to get to number 2, namely the library where *The Treatise on the Thirteen Virtues of Magic* was hidden, Sam would have to get into the city, and the illustration didn't show any gate nearby. Number 3, his rendezvous with Captain Diavilo, lay on the other side of a river called the Tiber. But distances and perspective were drawn so crudely that it was hard to set much store by them. It was as if the artist had decided to represent Rome through its notable architecture while ignoring the rest of the city — hardly the reliable, accurate map Sam would need to find his way.

He decided to try his luck by following the wall to his right. After a few minutes' walking, he reached the banks of a river that flowed right along the ramparts. The only way to go farther would be to swim. In the distance, he could hear a strange clamor of muffled shouts and occasional jingling. Was it morning or evening? Had the attack begun or was it already over? Whatever the case, no one seemed to be around.

Retracing his steps, Sam could see through breaks in the fog that the wall was hardly uniform. Brick alternated with stone, and parts of the ramparts were topped by roofs, as if they'd been incorporated into houses. Out on the river, he spied what looked like jetties, with long black shapes that might be boats tied to them. Sam thought he might be able to borrow a boat to cross to the far shore and Captain Diavilo's camp — provided he was first able to reach the library, of course!

He passed the place with the Hathor sign, climbed a hill-ock where the wall made a right angle, and found himself on a paved road lined with gardens and huts. Now that Sam was higher, the fog was less dense, and surrounding noises reached him much more clearly. Rumblings, distant whinnying, and metallic clanking all merged into a huge roar, as if a storm of soldiers and horses was preparing to break over Rome. What would happen if he couldn't take cover before Charles V unleashed his troops?

"Over here!"

The voice seemed to come out of nowhere.

"Mamina, over here! They're already at the Torrione Gate!"

It sounded like a young man, standing somewhere atop the wall. Just then a woman in a hooded cape emerged from the fog carrying two big baskets. She looked quite old and was panting as she hurried toward the wall.

"Here I am, Enzo!" she gasped. "Hold the ladder and I'll —"

She stopped dead when she saw Sam.

"What are you doing here, *ragazzo*? Everybody's supposed to be inside the walls!"

In the course of his travels, Sam had mastered the art of giving vague yet plausible reasons to explain his presence in places he should never have been.

"That's just it, I was trying to get inside," he promptly replied, speaking a melodious language that ran trippingly on his tongue. "I fell asleep on the riverbank and when I woke up, the fog had come in. I got lost."

The unknown woman shot him a sharp glance. "You must have been drunk to fall asleep outside, considering what's about to happen!"

"Yeah, I guess I did have a bit to drink," lied Sam, looking shamefaced.

"Mamina!" called the voice from above them. "I have to go to my position on the battlements!"

"That's Enzo, my helper," said the old lady. "He's all in a hurry to get stuck with a pike or shot by a harquebus. Crazy boy! As if he'll keep Rome from falling all by himself! But I can't make him listen to reason. He loves his city more than he loves himself."

She held out one of her baskets, which was covered with a cloth.

"Lend me a hand, *ragazzo*. I may not be able to save Enzo's life, but maybe I can save yours."

Sam took the basket, and she hurried on again, trotting confidently through the fog. He followed her to a crude ladder leaning against the stone wall, its top lost in the mist. Despite her age, the old woman briskly climbed the rungs and disappeared into the grayness.

"Come on!" she ordered after a few seconds. "And be careful not to spill my plants!"

Sam slipped his arm through the basket handle and headed up the ladder, which felt dangerously rickety. As he reached the top rungs, a young man with long brown hair extended a hand to him, which Sam gratefully accepted. He climbed over a windowsill into a mansard room with two tables spread with plants and leaves. The mix of smells in the room was so powerful, it made his head spin.

"Pull up the ladder and bar the shutters, Enzo," said Mamina.

The young man did as he was told while excitedly talking to Sam.

"So you were outside, were you? What's the news? They say there are at least twenty thousand of them, maybe thirty thousand! Besides the Spaniards and the Germans, there are mercenaries from all over Europe: Gascons, Burgundians, Grisons — even Italians in the pay of those Colonna traitors, may they burn in hell! And that scum wants to kill every last one of us!"

"All this because our pope is allied with the king of France," sighed the old lady.

"And the king of France is fighting Charles the Fifth?" Sam guessed.

"That's right — Charles the Fifth and his dogs!" Enzo closed and secured the wooden shutters. "And if we don't stop them from entering the city, they're going to destroy everything! Everybody knows Charles can't pay his troops, so the soldiers will take it out on us."

"*And* on my botanical garden," added Mamina, who was examining what she had gathered by the light of a candle. "Those savages won't think twice about trampling my medicines!"

She held up a yellow root that looked like a wrinkled potato with arms, legs, and a head of hippie hair. It was ginseng, which Sam had seen at home when his mother was still alive and occasionally cooked an Asian-style meal.

"This is worth its weight in gold, *ragazzo*. I would hate to lose it. I even sell it to the pope; it helps his circulation."

"You're a doctor," guessed Sam.

"An herbalist, *ragazzo*. Haven't you ever seen my shop in the Borgo?"

"Er, no, I'm not from Rome," he stammered.

"So you're a novice pilgrim?" asked Enzo. "That would explain why you're wearing white. Well, you picked a bad time, friend. Our holy city has become a trap for all good Christians. And if we don't rise up together against those barbarians —"

"Easy, Enzo! If this boy is here for his devotions, don't try to make him take up arms! As for you, instead of being in such a hurry to die, you'd do better to follow me to the pope's palace and then to Castel Sant'Angelo. There, at least, you'd be safe!"

"There's no way I'm going to let my brothers face these unbelievers alone!" Enzo fired back. "If I have to die, it will be with a smile on my lips, because I've served my God! What is more glorious than to sacrifice yourself for the Lord?" he asked, looking at Sam.

Sam lowered his eyes, unsure of what to say. Mamina shrugged and slipped the ginseng into a little canvas bag with various other plants. "Let's go," she said.

They went down a trapdoor at the back of the room into the herbalist's shop. It was an extraordinary place, with a big mosaic of a tree on the floor, bunches of flowers and leaves hanging from blackened beams, and high shelves of pots bearing labels in Latin. The smells ranged from the floral notes of a perfume store to the reek of an old garbage can.

"I have to leave, Mamina," Enzo announced. "My comrades will think I'm a coward if I don't show up soon!"

Enzo put a coat of chain mail over his leather jacket, pulled his long hair back so it fit under his metal helmet, and picked up a rifle with a short stock. Mamina hugged him in silence, but he gently pulled himself free. He opened the door to an alarming din from the outside. On the threshold, he turned to Sam. "There's another helmet and a lance near the counter, if you don't want to rue the day you abandoned your pope and your Church."

He closed the door, returning the room to its fragile, time-less peace.

"What a pity!" moaned Mamina. "Under that man-at-arms bluster he's just a headstrong rapscallion! A child! I pray that his fervor will be rewarded, and our Lord will spare him. Really, the number of ugly things I've had to see in this life-time . . ." She picked up the helmet and lance Enzo had mentioned and tossed them with a clatter onto the worktable. "That said, if you want to accompany me to the Vatican, there's no reason why you shouldn't be armed. A lot of criminals and marauders have taken shelter inside our walls. I may have to abandon my shop to Charles's bully boys, but I intend to take a few treasures with me."

Using one of the keys hanging at her waist, she opened a drawer under the counter, took out a well-filled leather coin purse, and stuffed it into her bag.

"A year's worth of concoctions and poultices, *ragazzo*! Money earned by the sweat of an old woman's brow, by my faith. Since you're here, you'll serve as a bodyguard for me and my savings, won't you? At least keep us company as far as the pope's palace. In fact, it would be a good idea if you took ref-uge there too. I can get you in, if you like."

"Well . . ." Sam hesitated. First and foremost he had to get hold of *The Treatise on the Thirteen Virtues of Magic*. Pulling the map of Rome from his pocket, he said, "A friend told me about some places in Rome I absolutely had to visit — especially this library. I know the circumstances aren't ideal, but I'll never have another chance."

Mamina turned the map around and frowned.

"Mmmhh . . . I know this kind of print. You can buy one from any street seller in town. As for these numbers . . ." She pointed to the place where the stone was hidden. "This first one is outside the city walls, close to the Santo Spirito hospital. Except for orphans and the sick, I don't know that there's much to see there. Number 2 seems to be the pope's library, if that's the one you mean. It's inside the Vatican, and I hear they've got the most beautiful collection of books in all Christendom. As for this number 3 . . ."

Her mouth puckered as if she'd bitten into a lemon.

"That's the Colosseum, if I'm not mistaken. It's just for people who like ruins, and frankly, I wouldn't advise you to go there right now."

"Why not?" asked Sam, worried by the herbalist's look of disgust.

"Rumor has it the Colonna family has set up camp there."

"The Colonna family?"

"Easy to see you aren't from around here, *ragazzo*! The Colonna are a very old Roman family, and they've opposed Clement the Seventh ever since he was elected pope. They threw in their lot with Charles the Fifth when the war began, and they've stationed their troops a little to the rear, waiting to see which way the wind blows. But their soldiers are worse than most mercenaries, take it from me. More vicious than the Spaniards, greedier than the Germans, and nastier than either. I wouldn't give somebody like you much of a chance if you fell into their clutches." Lowering her voice, the herbalist continued: "Especially with Captain Diavilo, the man who commands them. To show how cruel he is, you know what his soldiers call him? '*Il Diavolo*' — the Devil! Imagine that!"

Mamina crossed herself, as if merely saying his name might summon the demon himself.

Sam figured it might be wise to accept the helmet and lance after all.

CHAPTER TWELVE

The Siege of Rome

Rome was now at war for real. The earlier distant rumbling had suddenly broken like a storm above the ramparts, and the battle to protect the city raged all around Sam and Mamina. Men busied themselves around huge pots set over blazing fires at the foot of the walls, filling buckets with a thick, hot substance to pour down on the attackers. A little farther on, a bucket brigade supplied the men on the battlements with big rocks and other missiles. A fine rain had started to fall, though without dissipating the fog, and the roar of the fighting seemed to drift down from the sky, as if invisible gods were clashing above the white clouds. Occasionally, more distinct yells ripped the air, giving the celestial violence a human dimension.

"The siege ladder! Shove away the ladder on the right!"

"Pitch! More pitch, fast!"

"I die in the name of our glorious Lord. . . . Ahhh!"

In these apocalyptic surroundings, Mamina walked quickly across the gleaming pavement, head bent. Sam walked beside her, loaded down with the bags she had peremptorily hung around his neck, his skull squeezed into a tin can of a helmet and his feet flopping in a too-big pair of sandals. He leaned on his lance and tried to look martial.

Leaving the fortifications behind them, they angled into a narrow street, then came out on a wider boulevard where panicked Romans were crisscrossing in every direction. Dozens of silent people seemed to be wandering aimlessly, like a swarm of insects confused by the racket. Some carried bundles, others pulled carts, still others stood stopped without reason.

Mamina, on the other hand, seemed to know exactly where she was going. She walked up a main street lined with barricaded shops whose wrought-iron signs dripped in the rain: baker, cabinetmaker, instrument maker . . . They emerged onto a square dominated by the powerful bulk of a palace with handsome arcades. Like a skittish flock awaiting its shepherd, a frightened crowd huddled near a gate in the north corner. Undaunted, Mamina strode over and started elbowing her way toward the building's entrance, with a somewhat embarrassed Sam at her side. A line of soldiers in blue, yellow, and red uniforms barred the way, ready to cut down anyone who dared to cross. Lowering her hood, the old lady planted herself in front of them.

"I am Mamina of the Santo Spirito herbarium," she announced firmly. "I am here to deliver my Marco Polo panacea to the pope, who ordered it specially."

She nodded to Sam, who opened the bag to display the ginseng root.

"I know your superior, Lieutenant Maladetta, very well," she told the soldier in charge. "And you must recognize me too, considering I've been visiting our Holy Father for the last four years."

Under his polished helmet, the soldier's large reddish mustache quivered in agreement.

"Perfect!" said Mamina with pleasure. "In that case, and given the circumstances, you'll understand that His Holiness mustn't be kept waiting. If he found out that his Swiss guards prevented his remedy from being delivered . . ."

Big Mustache glanced questioningly at his comrades, none of whom objected.

"This young man is with me," she said, pointing at Sam.

The Swiss guards raised their halberds to make way, and Mamina dragged her protégé through the gate as an angry murmur rose from the crowd.

"I've got medicine for Pope Clement too," yelled a young woman in a torn coat.

"Take us into Sant'Angelo under His Holiness's protection!" someone else demanded.

For want of more convincing recommendations, however, the guards remained unyielding. The gate closed, and Mamina took Sam's arm, whispering in his ear.

"I'm sorry, *ragazzo*. I had to bend the truth a little, I know. But what else could I do? Otherwise they'd never have let us through."

They crossed an outer courtyard full of activity. A platoon of Swiss guards raced toward a side doorway, groups of prelates in black and white conferred in the walkways, and servants by the dozen carried huge trunks here and there. It was clear that everybody expected the papal palace to be overrun, and it was urgent to move everything out.

"See that portico at the back?" asked Mamina, pointing to a covered passageway between two columns. "It leads to the

Parrot Court. That's the way to the pontiff's library. I don't know what kind of welcome they'll give you in these circumstances, but if you're really set on going there . . ."

She relieved him of the bags he was carrying.

"As for me, I'll try to make it to Castel Sant'Angelo. If you change your mind, climb those stairs on the right and cross the terrace; you might catch up with me. Even if I'm not able to see the pope, I have a few cardinals among my customers. There must be one of them who will help me reach the fort."

She gave his wrist an affectionate squeeze and tottered off toward the great marble staircase.

Sam headed for the portico, which led to another courtyard dominated by a huge church under construction, whose scaffolding seemed to reach to the sky. Faced with several buildings, Sam chose the one whose façade showed a book and two crossed keys. It had to be the papal library.

The door stood open, and in the vestibule Sam ran into a small man with thinning blond hair who was packing books into a large, ironbound chest. The man straightened up and stared at Sam, taken aback by his unconventional outfit.

"I asked for help, but I didn't expect this," he said. "Wasn't there a soldier or a Swiss guard available?"

Sam's mind raced to come up with an answer that would give away as little as possible.

"Many are on the ramparts," he said.

"The ramparts, of course," agreed the small man sarcastically. "All of my assistants rushed over there. What use are books when you could be at war, right? Man likes to destroy with one hand what he has built with the other. Well, that's just too bad," he said defiantly. "I plan to fight too, in my own

97

way. And the stakes are high; we're talking about saving our culture. Are you prepared to fight for books, my boy?"

Sam nodded, prepared to agree with anything that got him closer to Klugg's *Treatise*.

"That's perfect. In that case, come along."

Sam followed him into the library, which appeared to be a series of three richly decorated rooms furnished with imposing cabinets, several of which stood open.

"You've never been in here, I imagine?"

Sam shook his head.

"And what is your exact position in the palace? Kitchen boy? Stable groom?"

"Er . . . herbalist. That is, I help Mamina, the Santo Spirito herbalist. She insisted that we come here because of the battle. I came along because I wanted to see the library."

He spoke these last words with a candor that must have pleased the man, whose eyes now gleamed with wry amusement.

"So you wanted to see the library? A laudable curiosity, I must say! And one I wish all the inhabitants of this palace shared, including the most illustrious! My name is Patrizio Bocceron," he said, giving a mock bow. "I am the pope's librarian. And if you like books, you're in for a treat. This is the finest collection of manuscripts and printed works in the world!"

He spread his arms, gesturing at the space in front of him.

"This first room is devoted to Latin authors: St. Augustine, Tacitus, Seneca, and many others. The second is given over to Greek works on theater, philosophy, medicine, astrology, and so forth. The third room, which is called the Great Library, contains works that are fragile or ones that our Church does not want circulating freely. As you can imagine, I can't allow you in there. On the other hand," he continued with a smile, "I will need your arms for the two other rooms."

He walked to the center of the Greek room and pointed to an open cabinet housing dozens of volumes with intricately decorated bindings.

"Unfortunately, we don't have time to get all five thousand of our volumes to safety," said the librarian with regret. "So I have to sort through them and identify the ones that must be saved at all cost. For example, which of these should I save from our enemies: a rare edition of Aristotle's *Physics* or this only copy of Ptolemy's *Geography*? It's an impossible choice, like deciding which of your children should live and which should die! But it's a choice that must be made if we want to preserve what we are. After all, the war won't last forever, will it?"

He looked hard at Sam, as if to make sure he understood everything he was saying.

"I'll give you the books I've selected, and you'll pack them in the chest in the vestibule, being careful not to damage them. Then we'll take the chest to a safe place. Do you understand? And take off that helmet; it won't do you any good here."

"I'm glad to help," said Sam. In fact, he was beyond glad — delighted! He had vaguely hoped that the confusion of the war would allow him to get into the library one way or the other, but he would never have imagined being formally invited into the place and asked to look through the books!

So he went to work with good grace, using the greatest care in handling the beautiful volumes, some of which were bound with gold and precious stones. But despite Sam's eagerness, he hadn't lost sight of his goal: Klugg's *Treatise*. He could feel the pulse of Time in his chest grow stronger each time he approached the third room, the very one he was forbidden to enter. Moreover, after inspecting the cabinets in the Latin and Greek rooms, he saw that none of the shelved works looked anything like the *Treatise.* The book he wanted must be in the Great Library.

After half an hour of careful packing, Bocceron decided that the large chest was full, and they should stop trying to add more books. Moreover, the sound of fighting on the walls outside had grown louder, as if the attackers were getting closer to the palace.

"It would be dangerous to stay any longer," he said, adjusting his black cassock. "There are a hundred more books I would take, but . . ."

He closed the now overflowing chest and grabbed one of the metal handles on the side.

"The Sant'Angelo fortress has an annex where the pope's archives are stored," he explained. "The books will be safe there. Let's go, my boy!"

Sam took the other handle. They bent their knees and tried to lift the enormous chest together, but it didn't budge. They tried again, and then a third time, grunting louder, with no more result. It was as if the chest were bolted to the floor.

"Will you look at that!" exclaimed Bocceron. "Our forebears' thoughts are heavier than we imagined. I'm afraid that . . ." He raised the lid, briefly considered the packed books for a moment, then changed his mind. "No, it would be criminal to take fewer of them. We just need some help. Four men and a handcart can't be too much to ask for!"

He pinched his lips with his fingers, thinking hard.

"If I'm able to find Cardinal del Monte, I may be able to convince him," he muttered. "He's a book lover, a real one. At this point, he's probably somewhere over by the Belvedere." Bocceron turned to Sam. "We have no choice; I must get help. The Belvedere is right behind us; I'll be back very soon. Until then, don't let the chest out of your sight, and be careful no bandit enters the library. The scent of plunder has sharpened many an appetite these last days."

He gave his unlikely assistant a pat on the shoulder and ran outside with surprising speed. Sam watched as Bocceron disappeared into the foggy courtyard. He had just a few minutes to get his hands on Klugg's *Treatise*.

CHAPTER THIRTEEN

In the Lion's Mouth

Sam raced through the Latin and Greek rooms and burst into the Great Library. He'd only been able to sneak a few furtive peeks into the room before, and he was now struck by its atmosphere of study and contemplation: the warm light from the stained-glass windows, the smell of wax and old books, the great black table to which manuscripts were attached with silver chains, and the big velvet-covered armchairs. Various objects that reflected a search for knowledge filled the room: an unusual metal globe with a series of interlocking rings; a triangular hourglass two feet tall; calculation instruments that looked like compasses; and a big watch without hands, marked by mysterious gradations.

In addition to a handsome chimney flanked by a pair of stone lion heads, the room held five iron cabinets, four of which were open. Sam searched all the shelves he could reach without seeing anything that looked like Klugg's *Treatise*. He turned the locked cabinet's handle without success, but didn't insist, because the pulse of Time told him that the book was somewhere else. The intensity of the pounding in his chest varied depending on which side of the room he stood: weaker when he went to the right, where the locked cabinet was, stronger when he moved to the left.

Sam positioned himself exactly where the pounding was strongest, in front of an oval mirror whose elaborate frame looked like a golden starburst — a kind of sun, in fact. He glimpsed his own reflection: a young man of fourteen with a dirty shirt, tousled hair — the helmet had plastered it down — a hard face, and eyes that burned with fierce determination. He looked like some street tough out to steal money or food. Someone who didn't have much to lose, anyway.

Sam got a grip on himself; this was no time for brooding. The Arkeos man had spoken of a cabinet with a sun on it that held the *Treatise*. Sam was facing a mirror that could pass for a sun all right, but he didn't see any corresponding cabinet. Yet the rhythm of Time was strongest here, as if a stone statue were right at hand.

On an impulse, he lifted the mirror from the wall and set it on the floor. Hidden behind it was a safe about two feet square, with a sun and six rays right above a small keyhole. The sun was the size of the bracelet, but the slits were merely scratched into the surface, too shallow to accommodate coins. This sun must be meant for something other than traveling. "All right," whispered Sam. "I've got just what you need."

He took the Meriweserre bracelet from his pocket, unhooked it, and removed the six coins. He then set the bracelet on the solar circle. It flashed brightly, and something clicked somewhere. Sam would have loved it if the secret compartment had swung open, but it didn't. He tried pulling with his finger in the keyhole, but to no avail. The sun and the bracelet obviously weren't enough; he also needed a key.

He repeated his moves, trying to understand what was happening. The instant he set the bracelet in position, it blazed with light, and the sharp click sounded again, but it didn't come from the secret compartment. Nor did it come from any of the cabinets, or the frescos of cities and countries on the walls. The fireplace! Yes, it was coming from the fireplace!

The next time he positioned the Meriweserre bracelet, Sam watched the fireplace intently. At the moment of the click, the lion head on the right seemed to move. It was barely perceptible — like a blink of an eye, or a tiny blurry spot on an otherwise sharp photograph. Sam rushed over to the fireplace several times, but he wasn't fast enough to get there before the head stopped moving. After several tries, though, he was able to determine that the animal's jaws opened and closed incredibly quickly, and that something shiny lay inside them. Could it be the key to the safe?

He carefully examined the fireplace's side columns. The stone lion had a handsome mane, slanting eyes, and jaws full of impressive teeth. A tiny slit between the jaws showed that they could open, but the mechanism worked so fast that it was impossible to take anything from between them. Sam strained to open the jaws by hand, but without success. Perhaps he could use a tool, like one of those pointed mathematical instruments. . . .

He looked at the triangular hourglass on the black table and had a sudden flash of insight. The flow of Time, of course!

How stupid he was! The Arkeos man hadn't taken the *Treatise* himself because the lion moved too fast for him to reach the key. He had sent Sam to Qin's mausoleum to acquire the secret of slowing down time — the only way to outpace the lion and rob it of its prey.

Returning to the secret compartment, Sam tried to concentrate. He had to reenter the trance state that had allowed him to carve the stone statue and escape Qin's tomb. He closed his eyes and mentally descended within himself, deliberately slowing his heartbeat. His pulse slackened until it matched the venerable tempo of Time, and the two rhythms started to beat in sync.

Sam opened his eyes and realized that he was again seeing the world through a kind of green filter. He pressed the Meriweserre bracelet onto the sun emblem. At the moment of the "click" — which was now drawn-out and cavernous — he ran toward the fireplace. He felt he was floating through the air, his movements again setting off a series of vibrations that became vast concentric circles, as if he were moving through a liquid dimension. Sounds were amplified and distorted too. In the hushed atmosphere of the library, the sandals Mamina had loaned him thundered like buffalo hoofs, the clamor of fighting outside sounded like an orchestra of bass drums, and men's voices flowed slowly through the stained-glass windows. It reminded Sam of when he was a child and would hold his head underwater in his bath, listening as the noises of the house reached him with unusual clarity and strength.

In three strides Sam was at the fireplace, where the stone lion seemed to be giving a full-throated roar. A golden key glittered on its granite tongue, and Sam was just able to snatch it before the jaws rumbled shut. Success! Sam ran back to the safe, put the key in the keyhole, and turned it.

The door opened with a screech. Behind it, a shelf cut into the thickness of the wall was loaded with books of different sizes and shapes. Sam spotted one whose binding showed a network of thin lines. Its dark blue cover had a black 13 in a Middle Eastern style, exactly like Chamberlain the archaeologist's edition. It was *The Treatise on the Thirteen Virtues of Magic*.

Sam blinked a few times to allow his heart to resume its natural rhythm. His pulse suddenly raced ahead of the slower one it had been pacing. With a violent crack in the air, Time seemed to expand, then abruptly resume its regular course.

The green filter had vanished, and Sam could now admire Klugg's *Treatise* in all its splendor. He eagerly flipped through the book to be sure there was no mistake. It had the same engravings of various stone statues in odd places, alchemical recipes, and the horrible picture of the bat with the child's head. But unlike the last time, when Sam had looked at Chamberlain's copy, he could no longer read the Arabic texts. He had changed places and times, and so his dictionary had changed as well. . . . On the other hand, because he was speaking a language very much like Latin, Klugg's notes in red were now understandable, though a few words remained obscure. In this new dialect, the famous motto on the working of the stone statue came out this way: "He who collects the seven elements will be the master of the sun. If he can make the six lines shine, its heart will be the solution of time. He will then know the heat forever." Not the most elegant translation, but close enough.

Finally Sam turned to the last pages, the ones that had supposedly disappeared during Charles V's invasion. They were all there, and in perfect condition: a dozen pages full of drawings and commentary in red ink. A statue of the god Thoth, a detailed illustration of two Golden Circles, a picture of a man in a turban, coats of arms, cabalistic signs . . . Sam would have liked to examine it at leisure, but this was hardly the time. The librarian could come back at any moment, and he had to put everything away. Still, he had the talisman that would save Alicia!

"It won't be long now," he murmured, as if she were standing next to him. "Trust me."

A clatter of wheels on paving stones outside tore Sam from his reverie. Out in the Parrot Court, a cart or carriage was approaching; Bocceron must have found the help he needed. As Sam started to close the safe, he bumped a small, wax-sealed ivory box. He caught it just before it fell and put it back, then closed the safe. The rattle of carriage wheels was getting louder. Sam quickly rehung the mirror, hid the golden key in the back of one of the open cabinets for Bocceron to find later, and rushed to the vestibule with Klugg's *Treatise* under his arm. He slipped the volume under a nearby sideboard and reached the ironbound chest just as several men and the librarian emerged from the fog.

"Ah, you're still here! That's fine," said Bocceron absently. "Cardinal del Monte was good enough to give me reinforcements, but in exchange I must do a certain favor for His Holiness."

He looked ill at ease, clearly preoccupied by something other than the fate of his precious books.

"Come with me," Bocceron said to a man whose sharp profile suggested a bird of prey. To the four soldiers behind the man, he said, "You others, lift the chest onto the wagon and wait for my return. And I don't want anyone rummaging inside it, all right?"

The Swiss guards obeyed as Hawk Face drew a silver key from beneath his long brown cape and held it up to the librarian.

"Shall we go?" he asked. "Our sovereign pontiff is hardly inclined to patience this morning."

Am I dreaming? wondered Sam. Except for the color, the key looked exactly like the one he had just taken from the lion's mouth. Bocceron examined it in the dim light.

"This is the first time I've ever seen it," he whispered. "And it had to be at a time like this, when everything might be destroyed!"

"These are the circumstances that justify the Holy Father's orders," the other man answered. "Now if we can proceed . . ."

They walked deeper into the library without paying any further attention to Sam, who decided to follow them at a distance. Could there be a second key to unlock the secret compartment behind the mirror? And if their goal was indeed the safe, what could they be looking for there? Sam had an unpleasant feeling it might be *The Treatise on the Thirteen Virtues of Magic.* Hugging the walls, he tiptoed through the Greek room and got as close as he could to the door to the Great Library. The two men had stopped on the left side of the room, where the hidden safe was.

"I really don't know what's inside it," Bocceron was saying. "My predecessor, Nuncio Moretti, told me of the compartment's existence when I arrived. Pope Sixtus the Fourth had entrusted its construction to an Egyptian architect — an odd fellow, Moretti said, but with knowledge beyond compare."

Sam's heart almost stopped. An odd Egyptian — could it be Setni again? He heard a slight click on the tile floor and guessed that the two men had just set down the mirror.

"Amazing, isn't it?" said Bocceron. "I've often wondered what this compartment might hold. The nuncio said there were originally two keys, but one had been lost, and the other was locked in the pope's treasury in Castel Sant'Angelo. I never imagined I would hold it in my hand!"

"His Holiness entrusted it to me with instructions to only give it to you, and to return with the object immediately," said the other man. "What does this sun emblem mean?"

"I have no idea. As far as I know, this Egyptian architect was free to decorate it however he chose. It remains to be seen if this lock even works. . . ."

Some clicking and a now-familiar screech followed. The door to the secret compartment had just been opened.

"Books," exclaimed Bocceron ecstatically. "Books I've never seen before!"

"And the jewel box is on the shelf," said the pope's envoy happily. "Clement will be pleased."

Sam couldn't resist the temptation to look into the room. The librarian had picked up one of the volumes while his companion examined the little ivory box Sam had knocked over earlier.

"I'm going to bring it to him immediately," said the envoy, secreting the box under his cape. He turned to leave, but Bocceron was still absorbed in the new trove he'd discovered.

"We didn't come here to inventory the library," said the man sharply. "My men and I must leave as soon as possible, so if you want to use the cart, I suggest you hurry."

Sam realized that it was time for him to get out of there. He discreetly retraced his steps and, as he went, took one of the curtain tiebacks from the Latin room. Once in the vestibule, he retrieved Klugg's *Treatise* from under the sideboard and tied it to his stomach as best he could. His shirt now had a small bulge, but in the fog nobody would notice. He then went out to join the soldiers standing around the cart, just as a yell echoed from the palace walls.

"Fall back! They've entered the city! Fall back!"

CHAPTER 14

A Small Ivory Box

Word of the attack spread quickly throughout the Vatican. People at windows shouted the news to each other, and prelates quickly filled the Parrot Court, trying to estimate how long it would take the enemy to invade the pope's sacred precinct. The fog was starting to break up, and the rising sun gave the thinning mist an unreal, coppery glow. Most of the city's cannons had fallen silent, meaning that the resistance on the ramparts had ended and the fighting had now moved into the streets. This complicated things for Sam, who had hoped to leave the same way he'd come in, then cross the river and head for Captain Diavilo's camp. He would have to find another way.

Having locked the doors, Bocceron left the library with regret. From the black look that Hawk Face shot him, he seemed to understand that he'd better hurry if he didn't want to be left behind with his chest of books.

"The Holy Father may already have reached Castel Sant'Angelo, and I was supposed to return to him immediately," grumbled the envoy. "There's not a moment to lose!"

"I'm right behind you," said the librarian obediently.

Their little convoy started out, following a complicated route through the palace that would allow the cart to reach the gardens behind the main buildings without any obstacles. Sam lent a hand pushing and pulling the cart through the crowds. When Bocceron recognized a soldier heading down to defend the main gate, he stopped him. The man, who was barely older than Sam and looked badly frightened, paused reluctantly.

"Does anyone know what's happening, Aldo?"

"It's the Spaniards!" gasped the young man. "They overran the ramparts in Santo Spirito by breaking through a window in the walls. There are at least three thousand of them attacking us, and the Germans are right behind them! We have to defend the citadel!"

He waved and ran off.

"We mustn't weaken," said Hawk Face, "or we won't save either our skins or these books!"

They resumed their progress as best they could, moving through halls and courtyards until they came out on a wide gravel terrace. Threading their way between fountains and potted orange trees, they reached a low building that seemed to be the rallying point for the entire palace. Guards were stationed around the crowd of prelates trying to get in, which included richly dressed men as well as women and children. Joining the anxious sighs and animated discussions rising from the queue was an odd cacophony of bird cries. A large aviary was located nearby, and the birds, panicked by the noise, were shrieking and chirping loudly.

"Too many people ahead of us," decided Hawk Face. "We'll have to work something out. I'll need you, Bocceron."

As the two men set off to arrange a pass for the library's treasures, Sam turned to a Swiss guard on his right, who'd been pushing the cart.

"I'm not from Rome," Sam began. "Is this how we get to Castel Sant'Angelo?"

The soldier, a tall, friendly-looking fellow, nodded. "A covered passageway called the *Passetto* runs from this building to the castle. It's the safest way to get there. That's why all these people are waiting," he added, pointing to the people lined up in front of them. "Only the cream of the crop too! Look, that's part of the Orsini family over by the column, and a few of the Conti near the statue of Hercules. And that boy playing with the stick is wearing Frangipani colors. All of Rome's nobility is here!"

"But no Colonna men," Sam dared to say, remembering what Mamina had told him about Clement VII's sworn enemies.

"Not so loud, boy," warned the guard, shooting Sam a knowing look. "The Colonna aren't too popular around here. Though it's not entirely their fault, if you ask me."

"What about Captain Diavilo?" persisted Sam. "He's in charge of their troops, isn't he?"

"Diavilo? He's a beast!" exclaimed the guard, raising his arms to heaven. "My older brother spent some time with him when he was younger. You know what he did the day he turned ten, when his father gave him his first sword? He swung it through the air a couple of times, and then *chop!* He cut his dog's head off! With one whack. Yes, you can roll your eyes — his own dog! My brother says that Diavilo was crazy from the very beginning, and he sure didn't improve with time. You knew he's only got one hand, right? My brother says he lost it when he was captured by the Turks some twenty years ago. They stuck him in one of their filthy prisons without any food, planning to starve him to death. But when they came back after a few weeks, Diavilo was still alive. First he ate rats, then bugs, then moss, and when he didn't have anything else to eat, he cut off his left hand and . . ."

The Swiss guard's face twisted in disgust.

"Anyway, you can imagine what he did. When his jailers took him out, they were so impressed by his courage that they nursed him and let him go. Someone who kills his own dog and can eat a part of himself is no ordinary man, is he?"

Sam nodded, wondering how much of the guard's tale was truth and how much was legend. "If he's so clever and brave, isn't there a chance he'll capture the fortress?"

"Sant'Angelo's impregnable," said the guard confidently. "Take my word for it. For centuries now, none of the popes who took refuge here have ever been forced out. Don't worry, boy, once we're inside, no one else will be able to get in."

"What about getting out?" asked Sam, who was worried about how to reach Alicia.

"You'd have to be crazy to leave the castle when the city's about to be overrun! Besides, I don't see how you could do it unless you had wings. Sant'Angelo is also the toughest prison in Rome, in case you didn't know that. It's perfectly designed to keep anyone from escaping."

Sam forced himself to smile with the Swiss guard, though the prospect of locking himself in a prison no one could escape from was hardly reassuring. Well, too bad. He already had

Klugg's *Treatise*, and nothing was going to stop him from bringing Alicia home.

Thanking the guard, Sam stepped away from the cart to hitch up the *Treatise*, which tended to slide down under his shirt, and to consult his map of the city. On the engraving, Castel Sant'Angelo's impressive defenses made it look formidable, the perfect place to withstand a siege. But to reach the ruins where Captain Diavilo was encamped, Sam would have to cross much of the city — a tall order even in peacetime; perhaps impossible in war.

Sam had been studying the map for a few minutes, trying to work out the best itinerary, when shouts caused him to look up. Someone was walking toward the building, surrounded by a group of cardinals and soldiers and generating great excitement as he went.

"Clement! It's Pope Clement!"

"Bless us, Your Holiness!"

"Take my young son with you, for pity's sake!"

A dozen guards kept the curious at bay, and the pope reached the cart just as Hawk Face rushed over to him.

"Holy Father, forgive my tardiness," he said, bowing deferentially. "I thought you were already in the fortress and —"

"No matter," interrupted Clement VII, signaling his men to move away. "Do you have it?"

While Hawk Face fumbled under his cape, Sam observed the pope. He was about fifty, with a haughty air, prominent nose and cheekbones, and black hair pulled back under a red cap. He wore a spotless long white robe and a red coat over his shoulders and chest. Despite his arrogance, the pope's color was sallow, and heavy circles lay under his dark eyes. Hawk

Face held out the ivory jewel box he'd taken from the secret compartment, and Clement VII weighed it in his palm before opening it.

"So it really exists," he murmured. "I may have a chance of getting out of this after all!"

The onlookers on the esplanade suddenly fell silent, as if aware of the solemnity of the moment. Clement VII broke the box's wax seal with his fingernail and lifted the lid. His face hardened.

"Empty!" he said. "It's empty!"

He angrily threw the box away and resumed walking toward the low building.

"I'm sorry," said Hawk Face, backing away in embarrassment. "I followed Your Holiness's instructions to the letter, and I couldn't anticipate that —"

"I'm not criticizing you!" shouted the pope. "How could you even imagine what this thing contained? Go away now. I don't need you anymore!"

The pope's guards stepped in to push the dismissed man away, but Hawk Face continued. "Your Holiness, remember this chest of books? We need your authorization to carry them to safety in the castle."

Clement VII didn't bother answering, but one of the cardinals following him signaled to Bocceron that he would take care of it.

As the crowd gave way to allow the pope to pass, Sam, who had kept his eye on the jewel box the whole time, snatched it up out of the dirt. He wanted to examine it more carefully than he'd been able to in the library. It was an ancient square box, whose ivory had turned somewhat yellow, about the size of Sam's palm. The lid, partly covered by the red wax seal the pope had broken, was engraved with a kind of hieroglyphic: a crouching ibis-headed figure in profile, possibly Thoth. The box was indeed empty, but the round, inch-wide indentation at the bottom was unmistakable. It had once held a very special ring.

CHAPTER FIFTEEN

The Treatise on the Thirteen Virtues of Magic

Two of the Swiss guards had been sent back to defend the main gate, so Sam had to help carry the chest of books the full length of the passageway overlooking the city. Whenever he could, he glanced through the arrow slits to try to see Diavilo's camp on the other side of the river. But though the fog was still lifting, a steady rain had started to fall, adding a veil of water to the mist.

The *Passetto* was as jammed as a highway at rush hour, and more than once Sam was nearly bowled over by prelates imperiously ordering people out of their way. The chest's iron straps dug into his shoulders and its weight bent his back, but at least nobody paid any attention to him — or to Klugg's *Treatise* lashed to his belly.

As he struggled not to stumble, Sam thought back to the little ivory box, which he had left on the ground of the courtyard, and the jewel it must once have held. The sign of Thoth, the circular indentation, and the fact that the box had been locked away with the *Treatise* all suggested that it once held the Eternity Ring. But in that case, why hadn't the Arkeos man demanded that Sam bring it back to him immediately? Didn't he realize it was in the hidden safe? Or did he already know the box was empty?

"Turn left here!" ordered Bocceron.

They entered the citadel by way of a heavy, nail-studded door, and went up a narrow circular staircase whose high steps were terribly hard to climb. Bocceron led them to the library annex, which he opened with a key on his key chain.

"Set the chest down in the entrance. I'll take care of it."

The friendly Swiss guard straightened his lanky body and heaved a sigh of relief. Sam massaged his upper arms, feeling incredibly light. Fearing that the bump under his shirt would betray him, he planned to slip away, but Bocceron had other ideas.

"Shelving the books will go faster if you help me," he said to Sam. "Especially since you already know them a little."

Sam's gaze wandered across the vaulted room filled with cabinets, chests, and scrolls. It would be a big job.

"First I have to . . ." he began, holding his stomach. "I mean, I need a little privacy."

The guard gave a hearty guffaw, but the others grimaced and turned away. Sam excused himself, promising to come back.

Once outside, he went looking for a quiet place where he could focus on the *Treatise*. It seemed that Sant'Angelo was half palace, half fortress. The extraordinarily thick walls made it look like a military fortification, but inside, it was an elegant residence, with many rooms decorated with frescoes and carved caisson ceilings. The crowd — young and old, men and women — had dispersed throughout the castle;

some were sitting on the ground amid their hurriedly tied bundles, others stood talking about the day's misfortunes, and still others slumped in the few available chairs, dazed with fatigue.

After wandering around for a few minutes, Sam found an upstairs window seat where he could enjoy light and relative quiet. He untied the cord under his shirt and settled himself next to the mullion window. If he was going to have to give the *Treatise* to Captain Diavilo, he wanted to know its secrets first. Moreover, he needed time to study the map and decide how to get out of the citadel.

He immediately skipped to the book's back pages, which Chamberlain said contained crucial information about the Eternity Ring. The section of about a dozen pages contained yet more drawings, maps, cabalistic signs, and annotations in red. Their overall meaning was unclear, but some of the illustrations looked familiar. On the first page of the section, a charcoal sketch showed the ibis-headed god Thoth standing with his arms held out level, a large yellow bracelet on each wrist. Klugg had written a comment below, but Sam had to go over it several times before he could read it, since his "Latin" was only approximate. The paragraph was titled, "The two Golden Circles, the authentic and the impostor," which must be a reference to the bracelet that Thoth himself had fashioned and to the copy made by Meriweserre. "They are like two brothers, who seem close and yet are entirely separate," said the text. "This is why the god of days spreads his arms, one to the east where the sun rises, the other to the west where it sets, <u>to show that they both oppose and complete each other</u>." This last clause was underlined.

The next page had a black-and-white drawing of an imaginary cemetery on an isolated, overgrown hill. Four tombs were lined up, each displaying a sun carved in its base. But despite the artist's effort to make the picture realistic, such a gathering of tombstones was highly unlikely. The first two were clearly Muslim, the third was topped by a Christian cross, and the fourth was none other than Setni's sarcophagus, as shown by its hieroglyphic decoration. Three lines of tiny writing appeared below the drawing, but in a language that Sam couldn't understand.

The following pages didn't seem to have any direct connection with the Eternity Ring or even with the stone statues: They showed a chess board where a turbaned black king was in poor position; a half dozen circles with four triangles in each, which in turn were decorated with a number of dots; a beautifully drawn frieze of leaves that ran across a series of linked pages, and so forth. Was Chamberlain wrong in thinking this missing part of the *Treatise* was so important?

The next to last page was more promising, however. It was an ancient map that unfolded to the size of four full pages, elegantly drawn in purple ink on yellow parchment. Klugg had made many notes in the margin, an indication of how important he thought it was. Despite some irregularities, it clearly portrayed the eastern Mediterranean, from Egypt to modern-day Turkey. The map used symbols like pointed cones for mountains and stylized waves for the sea, and identified several cities by their Arabic names. Two lines, one yellow and one white, started in the same area of the Nile in Egypt and wandered north along different routes; the yellow one went inland toward Turkey while the white one followed the coast.

Sam might have remained at that superficial level of understanding if not for Klugg's commentary. He had to read the notes several times, but when he grasped their meaning, he realized the importance of what he had in his hands. It was a map that showed the history of the Eternity Ring.

Everything indeed started on the Nile, in Thebes. The alchemist had written: "In times immemorial, Hyksos invaders overran the pharaoh's great kingdom and its capital, Thebes. A new ruler named Meriweserre crafted the second Golden Circle according to instructions left by Thoth. Meriweserre's descendents were eventually driven from the throne. They fled the kingdom, carrying the second Golden Circle and the Eternity Ring in its white jewel box."

A white jewel box, just like the one in the library's secret compartment!

"Soon thereafter, the surviving Hyksos split into two groups. One made its way east carrying the second Golden Circle, also known as the Impostor. The second traveled to the coast with the ring."

This split would explain why the two routes separated on the map. The yellow one (gold) marked the travels of the Meriweserre bracelet; the white one (ivory) showed that of the jewel box. According to the map, each of the two objects had followed a distinct route through a series of different cities: to the east, Basra, Wasit, Babylon, etc.; to the west, Ramla, Tyr, Sidon, and others. In the margins, Klugg had written comments on the dozens of cities he had information about: a founding date here, the name of the local chief there, a citation of a work mentioning one or the other of the treasures.

But for Sam the most interesting part concerned the two itineraries' end points. According to the map, the Meriweserre bracelet had wound up after several centuries in the city of Izmit in Turkey. Vlad Tepes had said that when he stole the Golden Circle in Izmit in 1447, no one remembered where the bracelet came from or the extent of its powers. So the map showed the actual itinerary the Meriweserre bracelet had followed. If it was true for the bracelet, would it also be right about the ring?

With his finger, Sam traced the second itinerary, which was marked by a series of little white squares. It was much shorter and easier to follow than the first. Once out of Egypt, the line ran due north to Antioch, a city near the Mediterranean's eastern edge. Klugg had written several notes about it in the corner of the map.

"Antioch: After the Ring of Time made its way here, along the coast of Syria, it disappeared from all records for more than a century. The last person to attest to its presence was the great philosopher Awzalag-al-Farabi, who in his 948 treatise on the principles of music reports seeing in the treasure of the Qadi of Antioch a white jewel box marked with the seal of Thoth and containing a strange stone ring.

"In 1098, during the first Crusade, the soldiers of Christ who had set off to retake Jerusalem disembarked in Syria and seized Antioch from the Seljuks. Taking possession of the city, they discovered inestimable treasures, including a piece of the Holy Spear that pierced Christ's side and the ivory jewel box that held the Ring of Eternity. The box was sent first to Constantinople, the nearby capital of the Byzantine Empire, then to Rome at the demand of Pope Paschal I. A mention of this shipment appears in the log of the caravel *La Nonna*, which transported it to Italy.

"The jewel box and its contents are therefore held by the popes somewhere in their palace in Rome. *That is where it must be sought.*"

Sam refolded the map, a crowd of theories filling his mind. The most plausible one was that his research convinced Klugg he'd located the ring in Rome, so he traveled there during the period that seemed the most propitious to steal it, namely after the construction of the Vatican library. But Pope Sixtus IV had engaged an unlikely architect, Setni, and the high priest had devised a Time-slowing mechanism to protect the treasure. When Klugg reached the Vatican, he found the secret compartment but couldn't open it! And so, as a last resort, he decided to explore Qin's tomb in hopes of learning how to slow time — a decision that had cost him his life.

Which left Sam to ponder this: What role had Setni played in this affair, and why did he agree to devise a magical hiding place in the Vatican?

In a way, Clement VII had answered this himself two hours earlier, when he unsealed the ivory box and found it empty. Sam suspected that creating the system in the Great Library was actually Setni's way of discreetly appropriating the ring himself. Who else besides the pope would have a key to the secret compartment? Its designer, of course. Setni could very well have retrieved the ring, then sealed the box with wax to make it look intact. It would be the perfect way to hide the ring while actually covering his tracks.

Glancing out the window, Sam saw that the rain had stopped and the sun was finally burning off the fog. He could now make out the river and the castle's drawbridge, which had been drawn up to cut off access from the other shore. Soldiers and onlookers had gathered on the Sant'Angelo battlements around the courtyard and were yelling excitedly. It took Sam a few moments to understand what was going on. The fortress was now closed to the outside world, but many laggards were still trying to get in. People had landed in boats and run to the base of the walls. From the ramparts the Swiss guards threw them ropes, which they climbed as the crowd applauded.

Sam instantly made up his mind. If the Romans were desperately trying to get into the castle, he desperately had to get out. He hid the *Treatise* under his shirt again and secured it with the cord, then rushed to the nearest staircase.

After a few detours he reached the esplanade, which overlooked the formidable stone tower on one side and the raised drawbridge on the other. Several hundred bystanders crowded the ramparts, giving advice and encouragement to the soldiers straining to hold the ropes and the unfortunates trying to climb them.

"Hang on! One hand after another!"

"Breathe! Remember to breathe!"

"Heave, ho! Heave, ho!"

Sam muscled his way through the crowd to reach a wide, west-facing crenellation. Much of the city was still hidden by fog, but he could glimpse orange and red roofs, church steeples, ruined monuments, and entire sections of the palace walls. Sam pulled out his map and tried to figure the direction he would have to take to save Alicia. About three hundred yards away, the river curved to the left, near the number 1 on his map — the stone statue. There was another bridge farther on, and on the other bank — and this is what interested Sam — a maze of streets disappeared into the fog. Diavilo's camp was hidden somewhere beyond that neighborhood.

Sam leaned out into space, wondering how he could take advantage of the situation. Twenty yards below him, a group of a dozen people were standing with their arms raised, calling to be rescued. They were mostly young men, plus one old man with a shock of white hair and three women who had taken off their long-sleeved coats. Five others were already climbing the ropes or being pulled up. Sam wanted to go down, but how could he manage that? What with the crowd, the soldiers, and the general tension, he would have to improvise, to surprise everyone with a little playacting!

"Nonno! Papi!" he suddenly shouted, waving furiously at the white-haired man below. "Nonno, can you see me? Here I am, Nonno!"

He turned to the people around him and said, "That's my grandfather down there. Can you see me, Nonno? I'm coming for you."

Yelling louder, Sam cut through the crowd of onlookers and made straight for the Swiss guards who were handling the ropes. He stationed himself in front of two of them as they lent a hand to a refugee who had almost reached the top.

"That's my grandfather," yelled Sam, gesturing as if to grab the rope. "He's right down below! You've got to save him!" Then, to the old man down below: "I'm coming to get you, Nonno!"

One of the guards made him step aside as the other congratulated the latest climber to reach the fortress.

"He's the one with the white hair," Sam continued. "He's my grandfather! He's old and he has a bad arm. He'll never be able to get up alone. He'll die if I don't go down to help him."

The second guard leaned over to look. "He's no kid, but —"

"I'm begging you," Sam insisted. "It's his only chance. Otherwise the Spaniards will capture him!"

A middle-aged woman in a black hat promptly took up the cause. "I'd certainly like it if one of my sons was willing to risk his neck to save his old mother."

"You've got that right!" added another woman. "It's a fine thing to want to save your grandfather!"

The guard gave in, but pointed a warning finger at Sam.

"All right, but it's on your head. If you fall and break your bones, that's your business. And be quick about it; other people down below are waiting!"

"Thank you!" exclaimed Sam. "I'll go down and help him climb back up. It won't take a moment."

He grabbed the rope before the soldier changed his mind, checked to see that the *Treatise* was still firmly in place, and, when the Swiss guards gave him the signal, stepped over the crenellation. Then he rappelled down the wall, slowing himself with his feet as best he could.

He hit the wet grass amid a roar of applause. Sam rubbed his burning palms and seized the white-haired man by the shoulders.

"Nonno," he cried. "I'm so glad to see you're all right!

The old man gaped at him. "Er, what are you —"

"I'm here, Nonno. Everything's going to be all right!"

127

He passed the rope around the old man's waist, ran the end between his legs, tied it off, and told him to hang on. Then he kissed his aged protégé on the cheek and yelled to the soldiers on the battlements.

"You can haul him up now. But take it easy, he's my grandfather!"

The rope jerked taut and the old man began to rise, clearly a bit baffled but nonetheless pleased. He wasn't that helpless either, skillfully using his feet against the wall to speed his ascent. At the top, he was greeted by an ovation worthy of a star, and the guards quickly untied him so they could throw the rope down to his valiant grandson.

But Sam was already running toward one of the boats pulled up on the shore.

CHAPTER SIXTEEN

Il Diavolo

Sam allowed the boat to drift with the current, occasionally sculling to stay near the shore. Overhead, the Borgo ramparts rang with the clash of fighting. Eventually he recognized the little beach with the buried stone statue. He got ashore, pulled the boat up on the sand, and ran toward the Hathor graffiti.

Sam reached the little mound and dug in the sodden dirt. The Thoth stone was still there, intact and ready. Reassured, he then measured off a dozen yards to the right and dug another hole. To save Alicia, he needed the coin stamped *Candor illaesus*, the Meriweserre bracelet, and the *Treatise*. He knew that when he reached Diavilo's camp, he would almost certainly be searched and relieved of all his valuables. So it made sense to hide the other six coins here, especially the gray one that would bring him and Alicia back to their present.

He was about to return to his boat when three cavalrymen suddenly appeared next to the hillock, leading their horses toward the river. Two more followed, and then another four. An entire troop of soldiers was coming to water their horses!

Sam crawled to the boat and hid behind it. After what seemed like hours of struggling not to fall asleep, he finally heard a trumpet call and a drum roll from the road. The men on the jetties clapped and shouted joyously, then headed back up the hill. Something was afoot.

Sam risked a peek over the boat's gunwale. On the hillock a hundred yards away, a column of warriors in armor was on the march. Some were mounted, others were on foot, carrying red-and-gray banners, their yells joined by the beating of drums. They paraded along the Borgo ramparts by the hundreds, apparently seeking new conquests. They looked like an army of gleaming machines. Having seized the pope's palace in the west, maybe Charles V's army was planning to head east — toward where Alicia was being held. If Sam wanted to cross through the city to reach Diavilo's camp, he'd have to move fast.

Once the clanking, yelling horde was out of sight, Sam launched his boat across the river, then clambered inside. His muscles were stiff with accumulated fatigue, and he had to fight the current to reach the other side. He tied the boat up to an odd floating platform of wooden barges linked by gangplanks, empty except for some merchandise hanging from a crane. Sam crossed the gangplanks, cut through a warehouse, and started to climb some stairs up to the street-level dock. Halfway there, however, he was startled by the sight of more red-and-gray soldiers just ahead. The attackers had already occupied the neighborhood!

There was nothing for it: He would just have to take his chances. He continued climbing up to the dock, where he was

130

forced to dodge a group of soldiers drinking and bellowing in the middle of the street. He ducked into a shadowed alley, but almost immediately bumped against a limp shape dangling from a post — a dead body. Sam stifled a cry and walked faster, hugging the walls as he crossed the neighborhood. Some of the buildings had their doors smashed in; others had been burned. Except for the looters' impromptu banquets in the squares, there wasn't a sign of life anywhere. The real inhabitants seemed to have vanished. Sam did a little scavenging himself, nibbling a forgotten loaf of stale bread and stealing a drink of water from a dipper and bucket. In his ravenous state, they tasted delicious.

After a while the houses thinned out, and Sam realized he was at the edge of the city. A vast field stretched before him, dotted with half-buried columns and temples, as if a flood of dirt and dust had covered it for days. He also saw the famous circular amphitheater — the Colosseum. It looked like a monumental stone ship that had somehow been caught in quicksand, its past glory ravaged by time. Entire sections of its arcades had collapsed, leaving a tormented, lacy pattern in the moonlight.

Sam scuttled over to the base of a column. A tent city had been erected in the Colosseum's ruins — Diavilo's camp, apparently — bounded by an earthen berm with a single entrance guarded by three soldiers. Dozens of men came and went between the tents, or stood in groups near fires whose flames crackled as they rose to the sky. The calm and discipline of Diavilo's troops contrasted starkly with the scenes of drunkenness Sam had witnessed in the city. That was hardly reassuring, because he'd hoped that the soldiers' carousing would make it easier for him to rescue Alicia.

Sam studied the camp perimeter from a safe distance. He could probably climb the berm under cover of darkness, but what then? How likely was it that he would immediately find the tent where Alicia was being held, and that this tent would happen not to be guarded? And once he freed her, what chance did they have of getting out without raising the alarm? None at all, short of a miracle. All things considered, Sam had no alternative but to follow Rudolf's instructions to the letter and pray that Diavilo would hold up his end of the bargain.

Fearful, but determined not to show it, he headed for the camp entrance. One of the guards immediately rushed toward him, drawing his sword.

"Halt! Who goes there?"

"I have something for Captain Diavilo," cried Sam, raising his arms.

The guard was on him in three paces. Skipping the introductions, he brought his sword point within inches of Sam's throat.

"If you're after a handout or some sort of favor from the captain, you're as good as dead," he snapped.

"I have something for Captain Diavilo," Sam repeated, trying to keep his voice from shaking. "Here, in my hand."

He slowly lowered his hand and opened it, and the soldier cautiously took the coin.

"A gold ducat with a hole in it. What's this mean? So you aren't a beggar, in spite of your lousy clothes?"

"That coin must be given personally to the captain," Sam

insisted, glad that his throat hadn't been slit yet. "It'll prove I'm not lying. I have two really important things for him. He knows what this is about."

The guard hesitated for a moment, glancing from the coin to the large book that Sam held in his other hand. He called to a boy nearby.

"Fabio, come here! Take this ducat to the captain, and tell him this snot-nose wants to see him. He doesn't look very dangerous, but he could be a spy for the pope. If the captain thinks we should take his head off, tell him I'll handle it right away." The guard spoke without particular feeling, as if decapitating people were an everyday part of his duties.

The young boy ran off. Sam spent some minutes in this uncomfortable position, with one arm raised, the other one stretched out, and a sword under his chin, until Fabio returned.

"The captain wants the boy brought to him right away," he said, panting.

Score one for me, thought Sam, lowering his hands.

But the guard said, "Don't count your chickens too soon, kid. The captain likes to have fun with snoops like you. If you're a spy, you might've been better off having me kill you right away."

With these encouraging words, Fabio grabbed Sam's arm and led him into the camp. At least a hundred men were going about their business: oiling harquebuses, sharpening blades, filling mess tins from enormous cook pots, or tending their horses off to the side. Their faces evinced the battles they'd witnessed — missing eyes, zigzag scars, broken noses, and cauliflower ears — but the men went about their business with surprising calm, which spoke well of their leader's authority.

The guard led Sam to the largest of the tents, which was roughly in the middle of the camp, and handed him over to a pair of big bruisers guarding it. The two stood well over six feet tall, and their faces were so laced with scars that it took Sam a moment to realize they were twins. The first one held him by the scruff of the neck while the second snatched away his book and the contents of his pockets — the Meriweserre bracelet and the map. He vanished behind a heavy purple drape across the tent entrance and returned a good five minutes later to drag Sam in.

Inside, the tent was like Ali Baba's cavern. Soft cushions lay upon thick carpets around a jewel-encrusted hookah. Gold plates, crystal goblets, and sterling silverware were carefully stacked behind a diaphanous veil, perhaps in anticipation of the evening meal. The rear of the tent was part bedroom, part bazaar. A bed with a frame of curved wood sagged under the weight of swords, shields, and other bric-a-brac. Shimmering cloth spilled out of chests, and paintings stood casually propped against statues adorned with necklaces and rings. Was all this just one day's plunder?

In the only open space on the right, a man sat on a golden chair, seeming to contemplate his treasures: Diavilo. He was rather fat, his jet-black hair tied in a ponytail, and dressed all in dark cloth, with a dagger hanging by his side. As the Vatican guard had said, his left hand was missing, and a sharp hook emerged from his puffy sleeve. But the most striking thing about him was his gaze. As he carefully examined Sam in his ragged, mud-splattered clothes, Diavilo's yellow, reptilian eyes seemed to search his very soul.

"Bring our guest a seat," he said softly.

His voice was very low and surprisingly gentle. One of the two giants found a chair near the bed and forced a thoroughly rattled Sam down at the captain's right.

"Very well. Leave us."

The bodyguards bowed themselves out. Diavilo opened his right hand; the Clement VII coin lay in his palm. He had set Klugg's *Treatise* and the Meriweserre bracelet on his knees. Sam felt heartsick to see that the bracelet, which usually glimmered delicately, wasn't shining at all, as if it had lost its real owner.

"So it's true, you've come for the girl?" asked the captain, his eyes boring through Sam like a pair of golden knives.

Sam struggled not to blink or show his fear. "Where is she?" he managed to say.

"In the tent with the wounded. She hasn't been very well these last few days," Diavilo said. "A sudden fever. We feared the worst. I brought her my personal physician, and she seems to have recovered a little. To our great relief, as you can imagine," he added in a tone of mock concern.

"I want to see her," Sam demanded. He remembered the raging fever that incapacitated his cousin Lily when the two of them landed in Chicago in 1932. Setni had explained it was "Time sickness," an illness that sometimes struck novice travelers. It had almost killed Lily, who had received the best of care; what might it have done to Alicia?

"Easy does it, my boy," answered Diavilo calmly. "First we have to talk."

"There's nothing to talk about. The agreement's simple: the book and the bracelet in exchange for my friend."

"The agreement, of course," murmured Diavilo, as if it had slipped his mind. Skillfully, he snagged the bracelet with his hook and slipped it onto the arm of a marble cherub next to his chair. He then turned to the *Treatise*, becoming engrossed in some pages and skipping others. Sam didn't dare interrupt him.

After about ten minutes, Diavilo finished his study. He fixed his gaze on Sam again and asked, "Do you know how much our common friend paid me for doing him this little favor? I mean, getting the book and the bracelet?"

Sam shook his head.

"Five thousand gold ducats. A tidy sum, wouldn't you say, for an incomprehensible book of spells and a crude bracelet that isn't worth a tenth of any of the things here? Do you know why he gave me this task?"

Sam couldn't think of a reason, but he didn't like the turn the conversation was taking.

"That doesn't interest me," he said. "I just want you to free Alicia."

"You're wrong," Diavilo said with a snicker. "It's quite fascinating. Our friend needed someone who spoke the Mohammedan language — Arabic, if you prefer — to make sure the book was the one he wanted. As it happens, I've spent some time among the Ottomans; in their prisons, to be exact. A very enriching experience."

Diavilo's pupils shrank to gleaming dots of molten metal, and he raised his stump as proof of what he was saying.

"During my time there," he continued, "I learned exactly what awaits me in the afterworld — in hell, to be precise. And compared with the pain I will endure there, nothing I might suffer in this world can touch me. Mere money certainly no longer impresses me, not even the five thousand gold ducats promised by our common friend. So I began to wonder: What makes this book of spells so precious that he would pay such a fortune for it? And what does he plan to do with this bracelet?"

"You have the bracelet and the *Treatise*," interrupted Sam. "The book is written in the right language, as you can see for yourself. I've done my part of the contract; please do yours."

Diavilo leaned back with a predatory smile. "Are you sure you want me to do that, boy? Do you even know all the contract's clauses?"

"What do you mean?"

"Because there's a part of the agreement that our friend obviously didn't tell you about. Once I have the bracelet and am sure the book is authentic, I'm supposed to kill the two of you."

"What?"

Sam nearly jumped out of his chair, but before he could rise, Diavilo caught his neck with the point of the hook. Sam felt a stabbing pain under his jaw, followed by a trickle of warm blood.

"What did you expect, you little idiot?" hissed Diavilo, forcing him to bow his head. "That after daring to appear in my tent you could just go on with your stinking little life? You innocent fool."

He pushed harder with his hook, mashing Sam's nose against the chair's armrest. Diavilo held him at his mercy for a few moments, and then violently threw Sam back into his chair.

"But I may spare you if you explain what the *Treatise* is about, and do it convincingly. Understand? I want to know what these maps show and what kind of treasures they point to. I want to know the meaning of those drawings of bracelets that look so much like the one you brought. I want to understand those formulas and texts that talk about a fabulous ring and all the rest. If you satisfy my curiosity, I'll spare your life."

Sam's hand was on his neck, trying to stanch the flow of blood soaking his shirt. The wound stung, and he felt dizzy. He had to play for time. "And if I explain all that, you promise to free Alicia as well?"

Diavilo pondered this as he wiped the point of his hook on his trunk hose.

"If your information is satisfactory, she'll be free to go," he said ingenuously.

Sam trusted this sudden show of generosity about as much as he would trust a werewolf under a full moon.

"I'm not telling you anything until I have proof she's still alive. I want to see her."

Diavilo turned his inquisitor's gaze on Sam for a long moment. Then he abruptly called to the twins: "Castor! Pollux!"

The two gorillas stuck their heads through the purple curtain.

"Bring the girl here," he ordered. "And don't let any of the men near her."

Diavilo settled himself in his armchair, gazing at his guest with amusement, as if he was about to pull a good joke. For his part, Sam was frantically trying to imagine a way out. Should he give in to the blackmail? Tell him all about the stone statue and the Golden Circle? What if Diavilo then decided to start traveling through time? Or should he make up a story that might satisfy the captain's curiosity, with the risk that his malicious mind would detect the deceit and he would decide to kill both him and Alicia?

Sam was still racking his brains when the purple curtain parted and Alicia entered, flanked by the two giants. She looked haggard, with her long blond hair matted and tear tracks down her cheeks. Her beautiful blue eyes, which were usually so cheerful, were clouded with terrible distress, and she wore the same sort of nightgown that Sam and Lily had found themselves wearing after their first journey. Sam thought she looked like a saint in a religious painting, a doomed woman about to be put to death. He rose to embrace her, but Diavilo intervened, swinging his hook against his belly.

"One more step and I'll cut your guts out right in front of your young friend — not a sight I'd recommend, given the state she's in. Listen carefully, boy. I satisfied your demand by bringing her; now you have to satisfy mine. And to begin with, I suggest a little entertainment."

He drew the dagger at his belt and tossed it to one of his henchmen, who caught it in midair. Then he opened the *Treatise* to a page that showed two stone statues, one at the foot of an Easter Island monolith, the other behind a fountain.

"Here's what we're going to do. I'll point out a few of these mysterious drawings in the book, and each time you aren't able to explain what they mean, my dear Pollux will cut off some part of your girlfriend. Let's start with her left hand. Pollux, if you would . . ."

The giant seized the prisoner's left arm and pulled up her sleeve while his brother set the dagger against her wrist. Alicia tried to scream, but terror seemed to paralyze her vocal cords.

"So we're agreed?" asked Diavilo with delight. "Fine. Be good enough to first tell me about this image of a sun."

CHAPTER SEVENTEEN

Alicia

Sam looked at the picture of the stone statues that the captain had thrust at him. It was too late to make anything up. Closing his eyes, he breathed deeply. Calming himself, that was the key. Removing himself from his surroundings . . .

Captain Diavilo repeated his question, but Sam ignored him. He was forcing his mind down within himself, the way he'd done in Qin's tomb and the pope's library. The pulse of Time in his chest was almost imperceptible, but it was there, and Sam focused on slowing his heartbeat until the two rhythms matched. Gently, peacefully, the two pulses in his chest merged into one.

Sam opened his eyes. The tent's interior was now a handsome dark green. Diavilo was still scowling and pointing to the *Treatise*, but seemed to be suffering from a strange paralysis, as if his body weighed a ton and he couldn't move his mouth. All that came from his lips was a gradually modulated cavernous sound, and his eyelids blinked ponderously. Behind him, Pollux had raised the dagger, but his gesture was arrested in midair. Alicia herself was also caught in the general torpor, dramatically frozen as she shrank away.

Sam snatched the Meriweserre bracelet from the marble cherub, then shoved Diavilo aside. As he crossed the tent to the twins, he realized that the dagger had descended a few inches, Alicia had imperceptibly jerked her head back, and Castor had turned slightly to block her. The three weren't totally frozen, merely terribly slowed down. Sam treated Pollux to a kick in the stomach, which put his blade out of range as the man toppled backward with astonishing slowness. He then yanked at Castor, who was still clutching Alicia. Though nearly at a standstill, the giant still had all his strength, and Sam had to wrench his fingers back to free her.

Now it was Alicia's turn. "I don't know if you can understand what I'm saying," he muttered into her ear, "but you've got to help me."

He wedged her firmly over his right shoulder and straightened up, cradling her in his arms. Normally Sam would probably have trouble carrying Alicia, but altering Time had energized him, and he was feeling a rush of positive energy.

Parting the purple curtain, they emerged outside to an unlikely spectacle. Dozens of men stood nearly paralyzed at their evening activities around the tents. One was bringing a soupspoon to his mouth inch by inch; another was about to pound his neighbor on the back but seemed to hesitate; a third was unsuccessfully spitting on the ground. Even the flames from the fires hung motionless, and when Sam brushed by one, it didn't burn him.

He made for the camp entrance, zigzagging among the statue-like figures in his way. Again, everything he saw was wrapped in a greenish haze, and each of his steps set off powerful vibrations in the air. His gasping breath escaped in thin lines of bubbles along his cheeks.

He covered about a hundred yards this way, bent under Alicia's weight and finding it increasingly hard to keep his heartbeat in tune with that of Time. Though he felt an unusual twinge of pain in his chest, he had no choice but to go on. However long the phenomenon lasted, they had to use it to get as much distance from Diavilo as they could.

They finally reached the edge of town, and Sam lurched into the nearest alley. He stopped for a moment to catch his breath; his legs were on fire and his heart was starting to hurt. Without setting Alicia down, he leaned against a wall and focused on maintaining the pulse of Time. Then he got underway again, this time moving more slowly. They passed two burned buildings and made it to the next block of houses, but Sam then had to stop for good. His chest felt caught in a red-hot vise, and his heart was about to burst, unable to maintain its abnormal pace.

Sam saw a row of buildings with smashed doors and entered the first open one. He set Alicia down on the earthen floor and collapsed next to her, on the verge of passing out. He closed his eyes, and his heart lurched brutally when the sharp crack rang out and Time resumed its course. He immediately felt Alicia moving next to him, and clapped his hand over her mouth before she could scream.

"Helmpf!"

"Alicia," he whispered, taking her in his arms. "It's me, Sam. Sam Faulkner. You saw me in the tent earlier, remember?"

She nodded, but continued to struggle.

"I managed to get us out of there," he added, "but they'll be after us at any moment. If I let you go, do you promise not to scream?"

She mumbled something that sounded like an agreement and he took his hand away.

"SAM, WHAT'S GOING ON?" she yelled hysterically.

"Not so loud! They probably aren't far away and —"

"WHO THE HECK ARE THEY? AND WHERE ARE WE? WHAT IS THIS PLACE? IT'S FULL OF CRAZY PEOPLE WITH SWORDS AND THEY ALL WANT TO KILL ME. WHAT LANGUAGE ARE THEY TALKING? WHAT LANGUAGE AM *I* TALKING?"

She was shaking him, desperate for an answer, but he was completely out of breath and feeling as if he had a ball of hot steel where his heart should be.

"We're in Rome in 1527," he gasped. "I can explain —"

"WHAT? What did you say?" She jumped up and grabbed him by the shirtfront. "Have you gone crazy? 1527?" At that point, she must have realized that he wasn't in great shape, because her attitude changed completely. "Sammy, are you all right?" she asked anxiously. "Your breathing is weird. Are you hurt?"

"No, just tired. I'll catch my breath and we'll get going again."

She ran a cool hand over his forehead and felt his pulse.

"You're burning up," she concluded. "And your heart . . . It's like you just ran a marathon or something!"

"That's pretty much it," he admitted. "But don't worry. I feel better already." He leaned up on an elbow and forced himself to a seated position. "We have to get to the river, Alicia. After that we'll be safer and I'll tell you everything. We probably have a five- or ten-minute head start. That's something. Besides, they don't know which way we went."

"But who are all those guys, Sam? *And how can I speak this language I don't even know?*"

"Later, Alicia. I'll tell you everything later, I promise."

She helped him up, and they went out into the alley. Luckily, there was no sign that Diavilo's men were on their trail. Alicia slipped her arm under Sam's to support him, and they headed toward the Tiber, staggering more than walking. Sam suddenly felt five hundred years old. He was bruised all over, his chest hurt, and his legs were cramping from his recent effort. He remembered when he'd seen Setni slow Time to give the Sainte-Mary punks a memorable drubbing in 1932. Afterward, the high priest had looked pale, on the verge of collapse. Stretching Time like a rubber band had its downside, especially when it snapped back in your face.

They went the way Sam had come earlier in the evening, once almost running into a patrol on the dock. They avoided it by hiding in the shadow of a church. Sam was feeling much better by the time they reached the riverbank, but he was careful not to tell Alicia that — partly because silence was their best ally, but also because he didn't want her to release his arm. It was her hand on his, her hair that brushed his cheek, her steps that crunched along with his. They were united by the danger around them, and they would face it together, the two of them. He knew it was stupid under the circumstances, but Sam felt almost happy.

It took them about half an hour to reach the river, where they took shelter in an abandoned fisherman's shed. Then, at last, Sam told her the whole story, from the beginning, without leaving anything out. How he'd found the stone statue hidden in the bookstore basement; how he'd been suddenly transported to the island of Iona; his many journeys before getting home; the role of Lily, who had helped him so much; their adventures in Pompeii and Chicago; their meeting Setni, the high priest; his confrontation with Vlad Tepes; the way he had rescued his father from the Bran Castle dungeon; his astonishment at learning that Rudolf and the Arkeos man were the same person; his recent trip to Qin's tomb; retrieving *The Treatise on the Thirteen Virtues of Magic*; and finally his slowing Time to snatch her from the clutches of *Il Diavolo*.

When he'd finished his account, it was nearly dark outside. Alicia was silent for a long moment. She looked at the Golden Circle, which was gleaming in the milky moonlight, then she laid her hand on Sam's knee.

"That explains a lot of things," she said. "Including those books about Dracula that you were lugging around when you came to my place. Or the fact that you didn't want to say anything about your father's health. But why didn't you tell me all this before, Sam? Maybe I could have helped you."

Sam smiled grimly.

"It seemed like you'd already suffered enough because of me, don't you think? You looked so happy and relaxed with Jerry the other day. . . . I didn't want to bother you with my problems. Besides, be honest: Would you have believed me?"

She shrugged a little. "Maybe not. But like I said once, I have a sixth sense where you're concerned. I knew you were lying to me. And now I'm stuck here too. . . . If I'd known all this before, I would've been more careful, especially with Rudolf."

"How did it happen?" he asked. "Did he knock you out?"

"No, Lily sent me a text message."

"What?"

"I got a message from Lily on my cell. She wrote that you absolutely had to see me at seven p.m. at the cafeteria behind the skating rink. You didn't have any way to reach me, so you were going through her."

"But Lily's at summer camp," Sam exclaimed, "hundreds of miles from Sainte-Mary!"

"I thought it was strange too. So I dialed the number and it went to her voice mail. I had no reason to think it was a trap."

"The rat!" snarled Sam. "I know how he must have done it. When Lily loaned me her phone the other day, Rudolf accused me of stealing it. When he got it back later, he kept it as bait for you."

"And I fell for it," sighed Alicia. "I rushed to the ice rink, but you weren't there and neither was Lily — just Rudolf. He claimed you hadn't been able to come because of your father at the hospital and that you'd sent him to apologize. He asked if he could buy me a coffee, because he wanted to talk about you. We went to the cafeteria and got our drinks, and he explained that he was very worried about you, that you'd started acting strangely after Allan disappeared. He wondered if I knew anything. As the conversation went on, I started to feel dizzy."

"He drugged you!"

"Yeah. He must've slipped something in my drink when I went to the bathroom. Anyway, I started to feel worse and worse, and he offered to take me home. I don't remember much of anything after that. Well, yes, I do: At one point in the car I woke up a little and he gave me an injection. I tried to struggle, but I didn't have any strength. He gave me more shots later."

She pulled up her sleeve; the inside of her forearm displayed a line of bruises.

"Where did he take you?" asked Sam, who still didn't know where Rudolf's Thoth stone was hidden.

"To be honest, I hardly remember anything. In the beginning there was a car and the smell of leather. Then seats covered with tan fabric, with the roar of a motor in the background."

"An airplane?"

"Maybe. I was totally out if it. And then this terrible burning sensation. I thought the car had caught fire. I even thought I was dead."

"That's the leap through Time," said Sam thoughtfully. "It always happens, but it doesn't last long. I think the stone Rudolf uses must be a few hours from Sainte-Mary; far enough to require a plane or a helicopter, but close enough so he can get back quickly. He's the one who got me out of bed the morning after you disappeared. He told me your mother was there, and she was looking for you everywhere. So he must've just gotten back."

"You have to be a real" — she used a word that would have horrified her mother — "to pretend to comfort a mother when you've just kidnapped her daughter!"

"It was a way to give himself an alibi. Besides, by coming to my house, he could keep an eye on me and see if I took the bait. It's evil." He was quiet a moment, thinking, then added: "What surprises me is Aunt Evelyn's role in all this. She's really

148

hard to live with, but I didn't think she would be his accomplice!"

"If it makes you feel any better, she wasn't with him, either at Sainte-Mary or afterward. When I woke up here, there were only men around."

She shivered before continuing.

"I was really scared, Sam. They had chained me to this mat, and all these thugs were standing around, dressed up like medieval warriors, looking at me as if I were some strange animal. . . . At one point Rudolf showed up, dressed like the others, but he didn't say anything to me. I was actually relieved when they forced me to take sleeping drugs; otherwise, I would've gone crazy. After a while, I don't know how long it was, I got sick, which didn't make things any better. I really thought I was going to die. It was as noisy as anything, with screaming and shots being fired. . . . I just regained consciousness this morning, and all day, I tried to lie still and not have anyone pay attention to me. Then the twins came into my tent this evening to drag me out to see Diavilo . . . and you."

She fell silent, staring off into space. Sam put his hand on hers, only too aware that he alone was responsible for everything she had endured. She didn't pull away, and they remained motionless for a moment, watching the lights of the city reflected in the river, trying to ignore the distant bursts of laughter and the occasional cries to heaven.

"I know what you're thinking, Sam," she murmured after a while. "You think I'm just a little girl, it's all your fault that this happened to me, that once again you weren't able to come through. Well, I'm not made of glass. Of course I was afraid, terribly afraid, and yeah, I cried my eyes out. I'm only human. But I'm a big girl too. I've learned to hang on and fight back. You can count on me, Sam; that's what I want to tell you. And in the future, instead of always protecting me, I'd like you to trust me enough to be honest."

She rose to one knee and drew closer.

"Besides, I'm not sure anyone else would've done half as much to save me — definitely not Jerry! So I've really found my Prince Charming again."

She leaned over and kissed him on the forehead.

"Thank you, Sam, from the bottom of my heart.

"And now we better get home," she said in a more playful tone, "because you really need a bath."

His head in a whirl, Sam took her outstretched hand and they stood up together.

Setting out again, they followed the shore to the jetty where Sam had tied up his boat a few hours earlier. The good news was that it was still there. The bad news was that some soldiers had set up camp on the opposite shore near the stone. Their mounts were quietly grazing in the shadows a short distance away.

"What do we do?" whispered Alicia.

"We have to pull the boat upstream so we can float across on the current," answered Sam. "Let's hope they're too drunk to hear us!"

In fact, the mercenaries seemed very cheerful, singing at the top of their lungs and toasting each other with large earthenware jugs. With a little bit of luck . . . They untied the rope and quietly hauled the boat upstream to an old bridge piling. On the other shore, a few pathetic torches lit the Borgo ramparts, giving it a funereal look. To the north they could make out the glow from Castel Sant'Angelo, which rose above the water like a fat candle.

Alicia climbed into the boat first and stretched out on the bottom. Sam shoved off and followed her, crouching in the stern. They silently drifted across, with Sam sculling to move them closer to the western shore. Luckily, once they were past midstream, the current carried them smoothly to the right side.

They pulled up on the Borgo beach near where Sam had buried the coins, and immediately got out and hid behind the boat. About fifty yards away, the soldiers continued to carry on, oblivious, but one of their horses whinnied nervously. They crawled quickly to the wall, where Sam dug up his collection of coins. He swore softly under his breath as he realized what he was missing.

"What's the matter?" Alicia asked behind him.

He showed her the coin with the gray coating.

"Rudolf gave me this one to get us back to our present. The problem is, we need seven coins to be able to choose our destination with the bracelet, and we only have six! The gold coin is back in Diavilo's pocket."

"What does that mean?"

"Well, as far as I can tell, with only six coins, the stone sends you randomly to one of the six time periods."

"So we won't get home right away?"

"We have one chance in six. But wherever we end up, we might pick up another coin, and that would shoot us straight home."

"So there's just one thing to do. Why wait? Wherever we wind up, it can't be worse than here, can it?"

Sam didn't answer: He knew from experience that it could *always* be worse. Still, she was right about not waiting, so he strung the coins on the bracelet, and they crawled along the ramparts like a pair of thieves. Once at the Hathor graffiti, Sam parted the grass and dug down to uncover the stone statue. A second horse whinnied, then a third. Sam noticed that some of the soldiers had fallen silent.

Without wasting a moment, he slapped the bracelet onto the sun, and the coins obediently slipped into their slots. He then hugged Alicia and set his fingers on the stone's warm, rounded top. It was just in the nick of time: One of the horsemen was gesturing in their direction. Sam held her tighter as the ground under them began to vibrate and a familiar hum filled the air. The stone suddenly erupted with what felt like a geyser of burning acid, which ran up Sam's arm, filled his chest and legs, spread to Alicia, and dissolved them into nothingness.

CHAPTER EIGHTEEN

The Church of the Seven Resurrections

Sam was still clinging to Alicia when they landed — on a marble floor somewhere, under the glare of electric lights. She lay hunched over, unable to control her nausea, while Sam looked around to get his bearings. Not only were they in some cold modern building, they were surrounded by glass display cases, costumes, paintings, and posters. . . . Was it some kind of museum? As he retrieved the Meriweserre bracelet from the stone statue, which rose from a hole cut in the marble floor, he wondered which of the six coins had brought them here. Not the Chinese one, of course; nor the Bran Castle coin or the Thebes coin from 1980. That left only Rudolf's gray coin, Chamberlain's plain metal one, and the blue poker chip.

Whichever coin it was, it clearly hadn't brought them home. Though the stone statue in front of Sam looked exactly like the one in Faulkner's Antique Books, the room was nothing like Allan's cramped basement space.

"This . . . is . . . dis . . . gus . . . ting," spluttered Alicia. She was still kneeling head down, fighting the spasms that wracked her body.

"It'll pass," said Sam soothingly as he stroked her hair. "I was like you in the beginning, and then it got easier."

"I don't care . . . if it gets . . . easier . . . I just want . . . it to . . . stop!"

Sam waited for her to finish retching, then helped her up.

"Where are we?" she asked in a shaky voice.

"No idea. Not home, unfortunately!"

The objects on display included a collection of painted pottery, African and Asian statuettes mounted on stands, and cases displaying flint blades, frieze sculptures, and ancient manuscripts opened to brilliant illuminations. Along the walls stood mannequins in clothes from different eras: a samurai with armor and sword; a warrior wearing a colorful coat and sumptuous feather headdress, possibly Aztec; a knight in armor with enough equipment to conquer Rome all by himself; and a mummy lying in a mock sarcophagus. The place might be a museum, but it wasn't very well organized.

"Look at that!" exclaimed Alicia.

She was pointing to a door whose engraved panels bore a pair of black horns with a golden circle between them: the Arkeos logo.

"That can't be good," muttered Sam.

He cautiously opened the door. It led to a room with a domed ceiling lit by banks of overhead lights. Photographs hung on the walls, and a large model of a building stood on a table covered with black cloth. When they were sure nobody else was in the room, Alicia and Sam walked over to the model. It represented an architectural complex whose general appearance was clearly inspired by the Hathor sign: An outer ring of buildings formed a shallow *U* that enclosed a central unit under a glass dome. Each of the outer buildings was in an architectural style derived from a different period of history, each with its appropriate label: "Pyramid Passage," "Regeneration Temple," "Eternity Pagoda," "Cathedral of the Last Metamorphosis," "Pandit's Private Residence." The glass dome covered a cutting-edge business center decorated in ultramodern fashion, though here too odd names appeared: "Pilgrims Amphitheater," "Transmigration Passage," "Counter of Dates," "Auditorium of the Six Births," etc. The whole complex was surrounded by trees, pools, and flowered walkways. The columned entryway bore a name carved into its facade: CHURCH OF THE SEVEN RESURRECTIONS.

"Any idea what this means?" asked Alicia.

"Maybe," answered Sam as he took the grayish coin from his pocket. "The Hathor sign is the logo of Arkeos, the company Rudolf set up for his antiquities business. Something tells me he wanted to bring us here."

"You mean to his headquarters? What for?"

"I have no idea."

"Then don't you think we should leave right away?"

"To go where? Back to Rome? To Qin's mausoleum? No, first we have to find a way to get home. If we're really in Rudolf's headquarters, there must be some coins around here somewhere."

"What if he finds us?"

"If he finds us," said Sam through clenched teeth, "we'll just have a little chat."

They crossed the room to look at the images on the walls: ancient objects, sculptures, statuettes, necklaces, and a close-up photo of the Omphalos, the sacred stone that was supposed to indicate the center of the world. It had been stolen centuries earlier from Delphi in Greece, shortly before Sam himself visited there.

"This is Rudolf's place all right," he said. "That's a picture of the Navel of the World. Arkeos sold it a few weeks ago for ten million dollars. This must be kind of like his trophy room."

"What about the other side?"

The opposite wall was covered by six large, framed posters, each with a caption. The first was labeled "Djoser Pyramid, circa 2600 B.C.," and showed an Egyptian hieroglyph cartouche that included the Hathor sign. The second was a reproduction of a Chinese text that ended with a pair of stylized horns and the solar disk. Its caption read, "Ode to Ri-dhil-fi, *Canon of Poems*, circa 1000 B.C." The third, "Inscription on the Temple of Apollo at Delphi, 5th century B.C.," showed Greek letters carved into a marble slab, again with the sign of Hathor. The fourth read "Stained glass from Canterbury Cathedral, 12th-13th century," and showed an enlarged piece of colored glass where the Hathor sign appeared in a blue and red pattern framed by two letter *R*'s.

When he reached the fifth picture, Sam paused.

"Do you see what I see?" he murmured.

Alicia approached. The fifth poster stated that it was a reproduction of *The Cardsharps*, a 1595 painting by Caravaggio. It was a magnificent composition, full of life and color, but what had caught Sam's eye was neither its beauty nor its subject. The painting showed a young card player being cheated by two men. The first was pulling a six of clubs from his belt; the second was peeking at the victim's cards so he could signal to his accomplice. And the second cheater bore a striking resemblance to Rudolf — a dark-haired Rudolf with a goatee, plumed hat, and old gloves.

"Amazing," said Alicia admiringly. "It looks just like him. Think it's a coincidence?"

Sam pointed to one of the cards that the first cheater was hiding behind his back. It looked like a seven of hearts or diamonds, except instead of the usual red pips, it had small *U*'s with circles inside them.

"Rudolf time travels, thanks to the Hathor sign. What's to keep him from posing for a sixteenth-century painter?"

"So he can hang his ugly face on the wall? The guy's got an ego the size of a house!"

"That's not the end of it," said Sam. He was in front of the last poster, a handsome black-and-white photograph of a building under construction, its steel frame visible through the scaffolding. A group of four workers was posing on a girder, and Rudolf stood among them, in overalls and a cap. He looked a little older than in the previous painting, and was smiling as he held out a handkerchief embroidered with horns and a sun. The caption read, "Construction Site of the Home Insurance Building, 1885."

"I wonder why he needs to show himself with the Hathor sign," said Sam, perplexed.

"Maybe they're like his vacation pictures."

"There's got to be more to it than that. Rudolf doesn't do anything without a good reason."

They left the room with the model by another door bearing the Arkeos logo and found themselves in a huge library and office. Again, there were no windows, but there was plenty of artificial light. Alicia and Sam first explored the adjoining dressing room, which consisted of a marble bathroom and a closet that contained many linen outfits for time traveling, as well as a well-tailored dark gray suit, a starched white shirt, and a golf bag and clubs. To the left of the dressing room stood a steel door with an electronic card lock that Sam wasn't able to open.

"I'd sure like to take a look outside," he grumbled. "I'd love to know where this fancy headquarters is located."

Alicia, meanwhile, was walking around the library, which had dark wood bookcases with silver retaining bars and a rolling ladder.

"There's more than just books, Sam." Alicia sounded upset. "Come over here."

He joined her. She was right; an entire section of the wall was given over to newspaper or magazine articles, neatly clipped and framed.

"That one," Alicia said very quietly.

Sam looked over her shoulder, brushing her cheek as he did. She'd found a *Newsweek* interview titled "Time is Money." It was illustrated with a photograph of a smiling, suntanned Rudolf. But he looked strangely aged, with thinning white hair and crow's-feet around his eyes. Fearing the worst, Sam anxiously searched for the article's date. When he found it, he swore aloud.

"He sent us into the future!"

CHAPTER NINETEEN

A Blue Poker Chip

"We're in the future!" Sam said incredulously. "Seven years after our present! Seven years!"

"And it's not a joke or a gimmick," added Alicia. "All the other articles are after our time too."

"But what's the point? What's he trying to do?"

"Did you read the interview?" she asked.

Sam focused on the article, a one-page Q&A in which a *Newsweek* reporter named Rod Armor interviewed Rudolf about his plans for the Church of the Seven Resurrections.

Newsweek: After years of suspicion — not to say mockery — is the launch of your Church of the Seven Resurrections Foundation a kind of revenge for you?

Pandit Rudolf: I'm not interested in taking revenge on anybody. In fact, I'm surprised that everything has happened so quickly. When I decided to spread the word about the extraordinary experiences I have had and the precious lessons that humanity could derive from them, I didn't anticipate such excitement. Messages of support have come in from the entire world, and the few criticisms have been swept away by others' enthusiasm.

N.: *What explains the interest generated by the Church of the Seven Resurrections?*

P.R.: *The exceptional power of its message. Who wouldn't dream of having a better life for themselves, for their children, and for their friends and family if they could draw on the experience of the past, the experience of those thousands of lives lived before us? What more beautiful teaching could there be than the lives of all those men and women who for millennia before us have thought, loved, suffered, and hoped? This is what I offer to anyone who wants to listen: the inheritance of knowledge and wisdom from our ancestors. The inheritance of their lives! Because I have personally lived in several periods of history, I have become a bridge between people of yesterday and those of today.*

N.: *But people have made fun of your so-called resurrections through time.*

P.R.: *I think I have proven that what I claim is true. The greatest scientists in the world have examined the evidence I provided, and you know their conclusions as well as I do. Yes, I really did live in Pharaoh Djoser's Egypt, in ancient Greece, in China under the first dynasties, and in other periods as well. The creator has chosen me to bring the universal message of the past and help the birth of a happier future for humanity. I have been chosen. I can't help that.*

160

N.: So you're a kind of guru.

P.R.: The only title I claim is that of pandit, *which some Indian friends have been gracious enough to honor me with. A pandit is a man of knowledge, a sage, who is respected because he has great experience of people and of things. It suits me very well.*

N.: And how does Pandit Rudolf respond to the criticism of the church's finances? It's said that millions of dollars have flowed into your coffers.

P.R.: Money is not an end; money is only a means. And I have never pressured anyone to make the slightest donation. It just happens that many of the world's free citizens feel as I do, that my project will allow us to build a better future. Helping to carry out this project is helping to build this future. Is there anything wrong with that?

N.: Some people also say you are planning a political career someday.

P.R.: Then they should join the Church of the Seven Resurrections! They seem to know more about the future than I know about the past!

"Pandit Rudolf!" snapped Sam. "*Bandit* Rudolf would be more like it!"

Irritated, he quickly skimmed the other articles. They described the master's exploits, giving anecdotes from the different "existences" he had lived since his "initial rebirth"; details about his "resurrection," which made him a kind of messiah who had traveled through history to bring knowledge and happiness to his contemporaries; plus breathless testimony by followers who tearfully claimed that Pandit Rudolf had encountered one of their ancestors centuries ago, or cured them of some illness thanks to his knowledge of ancient remedies and so forth.

The most interesting article was from the magazine *History Today*. European and Japanese laboratories had apparently authenticated the Caravaggio painting and the photograph of the Home Insurance Building, thus proving Pandit Rudolf's presence in those eras. Similarly, the Hathor signs on the Chinese *Canon of Poems*, the temple at Delphi, and the Canterbury Cathedral windows were certified as "historically undeniable."

"He's founded some kind of cult, is that it?" suggested Alicia when Sam finished his reading.

"A cult that attracts money and power. But what puzzles me is why he would want to bring me here with this gray coin. Was it so I could find all this out?"

They continued their investigation with the tall cabinets that covered one wall of the library. The cabinet doors were made from the same wood as the bookshelves, but faced with sheets of frosted glass. When he leaned close, Sam could see dozens of coins with holes in them, carefully sorted and labeled with dates and places. Pandit Rudolf's treasure!

"I think I just found our ticket home," he said.

He tried the latch, but it was locked. He and Alicia checked the rest of the cabinets, but they were all locked as well.

"No problem!" said Sam, picking up a heavy steel ashtray from a coffee table. He was about to smash through the glass when Alicia grabbed his arm.

"Stop! They've got burglar alarms!"

Sam looked up; above each display case was a black box with a blinking red light.

"Before we break anything, we ought to see if there's a key around here somewhere," she suggested. "I'll search the clothes in the closet. Why don't you check the office?"

Shattering a few of Rudolf's glass cabinets would have greatly improved Sam's mood, but he gave up the idea and headed for the office. It certainly matched its owner's megalomania. A huge room with gleaming black walls, it was filled with all sorts of precious objects, but also books, letters, and bills. Pride of place was given to a book in a glass display case in front of the desk: *The Truth about My Seven Resurrections*, by Pandit Rudolf, with a suitably impressive photograph of said pandit against a setting sun. Sam didn't bother taking a closer look.

There were also photos of Rudolf in the company of celebrities with whom he seemed to enjoy lifetime friendships. Among others, Sam recognized a famous singer who was starting to show her age and a gray-haired actor who had once been a big box-office draw. Sam also noticed a replica Thoth stone about a foot high. It was made of an ugly blue plastic, but it had accurate versions of the sun and the transport cavity, plus a slot at the top, like a child's piggy bank. Was that deliberate irony? After all, that was how Rudolf thought of the stone statue: a big piggy bank that took in lots of money.

Sam turned to the desk drawers, which were crammed with letters, papers, and publications to be filed. In one he found a stack of newspapers that he immediately recognized: *The Sainte-Mary Tribune*, his hometown paper. Every copy in the stack carried some article about the Church of the Seven

Resurrections. Reading the headlines, Sam realized that Rudolf had decided to found his church right in Sainte-Mary! The front pages told it all: "Mayor Approves Seven Resurrections Building Permit"; "Barenboim Street Residents Vainly Protest Pandit's Plans"; and then, the following week: "Pandit Rudolf: 'Our Foundation is a Major Economic Boost for Sainte-Mary.'" And more recently, "Work Starts in Barenboim Neighborhood" with a photo of bulldozers leveling the little Victorian houses Sam knew so well.

Alicia came in from the other room, rousing him from his appalled silence. "Sam, I have something for you! I didn't find the key but . . ." On the desk pad she laid a white plastic card labeled "Pandit Private Residence."

"I found it in a suit pocket. You think it's the key to the main door?"

Sam nodded silently, still reeling from what he had read. He took Alicia's hand before she pulled it back, and looked her in the eye.

"What's the matter?" she asked.

He showed her the front pages of the *Tribune*.

"He's building his lousy foundation right here, Alicia. In Sainte-Mary, on Barenboim Street. He's destroying the neighborhood, knocking down our houses."

She read the headlines in turn, her frown deepening.

"How can he?" she cried. "You can't do something like that. There must be laws against it."

"Yeah, right! With all the money he's got, Rudolf could have bought off the mayor and half the city council."

"What about the bookstore? Do you think it's gone too?"

"Of course it's gone," he said bitterly. "In fact, we're right on top of it. And that's *my* stone statue in the next room; that's why it looked so familiar. Rudolf has taken over my house."

Alicia squeezed his hand gently.

"We have seven years to stop him. That's plenty of time, isn't it? If we can just get home to our own time. . . . Did you find the key?"

Sam shook his head.

"Did you look everywhere?"

"I went through every drawer."

"What about that blue thing over there; what's that?"

"A piggy bank, I suppose."

Alicia lifted the plastic stone statue and turned it over with difficulty. It was very heavy, and produced a metallic rattle.

"I think there's something in it."

"Of course there is, if it's a piggy bank."

Alicia ran her fingers over the carved sun, the transport cavity, and the slot on top without finding an opening.

"This looks like the same kind of plastic as one of your coins, right?"

The comment was so apt, Sam was startled. He took out the blue poker chip with the hole and handed it to Alicia.

"How did you get this one?" she asked, studying the poker chip.

"My dad left it for me with one of our neighbors — old Max — along with the Bran Castle coin."

"So it comes directly from Allan. . . ."

Alicia tried to push it into the opening at the top, but without success. She then pressed it against the sun. To their surprise, the sun yielded, the chip was abruptly swallowed into the depths of the stone — and a metal key suddenly dropped into the transport cavity.

"Awesome!" Alicia said.

She grabbed the key, ran to one of the coin cabinets, and promptly unlocked it.

"How about a nice little thank-you?" she teased.

"Thank you," Sam breathed, hurrying to join her. Seen up close, the cabinet was a model of organization. Sliding drawers a few inches deep each contained about fifty coins arranged alphabetically by place, by date, and in some cases, by time of day. They had unlocked the *H–L* cabinet, which contained about thirty coins related to London in a dozen different centuries. The ultimate travel agency!

"The *S*'s must be to the right," suggested Sam.

It took them only a few seconds to reach the correct cabinet. Except for a few drawers dedicated to São Paulo and Sydney, most of it was given over to Sainte-Mary, with a special focus on the last decade. There were at least five hundred coins. Sam and Alicia worked their way through each level until they reached their current year, which was the largest collection of all.

"Bingo!" said Alicia triumphantly, pointing at three coins that roughly corresponded to the moment of their departure. "Why don't we go back right before my kidnapping?"

"Can't do that," Sam said. "There would be two Alicias and two Sams in Sainte-Mary at the same instant, and Setni says we wouldn't survive that. So the next one we can take is . . ." He picked up a plain silver disk that was blank except for the hole and the roughly stamped date and time. "This is six days after we disappeared; that should do the trick. And the arrival is scheduled for midnight, so we can sneak right back in." Turning the disk over in his hand, he said, "Know what I think? I think Rudolf makes the coins himself."

"Really?"

"Yeah, this whole series of coins is identical. Same metal, same shape, same rough stamping; only the date changes. He must've found a way to make his own supply of Re disks."

"There's even one for your birthday," she said, smiling as she pointed to a coin in the back stamped, "June 5 at 5 p.m." in their present year.

"Talk about a birthday," sighed Sam, picking it up. "That's the day I found the stone statue in my father's basement. Definitely not the present I wanted! Anyway, it'll be a souvenir," he said, pocketing it along with the two other coins.

As Alicia looked at the next cabinet, Sam started searching for another date three years before his present — one that mattered a great deal more to him. What if by some chance Rudolf's cabinet held a coin for the day that Elisa Faulkner died? It would give Sam a unique opportunity to save her, just as his father wanted.

With a trembling finger, Sam found the year he was looking for, and his knees almost buckled under him. The car crash had happened on July 11, and there indeed was a July 11 coin — two of them, even, so he had a choice! One was labeled 10 a.m., the other 3 p.m. For once, luck was on his side.

He pocketed both coins and ran to Alicia.

"I adore you, you know that?" he said, slipping his arms around her.

"Hey, what's got into you?" she asked, smiling, but without pulling away.

"I found a way to fix everything."

"What is it?"

"I'll tell you when we get home. Come on, we're leaving."

"Before you go," she said, holding him back, "maybe you should see this."

She was standing in front of the *T* display case, fingering a coin covered with the same grayish substance as the one Rudolf had given Sam. The label on the box read: "The *Titanic*, April 15, 1912."

"That guy's a real piece of garbage," she said in a tone of disgust. "The gray stuff must be some sort of coral or something. He didn't want to send us home. He wanted to send us straight to the bottom of the ocean!"

"Doesn't take any chances, does he? This was in case we managed to get away from Diavilo. Which also means that Rudolf couldn't have anticipated our coming here —"

Sam broke off. Looking beyond the row of *Titanic* coins, he'd spotted a box labeled "Thebes." Among the dozen disks in it, he found one that was dear to his heart: the glass scarab ring that Setni's son Ahmosis had given him three thousand years earlier to allow him to return to his present.

"This one belongs to me," he decided. "I left it in Setni's tomb during my first trip to Egypt, and Rudolf doesn't deserve to have it. Now let's get out of here!"

He took Alicia by the arm, but they hadn't gone two steps before she froze.

"Wait!" she whispered, a finger on her lips.

With a panicked expression, she pointed at the door to Rudolf's private museum. Sam listened hard and heard muffled sounds. Someone was walking around in the room next door.

CHAPTER TWENTY

Serial Killings

"Go hide in the dressing room," Sam whispered. "I'll see what's going on."

"Hey! No way we're splitting up!"

"Do it," he insisted. "We'll be easier to spot if we're together."

Alicia reluctantly left the room while Sam searched for some sort of weapon. He grabbed the steel ashtray and tiptoed toward the door. The room with the model was empty, and Sam slipped inside. He skirted the long table covered in black cloth and went to put his ear against the second door. There wasn't a sound to be heard. Maybe it had just been construction noises from outside, or footsteps on some upper floor. But what about the lights left burning and the suit and shirt hung up with the key card in a pocket? It was as if Rudolf had put his things down for only a moment, maybe just long enough to use the stone.

Very slowly, Sam turned the handle of the second door. At first all he saw was part of a display case, then most of the museum, including the samurai and the knight. Everything seemed quiet. Reassured, he opened the door wider to check the rest of the room when something cold and hard suddenly touched his head: a gun barrel.

"Well, well, it's little Faulkner," exclaimed Rudolf, who'd been behind the door. "I thought you'd be twelve thousand feet underwater by now! Drop what you're holding and straighten up slowly."

The ashtray clattered to the ground. Sam felt the gun pressing harder against his skull.

"So we meet again," said Rudolf. "You haven't changed a bit."

"You have," Sam said coldly. As in the *Newsweek* photograph, Rudolf seemed to have aged far more than the seven years that had passed since Sam's present. He had the same square jaw and gunmetal-blue eyes, but he now had a tracery of wrinkles around those eyes, as well as receding, dirty white hair. He was dressed in linen clothes like those in the closet.

"It's your all fault, boy! If you'd followed my instructions seven years ago, I wouldn't be in this situation. Step back a few feet."

Sam took three steps backward and bumped into the glass case containing the mummy.

"That's perfect. Put your hands behind your back, and don't move. There are eight rounds in the clip, and I'm an excellent shot."

Without taking his eyes off Sam, Rudolf stepped to an open safe in a cabinet like the one holding the coin collection. The safe had roll-out shelves, and Sam could see packages and old books on them.

"I was straightening up when you interrupted me. I brought back a little souvenir from a quick trip to the Scythians, and I wouldn't want it to fall into the wrong hands."

With the same maddening, self-satisfied smile, he held up a magnificent gold pendant about six inches high that showed a rider on a rearing horse. Rudolf had to turn in order to set his prize on one of the safe's shelves, and Sam chose that moment to act. He closed his eyes and forced his heart-beat to slow down, to match the dull pounding of Time within him.

But he had barely begun to experience the movement of his blood when he felt a stabbing pain in his chest, as if his heart was misfiring. He staggered and had to lean against the glass display case to keep from collapsing.

"Well, well, feeling bad?" asked an amused Rudolf. "Too much pressure, maybe — our boy can't handle the discomfort of traveling. Stand up nice and straight, and keep your hands behind your back."

Sam opened his eyes and breathed deeply, releasing the tightness in his chest. He was no longer able to slow Time! He had lost the ability to focus, or his heart couldn't handle it any-more. Or maybe Rudolf was somehow stopping him.

"I've been angry at you, you know," continued Rudolf. "You were supposed to give Diavilo the Meriweserre bracelet, remember? I don't know what happened there. He told me some mixed-up story about a sudden disappearance and witch-craft — in any case, he let you get away. But since you never appeared in the present, I figured you'd used my pretty *Titanic* coin and I was rid of you at last. Apparently —"

"Apparently I'm still here," Sam said defiantly.

"You're here, all right," said Rudolf with a nasty laugh. "The last of the Faulkners."

The sentence hit Sam like a punch in the face. What did Rudolf mean, "the last of the Faulkners"?

"I can see you haven't heard the news," said Rudolf delightedly. "Besides, how could you? Allow me to extend my condolences, somewhat after the fact. There was an unfortunate fire at your grandparents' place. Everything went up in smoke."

"*What?* When?"

"It happened a few days after you left. The house caught fire during the night. Everybody died."

Sam stepped forward, but Rudolf stopped him with a flick of his pistol.

"Don't try it, boy! Getting yourself shot here isn't going to bring them back."

"What about my father?" Sam asked dully.

"Ah, poor old Allan," said Rudolf with a big sigh. "He never came out of his coma. After waiting six months, the doctors pulled the plug."

For Sam, this news felt like a second punch. His father hadn't survived. Sam had failed him. He had failed right down the line!

"Life is unfair, isn't it?" continued Rudolf. "That's what I often told myself. Especially when I realized that while I could travel across the centuries, the price of the ticket was high. The traveler ages quickly and dies prematurely. Hell of a paradox, isn't it? The stone statue lets us push back the frontiers of Time, but it shrinks the tiny boundaries of our existence with each trip. You know that the Hathor sign lets you move between two places where the sign is drawn. But there are dozens of

Hathor signs by now, and I've sometimes had to make fifteen or twenty trips before getting to the right place. And with each one, I lose a little more life. Disgusting, eh?"

What Sam really found disgusting was Rudolf's contempt for other people — especially the Faulkners.

"But experience did teach me a few helpful things," Rudolf was saying. "For example, I found that if you travel with a lot of Re disks made in a place with the Hathor sign, your chances of getting to that place are two or three times as good. It's as if you're able to steer your way a little in the flow of Time. Naturally, that got me interested in how to make Re disks myself. I found an old Indian book that said the coins of a given period could only be created in that period, and that you had to follow certain rules. By following these rules I started making my own coins, and that spared me some useless trips — though not all of them; far from it. So I continued to age, and much too quickly. Which is why I had to have the Golden Circle."

Rudolf pulled out one of the safe's shelves. It held a softly glowing gold bracelet that looked exactly like the one in Sam's pocket.

"So you have it," said Sam soberly.

"Yes, I have it, but it wasn't easy. Especially because of your parents."

"My parents!" yelled Sam, again ready to rush him. "They're dead! Don't you have any respect for anything?"

"How do you know they're not involved in this?" retorted Rudolf. "You don't know anything about it. Do you want to die trying to jump me, or do you want to hear the story?"

Digging his nails into his palms, Sam struggled to control himself. He couldn't give Rudolf an excuse to shoot him. That would leave Alicia alone with this monster and ruin Sam's only chance of saving anyone. He had to wait until Rudolf made a mistake.

"That's better," said Rudolf approvingly. "I know you've heard of the Golden Circle, which was supposedly found by the high priest Setni."

Rudolf's smile was a snarl.

"Setni the old lunatic, I should say. He thought he'd been given a divine mission: to keep travelers from changing the course of Time for their own benefit. What naïveté! As if he were able to watch over all of history by himself."

"Setni was a good man," Sam shot back. "He tried to use Time for the good of everyone, unlike you!"

"So fair and good that it made him stupid," said Rudolf sarcastically. "He managed to find the Eternity Ring but didn't think to use it himself! He hid it somewhere in his tomb and then, like an idiot, let himself die. That's wisdom for you!"

"He knew the ring would corrupt whoever used it," said Sam. "He did the right thing."

"Since you feel so close to Setni, ask him where he put the ring," said Rudolf with a laugh. "You'd be doing me a big favor. Go ahead, ask him. He's right here."

With his pistol, he gestured at the display case. Sam shrank back. The mummy in the sarcophagus!

"It can't be," stammered Sam. "That isn't him!"

"Oh, yes it is. Venerable old Setni himself. I paid the Thebes museum a small fortune for him, hoping he'd give up a few secrets about the Eternity Ring. But the old fool is still holding his tongue. I've had him X-rayed and scanned, and haven't found anything at all."

The sight of Setni's mummy came as a third blow to Sam. He stood dazed for a minute, torn between sadness and dismay at the poor body wrapped in its yellowing bandages. Sam remembered the last words he had exchanged with Setni: "Will we see each other again someday?" he had asked. And the venerable guardian of the stones had answered, "Probably not in the way you imagine, young man." Sam was standing before the body of the most illustrious time traveler of all, and it was on display in Rudolf's museum like just another trophy.

"If you read *The Treatise on the Thirteen Virtues of Magic* carefully, it's clear that he buried the ring somewhere in his tomb," Rudolf was saying. "Oh, yes, I've read the *Treatise* now, Sammy; you left it for me in Rome, remember? I'd already read Chamberlain's copy at the time I sent you back to get it, but I needed the whole thing. And my gamble with you paid off: The very last page has a drawing of Setni's sarcophagus and an explicit commentary. But where did he hide the ring, exactly? That's what I'd like to know. You don't have any idea, do you?"

"No, I don't."

"Well, too bad. We'll come back to that later. For now, I promised you a story, didn't I? It starts thirty years ago, when your father and I were working together on the Thebes excavation. We'd found some coins with holes in them in a cup, and while fooling around, he placed one on the stone's sun. I was right next to him, and that's how the two of us were shot through Time. I'll spare you the struggles we had to get back to our own time. It wasn't easy, as you can imagine. Once we made it back, we resumed working on the dig, and that's when I made a major find: a finely wrought gold bracelet that seemed to fit on the stone perfectly. We tried it one night, and again found ourselves launched many centuries into the past, except that this time, we felt we could control our movements better.

"But when we got back to the excavation, your father said he was quitting time traveling completely. I did my best to point out how wonderful the situation could be for us, but he wouldn't listen. The discussion grew heated, we had a fight, and . . ."

Rudolf shook his head and blinked, as if all these years later he was still mystified by what had happened.

"I don't know how your father did it, but he managed to knock me out. When I came to, I thought I could see a dark shape near the stone and a brilliant ball of light. Allan had disappeared, and he'd taken the Golden Circle."

Sam felt a small twinge of satisfaction: *He* had been the dark shape, and he had delivered the knockout blow. A pleasant bit of anticipatory vengeance, all things considered! But the Golden Circle? He remembered the young Allan kneeling by Rudolf's prostrate body, slipping something into his pocket.

"The watchman caught me leaving the tomb," continued Rudolf, "and when Professor Chamberlain learned what I'd done, he sent me home. I had no way to see your father again, and especially no way to get the Golden Circle! Maybe now you can understand why I was so angry at Allan. By taking the bracelet, he'd stolen an entire piece of my life!"

Rudolf's hand was shaking, and Sam was briefly afraid he might pull the trigger by mistake. But Rudolf controlled himself and continued.

"Of course at the time I didn't know the full power of the Golden Circle. All I wanted was to find a new stone statue so that I could time travel again. That took me two full years of searching the world's libraries, two years of false leads and blind alleys. But I succeeded. And then I made up for lost time, believe me. I spent the whole next decade traveling, stopping in the present only briefly, and accumulating a nice little wad of cash in the process. Because it wasn't just valuable objects that made me rich, you know. I also had priceless information. Think of how much you can make in the market if you know how a company's stock is going to behave over the next ten years! Or how valuable a gold mine can be when you know its location half a century before anyone else. I had a field day."

Rudolf looked very pleased with himself, which irritated Sam, but also encouraged him. Smugness might cause Rudolf to lower his guard.

"I soon saw the advantage of setting up a company to sell valuable antiquities. And that's how Arkeos was born. But the more I used the Hathor sign, the faster I aged. I had heard of certain objects that could limit the negative effects of traveling, and further research turned up descriptions of the Golden Circle and references to Setni. Naturally I made the connection with the bracelet your father had stolen from me."

Rudolf paused to put away the Scythian pendant and close the safe, but did it without taking his eye off Sam.

"It took me a few months to pick up your father's trail, but when I learned he'd moved to Sainte-Mary, I quickly figured out why. I knew about Garry Barenboim and his exploits, and I quickly identified the house he'd owned in the early twentieth century. I paid a call on its new owner, a kind of a drunken witch who lived with a pack of crazy dogs. And as icing on the cake, the place turned out to house a stone statue! The witch refused to sell the house, but we worked out an arrangement so I could use the basement from time to time."

He kicked the cabinet door closed and took a step toward Sam.

"Of course that didn't solve the question of the Golden Circle, as you can imagine. So that's when I started watching your parents. I did it discreetly, as work or travel allowed. I wondered what your father was up to, whether he still had the bracelet or had sold it, and whether he was planning something or if his being in Sainte-Mary was just a coincidence. I even saw you in the garden a few times. You were pretty wild, as I recall, and not especially well-behaved."

Sam felt his heart sink. Even in those carefree days, the Arkeos man was hidden in the shadows, watching.

"And then I saw it," said Rudolf. "It was late one afternoon. Your parents were going out with some friends, and your mother was wearing the Golden Circle on her wrist. Allan had given it to her! It didn't shine as brightly as I remembered, but I would've recognized it anywhere. I was parked at the curb, my window halfway down, and your mother walked right by me. I could've opened the door and jumped her, but there were too many people around, and I might have ruined everything. So I decided to wait and try something different."

He took another step closer, and his face hardened.

"One nice thing about time travel is that it makes it easy to cover your tracks. Suppose you want to rob a bank, and you need a cast-iron alibi. On the date planned, you make sure you're seen somewhere far from the bank, in some crowded place where people will notice you. Then, a week later, you return to the chosen day, put on your mask, take your gun, and take care of business. Whatever happens, no one could possibly suspect you, because twenty people will testify that they'd seen you at that very moment hundreds of miles away. It really is the perfect crime."

Sam felt as if he were swallowing a pincushion.

"And that's how you went after my parents?"

"The Golden Circle belonged to me!" Rudolf practically shouted. "Your father stole it from *me*! I was just putting things right. I knew he wouldn't hand it over. What if we wound up fighting, the way we had the first time? I had already aged so much — I couldn't afford to lose it again. I had to take precautions."

"What you really wanted was to take revenge on him," blurted Sam.

"Well — yes, perhaps! I'm just a man, and I have my weaknesses. And your father had it coming," Rudolf snarled. "In any case, I prepared everything in detail. I hired a Sainte-Mary jeweler to make a dozen Re disks to my exact specifications, with certain dates and times. Meanwhile, I took a trip to Australia to create an alibi. When I got back, I collected the coins and started trying to travel about eight days into the past. It took me six or seven attempts with the Hathor sign, but I wound up landing in the Barenboim Street basement on the day I'd chosen."

Inside Sam's throat, the pincushion had now turned into a porcupine, and he could hardly speak.

"Was that July 11, ten years ago?"

"Yes, I think so; midsummer, anyway. I went to your house in Bel View, but Allan wasn't there, just your mother. I followed her into the garage, but when I asked for the Golden Circle, she claimed it had been stolen a few days earlier. I didn't believe her, of course, and I made her show me her jewelry box. There was no sign of the bracelet. I got angry and shook her up a little, but she stuck to her story. How could I imagine she was telling the truth? It seemed unbelievable! It was only by putting the facts together three years later that I understood what had happened. Someone had indeed taken the bracelet: old Maggie Pye!"

"Miss Pye?" stammered Sam, who could hardly believe his ears.

"That's right, the nice neighbor lady with the high-minded family values. She has a dark side, that one. When she saw the Golden Circle on your mother's wrist, she couldn't resist. She used to come to your house to babysit you, remember? She told me later — that's when she stole it. But how could I know that then? Your mother kept saying that someone had broken into the house, and I lost my temper."

A murderous gleam flashed in his eyes.

"So what happened?" asked Sam, who could feel the spiky lump moving from his throat to his stomach.

"I hit her, a little hard. Not on purpose. She fell and hit her head on the corner of the table and . . . But why did she have to struggle?" he shouted angrily. "That's all your parents have ever done, gotten in my way! I had to get rid of the body, so I loaded her in her car, drove to Doomsday Hill, and set things up so it looked like an accident. After the car rolled down the hill, I had to walk all the way home."

Sam clenched his fists as his eyes filled with tears. It was all too much. This guy had killed his mother and maybe his whole family. And there he was, alive, enjoying what he'd done, pitying himself for his long walk home. . . . No wonder Allan Faulkner had been so obsessed with finding the Meriweserre bracelet: He figured he could save his wife with the Golden Circle, only to find it gone at the time of her death. So he went looking for the copy to restore Time as he knew it, and wound up paying with his health and his life.

"Did you enjoy my story, Sammy?" Rudolf said mockingly. "Now it's time to move on to serious things. I think you have a little present for me, one you were supposed to deliver to me seven years ago. Empty your pockets onto the display case."

The Meriweserre bracelet, thought Sam. *Rudolf wants it too.* And once he had both Golden Circles, he would certainly manage to find the Eternity Ring. But maybe Sam had one last chance. He knew from experience that the bracelet tended to entrance anyone seeing it for the first time; Rudolf was sure to relax his guard when Sam pulled the bracelet from his pocket, and that would be his opportunity.

He put his hand in his pants pocket, while looking Rudolf right in the eye, alert to the slightest sign of distraction. The instant his gaze wavered, Sam would kick him in the shins and knock the pistol aside.

But just as Sam was visualizing his next move, he heard a noise coming from the room with the model of the church. Alicia must have left the dressing room! Sam couldn't keep from glancing toward the open door, and the move gave him away.

"How stupid I am!" cried Rudolf. "Your little girlfriend is here, of course! I forgot all about her. You saved her from Diavilo and brought her back with you. That must have been very romantic. . . . Ah," he said in a tone of wonder and delight, "*that's* why you two never came back to the present! You didn't wind up at the bottom of the ocean at all. I killed you in the future!"

His gun still trained on Sam, Rudolf gestured him toward the double door with the Arkeos logo.

"That way, Sammy. We're going to play hide-and-seek."

CHAPTER TWENTY-ONE

The Sixth Day

"In the dressing room!" Rudolf cried. "I bet she hid in the dressing room. Am I right? That's what I would've done."

Sam didn't answer. Mechanically, he pushed the door open and entered the room with the model, with Rudolf right behind him.

"By the way, I didn't have time to introduce you to my new baby, the Church of the Seven Resurrections — a major success! It's the biggest moneymaker I've ever developed, and it's roaring right along. Under other circumstances I'm sure it would interest you."

Sam bit his lip, trying hard to think of a way to warn Alicia while keeping Rudolf from finding her. But with the gun barrel on his neck, he felt like a lamb headed for the slaughter.

"Keep walking," said Rudolf. "I'm anxious to see how your girlfriend's doing."

When Sam stepped into the office, he immediately noticed that the door leading to the outside, the one controlled by the key card, was ajar.

"Well, well, it looks as if your friend needed some fresh air. She must've found the card in my jacket. I'm afraid she may be out of luck. But we'll check the dressing room anyway, if you don't mind."

Rudolf pushed Sam into the dressing room and quickly searched it. Then they returned to the door leading to the outside. Rudolf popped open a plastic box on the wall covering the card reader and fiddled with the wires inside. An alarm began to shriek and the ceiling lights started to flash.

"She won't get far," shouted Rudolf over the alarm. "There are men with dogs all around the construction site. I'm afraid you've made the wrong choice again!"

Rudolf shoved Sam into a hall with flashing strobe lights that smelled of fresh paint and plaster. Where could Alicia be? And why had she taken off this way?

As they walked toward a staircase, Sam wondered if he could brace himself against the banister and use the change of level to kick Rudolf in the stomach. He resolved to try his luck when they were halfway up, at the point where the stairway turned. But before he reached the first step, he heard a kind of crunch behind him, followed by a dull thud. He spun around to find Alicia holding a golf club in both hands, with Rudolf lying at her feet.

"Alicia!" shouted Sam.

She was shaking. "I didn't kill him, did I?"

"He would have deserved it," said Sam, as he knelt to check Rudolf's pulse. "No, he's just knocked out. How did you manage it?"

"I used the key card to open the door to make him think

I'd gone outside, then hid under the table with the model. The two of you walked right by me. So I took one of the golf clubs in the closet and . . ."

Sam stood up and hugged her in delight. She was warm and trembling, and he couldn't resist kissing her on the corner of the mouth.

"Thanks, Alicia. You were great!"

"I said you could count on me, didn't I?"

A door slammed somewhere above them. Between blasts of the alarm, they could hear running footsteps on the stairs.

"Quick," said Sam. "Reinforcements are coming!"

They returned to the office, closed the door behind them, and raced to Rudolf's museum, where the alarm was also howling. Sam made a detour to the cabinet safe and spent a moment wrestling with the handle, but it didn't budge.

"The other Golden Circle is inside," he explained breathlessly.

"Sam, it's a safe!" Alicia yelled. "Do you think they're going to wait for you to figure out the combination?"

"All right," he said, giving in. "Let's go."

They ran between the display cases to the stone statue, and Sam kneeled to ready the Meriweserre bracelet for the trip. He threw the *Titanic* coin aside, replaced it with the two July 11 ones, and put the glass scarab and his birthday coin in the transport cavity. When he set the Meriweserre bracelet on the sun, each coin obediently settled into its proper slit. On the solar disk Sam put the final coin, the one that should bring them back a few days after their departure.

Alicia gave a cry of astonishment as little fountains of sparks shot from the six rays. Sam drew her close and they held each other, fascinated by the tiny fireworks display. Soon a brilliant ball of light enveloped the sun, as if it had suddenly come to life, and Sam watched its golden glow lighting up Alicia's eyes. They were like two suns, he thought, shining at each other.

Pounding from the office next door urged them to get going. Sam put his arm around Alicia's shoulder and laid his hand on the stone. In barely a second a flood of incandescent lava seemed to rise from the bowels of the earth, sucking the two of them into a fiery whirlwind.

Sam was the first to return to consciousness, but it was with the unusual feeling of not having moved at all. It was as if he'd been struck by lightning and come back to life at exactly the same place. He stood up and looked around. The basement of Faulkner's Antique Books looked the way it always did — namely, dusty, dark, and nothing like the riot of bright lights and antiquities that characterized the pandit's apartment. The same nightlight cast the same weak glow on the same stool and cot. It was a lot less chic than Rudolf's lair, but a lot more comforting.

He leaned over Alicia, who was crouched on the dusty cement floor, slowly gathering her wits, and helped her up.

"Where are we?" she stammered.

"We're home. Well, at my father's bookstore, in the basement."

"You don't need to repeat everything twice, Sam," she said in an accusing tone. Sam, who was very familiar with the echo effect caused by the stone statue upon a return to the present, stayed silent until she spoke again.

"So we're in our own time? You're sure?"

"Yeah, just a few days after we left."

Still dazed by the intensity of the transfer, she bent her head and put her arms around Sam's neck. She hung on him for a moment, her face buried against his chest, without saying a word. Sam didn't know quite what to do, so he just closed his eyes and hugged her tight. At last, she drew back and looked away.

"I have to call my parents," she said wearily. "This is when we pick up our lives again, right?"

"That's right," said Sam.

They went upstairs in silence. The clock above the front door read 12:34 a.m. — a half hour later than the midnight coin had promised. That was odd, but perhaps Rudolf's coins weren't all that accurate. While Alicia made her call, Sam went to his bedroom to change and to stuff his things into his judo bag. When he joined her, she was just putting down the phone.

"Well?" he asked.

"My father wasn't there, but I got my mom. Basically she said that this was the best day of her life. She's jumping in the car and coming right over."

"She was really upset the last time I saw her," he said. "What are you going to tell her?"

Alicia shrugged. "The truth, I guess. That's simplest, don't you think?"

She gave Sam a meaningful look, but he changed the subject.

"I've got to let my grandparents know we're back. Do you mind?"

Alicia yielded the phone and went to freshen up while Sam dialed the number. He let it ring at least a dozen times, but nobody answered. He tried again, then twice more. Everyone at the house must be sound asleep.

"Mind if I take a change of clothes?" Alicia called down. "If my mother sees me like this, she'll have a heart attack."

"Look in my father's closet. First room on the left. It's full of linen shirts and pants. Help yourself."

While she changed, Sam again tried to reach his grandparents, but with no more success. Alicia came back down a few moments later wearing one of Allan Faulkner's distinctive time-traveler outfits. Her hair was combed and her skin glowed. How was it, Sam wondered, that the white clothes that hung on him like old pajamas somehow made Alicia look like a fashion model?

"Did you reach them?" she asked.

"There's no answer. I tried and tried."

"Aren't your grandparents a bit deaf?"

"Aunt Evelyn should be with them, and she's not hard of hearing, as far as I know," he said.

"What about Lily? Is she home from summer camp yet?"

"We left six days ago, and Lily isn't due back until next month. But with or without her, Evelyn and Grandma should've woken up. Unless they all went out in the middle of the night, which really isn't like them."

"Do you think there's a problem?"

"I don't know. Did you hear what Rudolf was saying earlier?"

"Well, just the end, when he was talking about . . . about your mother."

"Yeah, my mother," said Sam flatly. "That wasn't an accident. He killed her. But there was something else even worse. He told me that my grandparents' house burned down a few days after I left for Rome, and that they all died."

"What?" exclaimed Alicia.

"There was a fire a few days after I left." A horrible thought struck him. "I don't know how many days . . ."

Alicia stared at him. "You mean it could be happening right now?"

A squeal of tires in the street broke them out of their reverie. They ran to the door to welcome Helena Todds, who burst from her car and rushed to her daughter's arms.

"Alicia! Alicia, darling!" She covered her with kisses, laughing and sobbing at once.

"Mom, Mom! Calm down! It's me, I'm here!"

"Are you all right? I was so worried! You're looking thin! You weren't hurt, were you?"

"I'm fine, Mom, relax. It's all thanks to Sam. He's the one who brought me back."

Helena Todds turned to Sam, hugged him so hard his ribs hurt, and burst into tears again.

"Sammy, you're back too! Your grandparents have been looking for you all week! Were the two of you together?"

"When did you last talk to my grandparents?" Sam said urgently.

"Well, they called me yesterday or the day before, I can't remember. They seemed fine. Why?"

Alicia and Sam exchanged a serious look.

"We have to drive Sam to his house, Mom. Right away."

"You should call them first! I'm sure they would be happy —"

Alicia interrupted her. "It's really important. Sam thinks they may be in danger."

"What? What the —"

"Please, Mom, listen to me! We're going to Sam's right now! I'll tell you everything on the way, okay?"

Helena Todds looked at them one after another, clearly puzzled, but led them straight to her car. Sam sat in back, listening with only half an ear to the beginning of Alicia's story and her mother's responses. Instead he focused on the passing lights, expecting at any moment to see flames rising into the sky over Sainte-Mary. He was now positive that the fire would occur tonight, and that the arsonist could only be Rudolf. Why else would he have bothered to fabricate a coin to take him to Sainte-Mary that very night? On the day of the tragedy — today, in other words — he must have been parading somewhere far from Canada, planning to have his future self go back in time to commit the crime. He would rid himself of the last Faulkners, and nobody would be the wiser.

But this time, Sam was on his trail — provided, of course, that it wasn't too late.

"We have to call the police right away!" said Helena Todds in a rage over her daughter's story. "I mean really, Evelyn's fiancé! Who can you trust anymore? And once he made you get in the car, where did he take you?"

Alicia was at the critical juncture where she was going to have to convince her mother she'd been time traveling, but they reached the Faulkners' neighborhood just then, and they started peering at the darkened houses. The street lamps cast pools of light along the sidewalks, and few windows were still lit up.

"Everything looks pretty quiet, doesn't it?" murmured Alicia.

"What do you expect?" asked her mother in surprise. "It's nearly one in the morning; people are asleep!"

Sam lowered his window to sniff the air, but didn't smell anything suspicious. As the car turned right into the familiar pine tree–lined street, however, it passed a large black SUV with its lights out driving quickly in the other direction.

"That's Rudolf's 4x4!" Sam shouted.

"What? Is Rudolf here?" said Helena Todds in a panic. "What should we do?"

"Keep driving to my place," urged Sam.

She sped up, and they finally saw his grandparents' house, about thirty yards ahead on the right. The downstairs and upstairs curtains were all drawn, but moving light shone through them, as if a bunch of TVs were all showing the same bright yellow and orange images.

"Too late," Sam groaned. "He's already lit the fire!"

CHAPTER TWENTY-TWO

Inferno

Sam jumped out of the car the moment Helena Todds rammed it against the curb.

"Call the fire department!" he shouted. "Quick!"

"Don't go inside!" cried Alicia. "You could get killed!" But Sam had already vaulted Grandpa's flower bed and was racing to the front door. When he stuck his key in the lock, it jammed, so he heaved a rock through the living room window. Reaching through the broken glass, he grabbed the latch and opened the window.

He stepped over the sill, pushing the curtain aside. Fire hadn't reached this part of the living room, but Sam could see flames in the kitchen and the hall leading to Aunt Evelyn's and his grandparents' bedrooms, and the air smelled of gasoline.

"Grandma?" he yelled. "Aunt Evelyn?"

Nobody answered. He would have to run through the flames to reach them. Sam yanked with all his might on the curtain, which popped off the rod. He wrapped himself in it like a toga, praying that the cloth had been treated with fire retardant.

"Aunt Evelyn? Grandpa?"

Everybody seemed to be asleep. Sam rushed toward the bedrooms, feeling the temperature around him rise as he went. Acrid smoke was coming from the kitchen — probably some plastic burning — and he had to cover his mouth before entering the hallway. Flames were licking the walls and scorching the wallpaper, but they weren't high enough to stop him. The fire had apparently just begun. Strangely, Sam wasn't as bothered by the heat as he would have expected, as if his repeated experiences with the stone statue had made him less sensitive to the flames.

He kicked open the first door on the left, which led to his aunt's bedroom.

"Aunt Evelyn!" he yelled.

To his astonishment, she lay sleeping peacefully in her bed. The bathroom was aflame, and broken bottles littered the floor, creating a pool of burning liquid that had spread along the baseboards and carpet.

"Aunt Evelyn!" he shouted. "Wake up!"

He slipped the curtain off his shoulders and used it to beat out the flames. Then he rushed to the bed and started roughly shaking his aunt.

"Aunt Evelyn, get up!"

A large wad of cotton lay next to the pillow, and when he sniffed it, Sam recognized the heady smell of chloroform. Rudolf must have waited until the Faulkners went to bed, then knocked them out for good. Sam had no choice but to slap his aunt to rouse her from her drugged sleep. She opened her eyes and sleepily asked, "Is it the toast? Did you burn the toast?"

"This is no time to eat! The house is on fire!"

194

"The what?" It took her a few seconds to wake up and realize what was going on. "Sam! The house is on fire!"

"It'll be okay, Aunt Evelyn. Put this on," he said, wrapping her in a blanket. "Keep it pulled tight; it'll protect you. Come on!"

In spite of her protests, he forced her to get up and cross the line of flames at the threshold.

"Everything's on fire," she screamed. "It's all burning!"

She started coughing and gagging from the smoke. Sam pushed her into the living room, where flames now licked up the armchairs.

"Hurry over to the window," he urged her. "Alicia will help you out. I'll get Grandma and Grandpa."

He turned back to the bedrooms, trying not to inhale the toxic fumes from the garage and the kitchen. He again crossed the overheated hallway to the back bedroom, where his grandparents must be asleep.

"Grandma!" he shouted. "Grandpa!"

When he entered the room, Sam immediately spotted a fire by the bed: a wastepaper basket filled with rags drenched in gasoline. Rudolf had set a small barbecue propane tank next to it. The fire wasn't enough for him, apparently; he'd planned to blow the whole place up as well. Sam kicked the wastepaper basket, sending it flying toward the bathroom, and shoved the gas canister as far from the flames as he could. In the darkness, Grandpa was leaning back against his pillow, eyes open, but silent and motionless. Sam rushed over to him.

"Grandpa, are you okay? You can't stay here!"

Donovan Faulkner seemed to be in a stupor.

"Did somebody yell?" he asked distantly.

"Lean on the night table," Sam encouraged him, once he'd gotten him upright. "I'll take care of Grandma."

He reached across the bed to his grandmother and gently slid an arm under her shoulders to lift her. He whispered in her ear, "Grandma, it's Sam. I need you to wake up, right away."

Her head nodded gently, and she eventually opened an eye.

"Sam!" she cried. "My God, Sam, is it you? I'm not dreaming, am I?"

"There's been a fire, Grandma," he answered as calmly as he could. "We have to leave."

"There's a fire . . . ?"

Despite the astonishment in her voice, she quickly gathered her wits. She touched her husband's arm, then pointed to the window to her right.

"We can go out through there," she said. "It's faster."

Sam strode quickly over to the windows. Evelyn's bedroom had bars on its windows, which Sam attributed to her neurotic fear of the outside world. But his grandparents' room opened directly onto the garden; you could just step over the windowsill. Sam parted the curtains and swung the windows wide. The fresh air felt like a caress on his face, and he thought he heard someone yelling his name.

"Sam! Saaamm!"

"I'm here! At the back of the house!" he shouted.

While his grandmother circled the bed to get Donovan, who was completely disoriented, Sam grabbed the propane tank and heaved it outside. That was one less danger, anyway. Then he took the chair from the dressing table and set it under the window as a stepping stool.

"Saaammm!"

Aunt Evelyn emerged from the garden shadows with Alicia on her heels.

"Sam!" she repeated, out of breath. "It's Lily —"

"What about Lily?"

"She's upstairs in her bedroom!"

"Lily's here?" Sam was dumbfounded.

"Yes, she came home yesterday," Evelyn moaned. "She insisted. She said you would never get back without her!"

Sam felt a sour taste fill his mouth. Lily had the ability to help bring Sam home to his own time by thinking hard about him. So she was upstairs because of him. . . . "Did you call the fire department?"

"Mom called them three minutes ago," Alicia answered. "They should be here any moment now." She didn't mention what they both knew, that the fire station was on the other side of town.

"There was a propane tank at the foot of the bed," said Sam. "You've got to warn them when they arrive; there may be others. I'm going to get Lily. Alicia, look after my grand-parents, okay?"

A wave of objections erupted, but Sam would have none of them. He quickly ran back along the hall, again wrapped in his makeshift fire suit. Steam was rising from the walls, as if the house were sweating a bad fever through its pores. The flames in the kitchen and living room were now much higher, and had started licking at the door to the garage. That wasn't good: Grandpa's car was parked inside, and its gas tank was probably full.

Sam raced up the stairs with no problem, but the fire had already reached his and his cousin's bedrooms. He thought of all his things, his computer, the photos of his mother on his desk, the little everyday items he would never see again. But none of those mattered compared to Lily's safety.

He took a deep breath and entered his cousin's domain. The burning curtains made a noise like crackling candy wrappers, and Lily's bookcase shot yellow flashes to the ceiling as the books caught fire. Fortunately, the bed was just to the right of the door, and Sam was relieved to see the flames hadn't reached it. He yanked off the blanket and found Lily curled up in a fetal position, drenched in sweat, with a wad of cotton next to her nose. He batted the chloroform away and rolled his cousin onto her back. She was completely limp. "Lily! Come on, big girl, we gotta get out of here!"

He shook her by the shoulder, but she didn't react. Was she dead? Had Rudolf used too much . . . ? Sam took a bottle from the night table and splashed water on her face. This produced a little hiss of steam, but Lily still didn't move.

He tried to estimate how much time he had to bring her around. The fire had apparently started in the wastebasket under the desk. It had spread to the curtains, jumped to the bookcase, and was now scorching the posters on the wall and the purple carpet next to the bed. A dark, round shape lay beside a stack of magazines under the window: another propane tank, with flames already moving toward it.

"Lily," he shouted, shaking her harder. "We gotta go! You have to —"

BOOM!

He fell on top of his cousin, feeling the explosion's hot wind on his hair and skin. He didn't look up until the walls had stopped shaking and the air was still again. Everything around him — sheets, furniture, floor — was covered in fine gray dust, and a blizzard of charred scraps of paper swirled in the air.

Sam spat out the dust filling his nose and mouth, then put his hands to his ears. His temples hurt terribly, and he couldn't hear much, except for a sort of background static. The propane tank across the room was still intact, so the explosion must have happened in the kitchen or the garage. Sam could see a bright reddish glow in the stairwell, which meant that the fire downstairs was spreading. He couldn't afford to wait for a second explosion, especially one that might occur just ten feet away.

He gently put his arms around his cousin's limp body and tugged her to the edge of the bed. Crouching down, he slung her over his shoulder and struggled to his feet, then shuffled slowly toward the stairs. Sounds from the outside reached him in an oddly distant way, as if he were wearing noise-canceling headphones. For a moment, he wondered if he'd gone deaf, but that thought was driven away by a more urgent one. The staircase was still intact, but the bottom steps were now ablaze, which put the living room out of reach. Sam considered turning back to wait for the firefighters, but that meant risking the much greater danger of the gas canister exploding.

He had one option left to him: the slowing of Time. Sam closed his eyes and concentrated on going inside himself, but he had just started to visualize the regular movement of his heart muscle when the pain he'd experienced in Rudolf's museum again stabbed his chest. He stumbled, but Lily's weight on his shoulder reminded him that he couldn't afford to fail. Gritting his teeth against the pain, he continued to slow his heartbeat until it merged with the pulsing of the stone.

He opened his eyes. The green sheen familiar to him from his previous time-slowing efforts hung over everything he saw. The living room furniture appeared as dark blotches below him, and motionless clouds of smoke billowed along the ceiling. But his heart throbbed in his chest with every beat of Time, and Sam knew he wouldn't be able to keep this up very long. He moved slowly down the stairs, pressing his thigh against the banister to keep from falling, and reached the sea of flames. Even though they looked frozen, they still radiated suffocating heat. He wrapped the blanket around his and Lily's heads, took a deep breath, and walked into the inferno.

They were five or six yards from the window, seven at most. He was relieved to realize that his hunch had been right: The heat was certainly intense, but the flames didn't have time to burn him as he passed. Indeed, the worst was happening inside him. In his superhuman effort to keep his pulse in tune with the rhythm of the stone, his heart felt caught in a red-hot pincer, and the pain spread with every beat. As it rolled through his neck and down his left arm, he had to fight an overwhelming desire to give up. But he knew he had to save Lily, and that idea guided him like a pole star through his agony.

Sam stumbled forward through the still waves of flame. He crossed the foyer, felt the living room carpet under his feet, almost bumped into the sofa, and turned left toward the window.

But six feet from the window, he stopped dead. Something in his chest was stuck. It wasn't exactly pain — more like a short circuit that brought all the machinery of his body to a halt. Lily still lay unconscious on his shoulder, and he could see lights glaring outside and frozen firefighters reaching through the window. Just two steps . . .

Somehow he managed one step, then a second. His entire body went into a spasm as he took a third. As Sam blacked out, he pitched headfirst to the ground, barely feeling Lily's weight as she crashed down on top of him. He heard the sharp crack as Time resumed its normal course, and at the same instant, he felt something infinitely long and delicious, an ultimate deliverance: his last and final heartbeat.

CHAPTER TWENTY-THREE

Visitors

If life was air, then death was water, a warm, comforting liquid through which Sam swam effortlessly. He glided along, free of gravity, free of all the pain he'd endured while in his earthly guise. He could hear voices, distorted by distance — the unbridgeable distance from life, perhaps — calling to him from some far-off shore. Hands ran over him, looking for something — a last breath or spark of consciousness. Glowing flares whirled through the dark sky like colored stars. But Sam was a sea creature now, floating far away, free of everything. Soon, he would be with his mother.

"We're losing him!" someone in the other world was screaming.

Then something gently brushed his lips, something alive with infinite promise. Sam thought he could make out Alicia's lovely face above him, in a vague mist streaked with red and yellow flashes — probably just an illusion generated by his new condition. But the kiss went on, and Sam felt as if he were being slowly drawn from his watery world, as if an irresistible force was pulling him out of his newfound paradise. As he regained the use of his body, he suddenly experienced all the suffering he had managed to escape, in a searing flash that coursed through his entire being. He jerked upright, opened his mouth to breathe, failed, remained gasping for a few seconds, and finally passed out for good.

It was much, much later before Sam regained consciousness. His mind emerged from a confused maelstrom of images, a swirling mix of his beloved family, the hated Rudolf and Diavilo, nightmarish scenes of fire and flood, and confused glimpses of white shapes, gurneys and injections, the smell of alcohol, and the beeping of machines. Blinking in the greenish light, he found himself lying on a hospital bed wearing blue paper pajamas, his chest studded with electrodes and an IV line in his arm. He cautiously moved his legs and fingers, and felt the tightness of his skin where it was covered with gauze compresses. Automatically, he touched his chest over his heart, but the feeling of unbearable pressure he'd experienced in the burning house had disappeared. All in all, he didn't feel too bad.

He glanced at the row of screens and diodes blinking by the bed, and recognized the Sainte-Mary Hospital logo on one of the machines. He was probably in the same building as his father.

"I'm glad you're doing better," said a voice behind him.

Sam turned around. Someone was sitting behind the head of his bed, in the darkest part of the room.

"Aunt Evelyn?" he asked in astonishment. "Is that you?"

"I've been sitting with you for the last two days, since they brought you to the hospital. I didn't want to miss your waking up."

"Two days . . ." repeated Sam, who was less surprised by the amount of time than by his aunt's unusual solicitude.

"How do you feel, Sammy?"

"Well, a little as if I'd swallowed a bus, but otherwise not too bad."

Evelyn pulled her chair closer and — incredibly — put an affectionate hand on his arm.

"The doctor says you have to rest, Sam. You've had . . . a kind of a heart attack."

He frowned. "A heart attack?"

"Well, the tests say you had all the symptoms of one, anyway. But the doctor isn't worried; he doesn't think you'll have any aftereffects. The ambulance technicians were right there, and they took care of you, saved your life. Now you've just got to get your strength back."

For the first time in a long time, Aunt Evelyn didn't seem angry at the world at large or her nephew in particular. Her face was still a bit tense, but it had softened, and the way she was talking and smiling made her seem almost motherly.

"How's Lily? And what about Grandpa and Grandma?"

"Lily — it's a miracle. I don't know how you did it, what with all the flames and the explosions, but she's unscathed. A real miracle . . . Your grandmother is doing well too, except for the house burning, of course. The whole family has set up camp in the bookstore. You'll see, it's almost funny. As for Grandpa . . ."

She hesitated for a second before continuing.

"He's had a terrible shock. The fire, waking up in the middle of the night, his house burned to the ground . . . He still isn't in his right mind."

"What do you mean?"

"He's deeply . . . confused, let's say. The clinic held him for observation for twenty-four hours, but without result. Most of the time he just lies in bed, staring into space. And when he talks, he doesn't make sense."

"Is there any hope he'll get better?"

"Well, Grandpa's always been pretty strong. He just needs a few days."

"What about my dad?"

"He has ups and downs. I won't try and tell you he's doing better; that wouldn't be true. But as long as there's life, you know . . ."

Sam resolved to visit Room 313 as soon as somebody removed his electrodes and IV. And if nobody did, he would pull them off himself!

"There's something else you need to know," Evelyn added seriously. "Grandma, Lily, and I have done a lot of talking recently, and I realize how wrong I've been about you. I owe you an apology, Sammy. I haven't always behaved well toward you. I've been blind and unfair. Rudolf had me under some sort of spell, and I was seeing everything through his eyes. If I had a little more common sense, none of this would've happened."

For a moment Sam wondered whether he hadn't really died and gone to some heaven where aunts named Evelyn were nice. But the two of them were both alive, and his aunt's apology seemed sincere.

"Rudolf is the one who set the fire, isn't he?"

Evelyn bowed her head.

"I feel terrible, Sam. You can't imagine . . . I was so blind. He was always so kind and attentive toward me, he listened to all my worries — he really seemed to want to take care of me. But for the last ten days or so, he was distant and cold, as if he didn't need me anymore. The day after you disappeared, he announced that he had to go to Tokyo on business and wouldn't be home for a week. Then he suddenly showed up just as we were about to go to bed. He's usually so calm, but that night he was nervous — on edge, even. He had gifts for everybody, and while we were unwrapping them, he insisted that we try a Japanese drink he'd brought back, a sort of sweet milk-and-fruit drink."

"With a strong flavor to hide the sleeping drug, I bet."

"Lily said the same thing yesterday," she admitted bitterly. "Then we all started to yawn and quickly went to bed. After that . . . After that I just remember that my body felt numb, and I fell into bed like a rock. The firefighters found six propane tanks," she continued, "plus the one that exploded in the kitchen. Another twenty minutes, and the whole house would have blown up. We owe you our lives." Evelyn leaned over and kissed his cheek. "Thank you, Sam," she said in a voice full of emotion. She stood up. "Now I know your cousin wants to come in and talk to you — I'll go get her, shall I?"

She left the room. Not thirty seconds later, Sam spied Lily framed in the doorway. When she saw that he was awake, she raced over to his bed.

"Sammy!" she shrieked. "Sammy, I'm so happy!"

Lily hugged him so hard she practically crushed him.

"Hey! I'm sick here, remember?" he protested with a smile. "Are you trying to finish me off or what?"

"Sammy, you saved my life! You came up through the flames and you carried me through the living room in spite of the explosions and —"

"All right, all right!" he interrupted. "I'm a superhero, okay? But you would've done the same thing for me. Remember when we landed in prehistoric times and I got taken prisoner? You rescued me then, so . . ."

Lily shook her head as if he was talking nonsense, but her eyes were shining with joy and emotion.

"I'm so glad to see you're better, Sammy! The doctor told my mom that you showed signs of bradycardia." Lily said the word with a touch of self-importance, as she sometimes did in her Miss Know-It-All mode.

"Signs of what?"

"Bradycardia. It's a condition where your heartbeat tends to slow down a lot. That's probably why he wants to keep testing you."

"And is bradycardia dangerous?" asked Sam, who had a pretty good idea what caused the problem.

"Mom said the doctor didn't seem too worried. Except that with you it's pretty spectacular, apparently." She hesitated. "Are you sure you feel strong enough to talk? I want to hear everything that happened while you were gone."

"I'm fine," said Sam. "A little hungry, but . . ."

Lily went outside to ask the nurse to bring his dinner. Then she came back and sat down next to his bed. She opened the large colorful messenger bag she had slung over her yellow dress. "I didn't know if you would be awake, but I brought you this."

She pulled out a charred book, whose blistered red cover showed ash smudges and water stains.

"Our Book of Time!" Sam exclaimed. "You saved it!"

"It was in the back of your closet. It was burned, unfortunately, and then got wet when the firefighters hosed the place down. A few passages are still readable, though."

Sam took the book reverently. It smelled moldy and scorched — almost like burned flesh, he thought; a bruised little corpse pulled from the rubble. He spent a long time gazing at it in dismay, unable to express what he was feeling. An irreplaceable, sacred object had been sullied and destroyed. And Sam, who'd been told to guard it by Setni, hadn't been able to protect it.

He opened what remained of the book and turned the crumpled, wrinkled pages, some of which turned to fine black ash the moment he touched them.

"Look toward the back," Lily suggested.

The last pages were in better condition, though dark stains sometimes blotted out the text, and the paper had turned a caramel color that made it hard to read. But thanks to the identical double pages, Sam was at least able to reconstruct the title of one spread, "Year I of the Church of the Seven Resurrections," and scraps of text here and there: ". . . the birth of a new religion whose astonishing success . . . the pandit hopes to live another thousand years, to show that his work can take on the universal dimension that alone will give it its place in eternity . . . Sainte-Mary became the headquarters of a faith rooted in time and history greater than any . . ." etc.

"What do you think?" asked Sam, when he had deciphered all he could.

"It sounds as if Rudolf won, doesn't it?" Lily said glumly. "Alicia told us what you saw in the future: the construction site for the Church of the Seven Resurrections, the museum he built, the articles where he explains what he wants to accomplish with his cult."

"Yeah, he passed himself off as a kind of time guru, and thousands of people believe him; hundreds of thousands, maybe. Exactly the sort of thing Setni wanted to avoid."

"My mom feels really bad about all this," said Lily after a hesitation. "She's sure that if she'd been a little sharper she could have avoided this disaster. And if you hadn't regained consciousness, she would have never forgiven herself. We talked a lot over the last two days, Grandma and Mom and me, and Alicia too. . . . She told us everything you told her about what happened in Egypt and China. So you remember when we went to Chicago in 1932, how we thought the stone statue there got destroyed? Well, it turns out it didn't — it just got buried in the rubble. And Rudolf built his Arkeos headquarters right over that stone! He would take Mom there and have her just sit in the building and think about him. She thought it was kind of romantic," Lily said, making a face, "but now she realizes she can do the same thing I can — bring time travelers back to their present. And that was why he wanted her all this time."

Sam remembered that Setni had said Lily's talent was

passed from mother to daughter, and that their grandmother's thoughts about Allan seemed to have brought him back when he traveled long ago.

"Plus apparently he was always asking her questions about her family, especially your father, even though he never wanted to meet us. Remember how he wouldn't come for Christmas or any other family gatherings until your dad disappeared? She thinks he must have been avoiding Uncle Allan. Anyway, Mom figures she knew too much, and that was why Rudolf set the fire."

"He must have found something that would let him come back to the present without her," Sam said slowly. "And Pandit Rudolf in the future had the Golden Circle. . . . I bet I know what happened ten days ago, when he started to be cold to her again. He must have gotten the Golden Circle from old Maggie Pye, and he could travel freely without your mom's help!"

"The Golden Circle, of course! Alicia told me Miss Pye stole it from your mother! And maybe it was even her fault that —" Lily stopped short.

"Her fault that my mom died, right?" said Sam, completing Lily's sentence. "I thought of that too. If Maggie Pye hadn't stolen the bracelet, Mom could have given it to Rudolf when he came to the house. They wouldn't have struggled, he wouldn't have hit her. . . . But in the end, it was Rudolf who killed her, right? He's the only person responsible."

During the heavy silence that followed, Sam tried to chase away images of the fight, his mother's head hitting the corner of a table, a car tumbling end over end down a hillside.

"I went to the bookstore basement," Lily continued in a low voice. "I saw the coins you brought back from the future. There are two from July 11, the day your mom died. You're planning to go back and try to save her, aren't you?"

Sam stared at an invisible spot on the wall.

"I'm going to try," he eventually said. "I can't just let her die like that, with Rudolf hitting her, and . . . It would be too unfair. And if I bring her back here, to our present, that might give Dad the will to live."

Lily took his hand, as if she were comforting a distraught child.

"I know what you're feeling, Sammy, but you can't do that. You mentioned Setni earlier. There was one point he was really definite about: Going to a time and place where you're already alive amounts to suicide. 'Two identical souls can't be in the same place at the same time,' remember? 'If that were to hap-pen, the soul would inevitably consume itself.' You know what that means, don't you? If you went back to Sainte-Mary three years ago, you could die instantly!"

Sam shifted his gaze away from the wall.

"There's a way, though" he said, weighing each of his words. "A way Setni himself suggested. He said no one could go back, 'Unless the traveler were in a hypnotic trance or a magic sleep.' Am I wrong?"

"No, you're right; I remember that really well. But so what? Are you going to tell me that you now have superpowers when it comes to a magic sleep or a hypnotic trance? You don't even know what that means!"

"Yeah, but I know exactly where I was three years ago. At the moment my mom was killed, I was already asleep — a magic sleep, even — because that was the afternoon I had my appendix out!"

Lily gaped at him. "Your appendix!" she said. "I hadn't thought of that! But how can you be sure of the times? How do you know that you were under anesthesia just when your mother . . . had her accident?"

"I'll have to check out the times to be sure. But they'll be in my medical records, won't they? In any case, I took two coins for July 11 from Rudolf's cabinet. One was marked ten a.m. and the other three p.m. The police found Mom's smashed car below the hill around five p.m., so everything must've happened earlier that afternoon, during the time I was under anesthesia. So if I don't waste any time, I should be able to stop everything."

"Okay, but can you trust Rudolf's coins? What if you land in Sainte-Mary an hour too soon or too late?"

"Well, the one me and Alicia used for coming back to Sainte-Mary was stamped 'Midnight,' and we reached the library at about twelve thirty. Not totally accurate, but pretty good!"

"And then if you manage to reach your mom, you'll try to get her to come to the present?"

"That's a lot better than dying in the past, isn't it?"

"Well, sure . . ." Lily was quiet for a moment. "But remember Setni also said you absolutely mustn't change the course of time, because you could cause some huge catastrophe? It's a crazy risk."

"I know," answered Sam, who had been thinking about this ever since he learned his father's hope of saving his mother. "But you brought up the Church of the Seven Resurrections. Did Alicia tell you that in that version of the future, Grandma's house burned down and all of you died? We've already started changing things — fixing the future that Rudolf destroyed.

212

And if you think of it that way, in going back those three years, I won't be upsetting the past, I'll be restoring it."

"What?"

"It's simple. The past we're talking about, the one in which my mom died, isn't the real past. It's a past that Rudolf has already changed."

"Can you be a little clearer?"

"Sure! The Rudolf who came for the Golden Circle on July eleventh three years ago — let's call him Rudolf One — had actually come from the future. Not by much; maybe a week or two. Meanwhile, the real Rudolf of that time period — we'll call him Rudolf Two — was far away, creating an alibi. If Rudolf One had never time traveled, Mom wouldn't have died. But because he *did*, he erased the original version of how Time should have gone, and replaced it with a second, awful version where he kills her. So in saving my mother, I'm not really changing the past, you see? I'm just restoring it to its original version, where Mom never would have met Rudolf One at all." He paused. "A version where she doesn't die."

Lily looked as if she would have liked to argue further, but at that moment, the nurse came in with Sam's tray of food. After she arranged his table, propped him up to eat, and left again, an incongruous tune started playing somewhere in the depths of Lily's colorful bag:

I hope he's not out of reach.
Oh, yes, the boy on the beach!

"I can't believe it!" said Sam, laughing. "Don't tell me you still have that ringtone!"

"Shhh!" Lily hissed. She rummaged in her bag and pulled out a white cell phone that was now blaring:

> *He's so cute,*
> *He's so sweet.*
> *He makes my heart skip a beat.*
> *Oh, yes, the boy on the beeeaach!*

Sam was bent over with laughter while his cousin checked the incoming number. Then she thrust the phone at him.

"Take it, instead of laughing like a hyena. It's for you."

CHAPTER TWENTY-FOUR

Speaking Up

Sam took the phone and put it to his ear as Lily ostentatiously left the room.

"Hello?"

"Sam? It's Alicia. How are you feeling?"

"Alicia!" Sam's heart started going a million miles a minute. "I — I'm fine. Yeah, fine! I should be out of here soon. What about you? Where are you?"

"My parents decided to keep me away from Sainte-Mary until the police get hold of Rudolf. We just got to our summer house at the shore. The kidnapping shook them up a lot. . . . They're almost afraid to open the windows!"

"Did you tell them where Rudolf took you? Rome in 1527, and all the rest?"

"Well, pretty much. In fact, I think that's partly why they decided to take me up here. Mom seems to believe me, but my dad's been looking at me like I've fallen on my head. They're even planning to send me to a local psychiatrist as soon as possible."

"I can understand. It's not the sort of story people like to hear."

"Okay, but I didn't call to talk about my parents, Sam. Lily says you have heart problems."

"You and Lily seem to be talking a lot these days," he said teasingly. "You should have seen how conspiratorial she looked when she handed me her phone."

"This was the best way I could think of to talk to you and be sure no one could overhear us. If there was somebody else in the room, I told her to just hang up."

"Two James Bond girls!" cried Sam, flattered by the precautions. "This must mean you have lots of important stuff to tell me."

"Or just to talk about — like those coins from the future, for instance. Lily thinks you plan to use them to keep Rudolf from hurting your mom. Is that right?"

"That's why I took them."

"But she also thinks you'll die for sure if you go back three years."

"We talked about that, and I think she's changed her mind. Actually, I don't risk much more than I would for any other trip."

"What you mean by 'much more'?"

"It just means that I'll have to hurry. Of course if I run into Rudolf, there's no telling what'll happen."

"I guess *I* can't make you change your mind?"

"I know it doesn't seem all that sensible. But I've done stupid things before, like going to save you or running into my grandparents' house when it was on fire, and they've turned out okay." Sam realized this wasn't the best possible argument he could make. "Besides, it's like . . ." He groped to find the right words to explain how he felt. "I don't have any choice. My mom needs me, and I can't let her down. Do you understand?"

There was a short pause, and for a few seconds Sam heard only the faint hiss in the background of their conversation. Then Alicia sighed with what sounded like resignation.

"When I saw you unconscious the other night," she said in a low voice, "that terrified me, Sam. I thought that you'd . . . that you'd left me again, but this time for good. And it felt really awful, like this terrible emptiness. . . . There were the sirens, the yellow and red lights, Evelyn screaming, the neighbors talking . . ."

Alicia's voice died away and she didn't finish the sentence. When she continued a moment later, she was sniffling.

"At some point, one of the firefighters shouted that they were losing you or something. I just couldn't stand it. I threw myself on you to wake you up, to end the nightmare. I was sure I could do it . . . I was just able to touch you before they dragged me away. Finally when they put you in the ambulance, one of the technicians told us you were breathing better and you'd be okay."

Alicia was almost sobbing now, and Sam wanted badly to be able to hug her, even kiss her again. But she was so far away! Miles and miles . . . And he would be going away too, putting not just distance but Time between them. It occurred to Sam that he might never have another chance to tell her what he had to say — so he did.

"I love you, Alicia," he said with an openness that surprised even him.

She was silent, and he went on.

217

"I've loved you from the very beginning, since we were little. And I've never stopped loving you, not for a second. Even during those three years when we didn't see each other. I'll love you forever, Alicia; it's as simple as that." He swallowed. "The time we spent together in Rome, and watching the stone glow in Rudolf's museum — those were the best moments I've had in a very long time. Because we were together, just the two of us."

"Thank you, Sam," she answered tearfully. "I . . ."

She sounded too moved to add anything else.

"That's not all," he continued. "The other night, when I lost consciousness after getting Lily out of the house, I found myself in this strange state, as if I were floating between two worlds. At one point I felt I was leaving — leaving for real, I mean. Dying. And it's at that moment that you leaned over me and . . . and you kissed me. Or at least that's how my brain understood it," he said quickly. "Please don't take it the wrong way. And right away I knew why I had to live, so I came back to this side. To your side."

Sam fell silent, terrified at what she might say in response, but happy to have won this little victory over himself. He had opened his heart with all the sincerity he could muster, an honesty Alicia had often reproached him for lacking. After this, it would be up to her to choose. And regardless of what she decided, he would still love her just as much.

Alicia's breathing sounded a little ragged, as if she was hesitating about what to say.

"Things . . . things are complicated, Sam," she finally managed. "Jerry and I split up yesterday, and I'm not thinking very clearly."

"You broke up?" asked Sam, trying to keep the joy out of his voice.

"We just had too many fights these last few weeks. You know how jealous Jerry is. I got really tired of him treating me like his property, his *thing*. And then when you showed up . . . I don't know. . . . Things weren't the same between Jerry and me."

She stopped speaking again, and Sam closed his eyes tight, trying hard to somehow influence what she would say next.

"If I'm honest with myself, I think I love you too, Sam. But I want to be sure of my feelings and . . ."

Her voice suddenly dropped.

"Wait; I think someone's coming upstairs. It must be my father. He's afraid I'll go crazy and jump out the window or something." She called loudly, "Is that you, Daddy? Just a minute, I'm getting dressed."

Sam could hear footsteps, then Alicia whispered: "I'm really sorry. I'll call you again as soon as I can. If you have to leave before we can talk again, just promise me you'll come back. I trust you, Sam. I know you'll succeed." He could hear a little smile in her voice. "And by the way, the next time I kiss you, I want you to be awake, okay?"

The doctors were astonished by Sam's improvement after that. They spent most of the next day conducting tests on his heart, but didn't find anything out of the ordinary. The following day, the doctor finally unplugged Sam's wires and IV line. As soon as he left the room, Sam headed out as well, striding through the hospital hallways so fast that people turned to stare as he passed. He crossed the surgery department, reached the main lobby, and turned the corner toward Allan's room.

But Sam had barely entered Room 313 when his good mood abruptly evaporated. He'd forgotten how chilly the room was, more like a morgue than a place of rest and recovery. Now he was struck by the absence of organic life. Blinking readouts and monotonous beeping were the only activity in the place. Allan lay inert on the bed, and his health seemed to have worsened. A complex system of blue tubes now led to his nose and mouth from a big device that looked like a metal octopus with screens and colored bottles, which ventilated and fed him. His body was alarmingly thin, and gauze pads covered the sores on his chest and neck. Not only was he not gaining weight, but his wounds were apparently not healing.

Sam glanced at the heart monitor: fifty-two beats a minute, the lowest ever. He touched the emaciated wrist protruding from the sheet and couldn't repress a shiver; his father was cold as marble. But Sam had to talk to him, make contact again.

"Dad, it's me, Sam. I'm so sorry. I haven't been able to bring Mom back yet. A lot of things have happened these last few days. I had to take care of Alicia. . . ."

He told his father in detail how Rudolf had kidnapped Alicia and how he'd traveled from Egypt to Rome in order to save her, only to wind up in the future. He was careful not to say anything about the fire at Grandma's or his own hospitalization. But unlike the last time, Sam's account produced no reaction. He rubbed his father's arm, stroked his cheek, whispered in his ear, but Allan seemed tragically elsewhere.

Undaunted, Sam continued: "I really need to know what you think about something, Dad. If for some reason Mom refuses to follow me to our present, I have another idea: the Eternity Ring. You know what I'm talking about, don't you? Anyway, Chamberlain said that not only can the ring make you immortal, it can also cure any illness. So if the story is true and I'm able to bring it to you, that could help, wouldn't it? I know Setni hid the ring somewhere in his tomb and that you need both Golden Circles to find it. I already have the Meriweserre bracelet and I ought to be able to get the other one, the bracelet you gave Mom. What do you say? If I can get the Eternity Ring, would you use it?"

Sam held his father's hand and looked at the heart monitor: Fifty-two . . . Fifty-two . . . Fifty-one . . . Fifty-two . . . Hardly any change, not a flutter, nothing. If he had hoped for a reaction, he had failed. Or maybe Allan no longer had the strength to communicate, in which case Elisa Faulkner's return might come too late.

Sam had to act, and fast.

Sam was allowed to leave the hospital late that afternoon, having promised to return for further tests. He kissed his father one last time, thanked the nurses, and left with Lily and his aunt.

When they reached the bookstore, the first person he saw was Max, who was unchaining his bicycle from a lamppost. The old man gave a shout of joy and grabbed Sam's outstretched hand — practically crushing it — as he explained that he had helped his grandparents settle into the Barenboim Street store. As Sam watched him unlock the bike, he had a sudden inspiration.

"Max, I've always wondered: Why do you bother locking your bike here, since the neighborhood is so quiet?"

The old man, whose deafness was legendary, looked at him in confusion.

"*Thieves will buy it?* Of course they won't buy it! They'll steal it, that's all. There are plenty of thieves in Barenboim Street, and they never buy anything! I had a bike swiped from my yard a couple years ago, and that's why I lock this one up!"

"Could you give me the combination, Max?" asked Sam innocently.

"To you, of course!" he answered without hesitation. Max gestured to Sam to come closer and spoke into his ear: "Just turn the lock to 1937; it's my birth year. Clever, eh?" He winked.

Sam winked back, then waved as Max climbed aboard and pedaled vigorously for home. *Very handy, having a bike . . .*

He had barely crossed the bookstore threshold when Grandma ran to him, her eyes full of tears, and hugged him, murmuring, "Sammy, my Sammy!"

When she'd finished clucking over him, she gave Sam a tour of the new layout of Faulkner's Antique Books. The large sales area had been rearranged to accommodate the whole family. The bookcases had been pushed against the walls, a table and chairs set up in the middle, and a TV installed in a corner near a window. It felt temporary yet cozy, and actually kind of nice. Upstairs, the hallway was crammed with boxes, and the bathroom overflowed with salvaged linens that still smelled of smoke. Lily and Evelyn had moved into Sam's bedroom, which looked like a cross between a dormitory and a storage room for knickknacks from the old house. Grandma and Grandpa had taken Allan's quieter room.

"How is Grandpa?"

Grandma shrugged, her face sad. "Today he's practically raving, unfortunately. But go say hello anyway. He'll like that."

Sam opened the door apprehensively and found his grandfather sitting on the edge of the bed, staring at the sky through the open window.

"Hi, Grandpa. How are you feeling?"

Donovan Faulkner turned slightly and looked over his shoulder. He was thin and unshaven, his eyes vacant. Sam was so shocked to see him this diminished, he couldn't think of a thing to say. They stared at each other in silence for a while, until Donovan started to speak in a hoarse, quavering voice.

"I saw him."

"You saw him?" repeated Sam, mystified. "Who did you see?"

"The devil," he said very seriously. "I saw him."

"The devil?"

"Yes, the other night. He was standing in front of me, just like you! He brought the fire. The fire of hell. He wanted to burn us all!" he added angrily.

Rudolf, thought Sam. He must have seen Rudolf the night of the fire!

"It was Rudolf that you saw, wasn't it, Grandpa?"

But his grandfather didn't seem to hear, and went on: "The devil. He was there. He approached with flames and had fire in his hands. It was the devil, I saw him!" He was shouting now. "The devil!"

Grandma rushed into the room.

"Take it easy, Donovan. Take it easy."

She walked over, draped an arm around his neck, and gently

223

rocked him, talking quietly. In a minute Grandpa went back to watching the sky as if nothing had happened, his gaze lost in the distance.

"He's been like that since this morning," sighed Grandma. "One moment he's angry, the next he's completely apathetic. The doctors say there's nothing they can do."

Evelyn and Lily had run in, and from their stricken expressions Sam realized that they weren't any more hopeful. Rudolf had taken yet another victim. Sam felt a dull rage overcome him. He headed straight for Allan's closet, yanked it open, and grabbed a shirt and a pair of pants from the shelf of time-traveler outfits.

"What are you doing?" asked his grandmother, frowning.

"All this happened because of Rudolf!" Sam growled.

"That's true, but what do you have in mind?"

"I'm going to go get Mom."

"What are you talking about?" she asked, stepping toward him.

"Lily will explain," said Sam firmly. "I'm going to bring Mom back. That should bring Dad out of his coma. And who knows, maybe it'll even help Grandpa."

"Bring Elisa back?" blurted Grandma in astonishment. She looked at Evelyn and Lily, but the two simply lowered their eyes and said nothing.

"It's just a matter of a few hours," said Sam reassuringly. "The only thing that I'm asking you" — he looked at each of them in turn — "is that you think of me after I leave. With the gift you three share, I'm sure to come back!"

*　　*　　*

224

Sam knelt in front of the stone statue in the secret basement room. He had put on his linen outfit, taken the Book of Time, and hugged the three women. All he had left to do was ready his coins before leaving. He now had nine of them: the one from Bran Castle, the one from Thebes, Qin's Chinese coin, Chamberlain's very plain one, and the five he took from Rudolf's cabinet in the future: the two from the date of his mother's death, the one that had allowed Alicia and him to return to the present, another stamped with his birthday, and finally the glass disk from the Ahmosis scarab.

The coin stamped "July 11, 3 p.m." would determine his destination. He slipped six of the remaining coins onto the Meriweserre bracelet and brought it over to the stone, where they obediently took their places in the slits. He set the coin that would take him to his mother on the sun. It began to glow, and a bubble of clear golden light formed over it. Sam put his hand on top of the stone. Just before being swallowed by the rush of heat, he murmured:

"It's me, Mom. I'm coming."

CHAPTER TWENTY-FIVE

A Fish in a Drowned City

Sam came to in a dank, dark place that felt strangely familiar. He quickly got to his feet, retrieved the coin from the sun, and held up the Meriweserre bracelet to light his surroundings. The decor had changed — the big white wardrobe against the wall was a new addition — but Sam had no trouble recognizing the basement of Faulkner's Antique Books, or rather that of Garry Barenboim's house before it was abandoned. The great time traveler's basement looked pretty much the same as when Lily and Sam landed here in the early 1930s, full of useless trash, rusted machinery, and old boxes. That meant that Sam had arrived at the right place, some time between the 1930s and his present. With luck, it would be exactly three years back.

Before Allan set up his bookstore here, the house was owned by an old nutcase named Martha Calloway who lived with a bunch of dogs and was as friendly as a piranha on amphetamines. Sam would need to be very careful in order to get out of the house safely.

As his eyes grew accustomed to the dark, Sam saw a brighter area that must be the staircase. But in his hurry to get there, he tripped on a tangle of steel hoops, breaking the silence with a deafening clatter. He froze, but the damage was done. A long howl sounded upstairs, followed by a second howl and the clicking of claws on floorboards. Sam remembered the nightmarish photos Chamberlain had taken of Martha Calloway's dogs: the slavering jaws, the teeth sunk in the fence, the crazed, bloodthirsty glares.

A chorus of barking thundered toward the staircase, and in spite of the risk, Sam was forced to use the only weapon he had. He closed his eyes, concentrated, and tried to empty his mind of all thoughts — especially those relating to his recent heart problems. He descended into himself as quickly as possible, slowing his heart to match the Thoth stone's tranquil pulse, feeling his body yield to the rhythm of Time.

Sam opened his eyes to find a faint greenish light filling the room. An enormous pit bull was crouched less than a yard from him, lips drawn back and hind legs bent as if to spring. Behind it, four slightly smaller dogs seemed to be frozen into immobility as they tumbled down the steps. One was even suspended in midair, just about to land.

Sam didn't waste any time. Dodging the dogs, he rushed up the stairs to a hallway and kitchen that smelled like a zoo cage. Turning into the living room, he found himself nose to nose with Martha Calloway herself. She was wearing a long striped dressing gown and carried a double-barreled shotgun, clearly prepared to blow away whoever had dared break into her basement.

He stepped neatly around her and headed for the front door. A ring of keys with a dog-shaped address tag hung by the door, and he pocketed it before stepping outside. Three more dogs stood in the middle of the walkway, teeth bared, apparently ready to attack. A ten-foot cyclone fence had been added to reinforce the picket fence enclosing the yard. He walked to the gate to the street, unlocked it, and ran out onto the sidewalk, locking the gate behind him.

Sam wondered if he should consider releasing the pressure on his heart. His ability to slow Time would be invaluable if he ran into Rudolf, so he probably shouldn't exhaust his meager reserves now. On the other hand, if Calloway's dogs caught him or if he didn't reach the Bel View neighborhood in time, he wouldn't see Rudolf at all!

He ran to Max's place. As usual, the old man's bicycle was chained to a tree in the yard. Sam set the bike lock to 1937 and the metal bar snapped open, freeing the chain.

"Sorry, Max," he muttered. "It's for a good cause."

He climbed on the bike and covered a few hundred yards with the feeling that he was swimming through a drowned city. Sainte-Mary looked as if it had sunk below a murky green sea that Sam was churning with each pedal stroke. Once he was a safe distance from Calloway and her pack of dogs, he closed his eyes, released his heart from Time, and waited for the sharp crack. When he opened his eyes again, Sainte-Mary looked as the way it always did: houses with colorful shutters, flowers in the yards, children playing on swings. The sun was high in the sky and it felt like a warm July day. A moment later, Sam passed a drugstore with an electronic sign reading JULY 11, 3:12 P.M. He was right on target.

228

Elated by this new certainty, he pedaled so hard that he began to get a stitch in his right side. He would be seeing his mother in a matter of minutes! She must be somewhere in town right now and . . . He remembered the scene at the hospital with new clarity. Sam had been eleven, and as the aide wheeled him into the operating room, Elisa promised to fetch his favorite pajamas from home and said she would stop downtown to buy him some comic books and candy. Sam could still feel the sweetness of her kiss on his cheek when she said goodbye: "You'll just feel like you're going to sleep, Sammy. And when you wake up, it will be all over." He even remembered the squeaking of the gurney being rolled to the elevator, the comment by the aide who was pushing it — "There's a short wait for the operating room, but we'll take good care of you" — the slamming of a door on his left . . . Maggie Pye had visited him earlier that morning, bringing a box of candy, and he could still taste the one chocolate he'd been able to snatch before she tried them all herself. The images and sounds had never come back to him so intensely.

In a quarter of an hour Sam reached the hill below Bel View. His stitch hurt more and more as he slowly pedaled up the familiar curves. With difficulty, he reached the avenue of maple trees that led to his old neighborhood and heaved a sigh of relief: Everything looked normal. The handsome white houses stood next to lawns and flowers; birds were singing in the trees. Nothing suggested that a tragedy might be about to happen.

Sam passed number 18, where old Miss Pye was pruning her rosebushes, continued to the corner, and casually rode by his house — his former house, that is. Here too everything seemed quiet. He felt a twinge when he looked into the yard and saw their old barbecue. . . . They had been having dinner outside — with Alicia, in fact — when Allan said he was going to Toronto for business, the day before Sam's unanticipated surgery. That had been their last meal together. But Sam resisted this new wave of memories; he couldn't afford to let himself be overcome by emotion.

Reassured that Rudolf was nowhere to be seen, he leaned the bicycle against the hedge and spent a moment massaging his painful stitch. He'd clearly neglected the bike since taking up skateboarding, and was paying the price. The garage was locked, as was the front door, and when Sam put his ear to it, he didn't hear any suspicious noises inside. His mother must not have gotten home yet.

For a moment he considered breaking in — smashing a window, maybe — but the house had an alarm, and he certainly didn't want the Sainte-Mary police to arrest him for burglary. Maybe Sam could use the time until his mother arrived to retrieve the Golden Circle, as he'd promised his father. After all, Maggie Pye had some explaining to do to the Faulkner family.

Sam rode back to number 18, a few houses down. "Hello, Miss Pye," he called out as he dismounted.

Startled, the old lady jumped back from her rosebush. "You frightened me, young man!" she snapped. "What do you want? And who are you, anyway?" she added, peering at his clothes suspiciously. "If you're fund-raising or something like that, you're not getting a thing from me."

Sam reflected that he was lucky Miss Pye was so near-sighted that she couldn't recognize him. Otherwise she might be very surprised to see him out of the hospital and three years older!

"I could tell you who I am, but you wouldn't like it," Sam said as he approached. "I'm here to help you redeem yourself."

"You belong to some religious cult, is that it?" said Miss Pye more loudly. "I'm not interested in whatever you're peddling. Get out of my yard immediately!"

"I don't think you're really a thief," Sam said calmly. "I imagine you just acted on impulse. You saw Mrs. Faulkner wearing the bracelet, and you couldn't resist. You absolutely had to have it. But now she would like it back."

"Whatever are you talking about?" Miss Pye was shouting now. She took a step back and raised her pruning shears. "You leave right away or I'm calling the police!"

"That's a great idea. I'll tell them how you spend your time when you're supposed to be babysitting. Stealing jewelry, for example."

Miss Magpie, as Allan called her, looked shaken. She opened her mouth to protest, but seemed to think better of it. "Who are you?" she repeated more quietly.

"I was at the hospital this morning," said Sam, turning the knife a bit. "You were wearing a green dress with a wide collar. You told Mrs. Faulkner that her polka-dot blouse looked lovely, and that you would be happy to keep her son company after the operation. The perfect neighbor, right? But then you ate half the box of chocolates you brought, which seems kind of rude."

The old lady had turned as pink as the roses she was pruning. She fussed nervously with her checked apron.

"What is it you're after?" she stammered.

"I want to ease your conscience, Miss Pye. But to do that, you have to give me the bracelet. I'll return it to Mrs. Faulkner, and I promise she'll never know who took it. I bet that would make you feel better."

Miss Pye hesitated and glanced at the surrounding houses to make sure no one was watching. "Come inside," she said.

Sam followed her into a living room that was too full of everything: too many chairs, too many clocks, too many ceramic cats on too many tables, too many brown-and-yellow flowers on the wallpaper. It was as if the old lady needed to surround herself with excess to keep loneliness at bay.

"I only borrowed it," she said in a rush once they were indoors. "Of course I was going to give it back. I just wanted to have it for a while, that's all! Besides, Elisa must not like the bracelet that much; she hardly ever wears it. I didn't think she would even miss it."

Sam held his tongue. Things were going well and he didn't want to risk ruining everything. Besides, with her purplish hair, lined face, and guilty expression, Miss Pye inspired more pity than anger.

"I'm very fond of the Faulkners," she continued. "This is the first time I've ever done something like this. And you're right; it has been on my mind. Still, there's something about that bracelet," she breathed.

She started for the staircase but stopped with her hand on the banister.

"How do I know you're really going to return it to them?"

"I showed you I was telling the truth when I talked about the hospital," Sam said firmly. "You'd be surprised at all the things I could tell you about the Faulkners and yourself.

Things nobody in the world would know. That bracelet belongs to the Faulkners, and it has to go back to them."

The old lady stared at Sam for a long time, then she muttered something like, "Blasted bracelet," and climbed the stairs. Sam followed her into a little office, where she unlocked the drawer to a worktable piled high with seed catalogs. She reached into the drawer and took out a blue velvet bag, untied it, and slowly, very slowly, turned it over her palm. The Golden Circle slipped into her trembling hand.

"It really is beautiful," she sighed.

Sam took a step closer. The Golden Circle looked exactly like the Meriweserre bracelet, except that this original was slightly more refined, as if it had been polished by the passage of additional centuries. But though it was a handsome golden color, it didn't give out any light.

"I know how you feel," Sam said. "But you and I both know that it has to go back to Mrs. Faulkner."

"You promise you won't tell her it was me?"

Sam nodded. "If I'd wanted to turn you in, Miss Pye, I could have just called the police. I'm happy to keep this quiet."

Just as his fingers closed on the Circle, the sound of a car rose from the street. Sam rushed to the window overlooking the garden: His mother was driving up the street toward number 26. He stood petrified. She was there; she was alive! He couldn't see her, but it was her car! He had to get to her before Rudolf did.

"I have to leave," Sam cried. "Thanks a lot, Miss Pye. This'll stay between us, I promise."

He slipped the Golden Circle into his pocket and raced down the stairs. He ran out of number 18 and grabbed the bike. But as he was about to climb on, he suddenly felt a sharp pain just above his right leg. He gave a muffled cry and stopped. This couldn't be a stitch; he must've torn a muscle. That had once happened to him in judo class, when he'd torn a calf muscle and had to stay flat on his back for two days.

It would hurt too much to ride, so Sam continued on foot, clutching his right side. He limped up the street to where it curved, and noticed a small motorcycle on the sidewalk that hadn't been there earlier. It was just an ordinary black motor-cycle — nothing special. Except that it was parked right in front of the Faulkners' house.

CHAPTER TWENTY-SIX

So Near and Yet So Far

Sam hobbled up the walkway at number 26 as fast as the pain in his side allowed him. The motorcycle's engine felt hot, which meant that its owner had just parked it there.

The garage door was still open, so Sam slipped inside, past his mother's pretty red Chevrolet. From there he crossed through the laundry room into the kitchen, which smelled deliciously of cinnamon and cake. How many times had he sat at the oak table doing his homework while his mother made crepes or cookies? He stepped into the big colonial-style living room and listened carefully. He could hear voices upstairs, coming from one of the back bedrooms.

"I'm not joking," a man's voice said menacingly. It was Rudolf.

"Neither am I," his mother replied coldly. "The bracelet was in that jewelry box, I tell you."

"So where is it NOW?"

"I don't know. I —"

A closet door slammed and Sam rushed toward the stairs, but he didn't get very far. The dull pain in his belly had suddenly become sharper and more localized, as if a razor blade was slicing into his skin. Caught in mid-stride, he collapsed against the banister, clutching his stomach.

"What about there, in that drawer?" snapped Rudolf.

Sam gritted his teeth, his eyes full of tears. He lifted his shirt and looked at his belly, but there was nothing to see: no cut, no blood. Yet it hurt so much he wanted to scream. It was as if an invisible knife were sinking into his belly right over his appendix scar. His scar . . . Appendicitis . . . Of course! He was experiencing what his other self was undergoing at the same moment at the Sainte-Mary hospital: appendicitis — and the surgeon's scalpel!

Sam struggled to keep from crying out. Yes, it had to be that. Somehow, he was connected with the body or mind of the Sam he had been three years earlier. That would explain those vivid memories that had surged up as he rode the bike. The fact that his double was now under anesthesia was saving him from a cerebral implosion, but it apparently didn't keep him from experiencing the physical aggression of the surgery.

"I'm warning you," Rudolf was saying, "if you don't find that bracelet right away, things are going to get ugly."

Sam took a breath and strained to stand up. The stabbing pain was still there, but he told himself that it had no real cause. He'd already been operated on, and he had the scar to show for it! The pain was an illusion, and if he mustered the willpower, he could overcome it. Bent double, he managed to climb a first step, then a second. His mother was upstairs; that was all that mattered.

"You're lying!" Rudolf was screaming. "You've been lying from the start! Just like your husband!"

"You know my husband?" Elisa asked in surprise.

"Of course I do! And if something happens to you today, it'll be entirely his fault!"

Sam bit his lip and lifted his right leg with both hands to help himself climb the last steps. The distance to his parents' bedroom at the end of the hall seemed endless.

"How do you know my husband?" said Elisa, sounding astonished.

"Too long to explain. All I can say is, Allan owes me. He owes me big time. And you're going to pay for him!"

A sharp noise like a slap rang out, followed by a cry that chilled Sam's blood.

"That's just a taste of what you've got coming," continued Rudolf. "I'm going to count to three. If by three I don't have that bracelet, you can tell your darling husband good-bye. One . . ."

Sam made his way along the hallway, leaning against the wall for support. He would never get there in time. Rudolf was going to kill his mother, and he wouldn't be able to lift a finger. At his wits' end, he closed his eyes and summoned his last ounce of strength to try to slow his heartbeat. It was a waste of time. The pain in his belly was so all-consuming, it made it impossible to concentrate.

"Two . . ."

"I don't know where the bracelet is, I swear!" she cried, terrified. "If I knew, I —"

Sam tried to shout, to say that he had the Golden Circle, but the weak cry that rose from his throat was drowned out by a scream from Elisa and the sound of furniture being knocked over. Rudolf must have hit her again.

"Three," he said in a cold, satisfied tone.

The door was ajar, and Sam could see his mother lying on the carpet between an armchair and an overturned end table. She looked unconscious.

"Mom!" he croaked. "Mom!"

Ignoring the pain in his stomach, he burst into the room and rushed over to his motionless mother.

"What the — ?" Rudolf roared.

Sam paid him no heed. He fell to his knees next to Elisa, who was sprawled on the carpet with a bloody bruise on her temple, and put his ear to his mother's chest. Under her polka-dot blouse, her heart was still beating. She was alive!

"Turn around right now or I'll shoot!" Rudolf shouted.

Sam hesitated, still bent over his mother's body. She wasn't dead; that was the most important thing. He would eventually find a way to get her out of here, but for now he had to do what Rudolf said. So he turned around very slowly, trying to hide his fear and his pain.

The Rudolf standing before him seemed younger than the one he knew in his present; he had fewer wrinkles at the corner of his eyes, and he was slimmer. But he still had the same hard look and the same predator's jaw. He was wearing a light gray summer suit and carrying a pistol with an unusually long barrel — a silencer, Sam guessed.

"She's bleeding," Sam said as forcefully as he could. "We have to get her to the hospital."

"You said 'Mom' when you came in, right? What is this crap?"

Sam struggled to maintain his composure in spite of the pain in his belly.

"Answer me! Why did you call her 'Mom'? She only has one son and he's about ten or eleven. I've seen him a few times and — " He looked at Sam sharply. "Where did you get those clothes?"

"She's hurt," Sam managed. "She needs a doctor."

Without lowering his pistol, Rudolf leaned closer. "Amazing! You look exactly like him, only older!" Then he stepped back quickly, as if he'd suddenly understood something. "Get up!" he ordered. "Up!"

Sam grimaced and awkwardly got to his feet.

"Tell me where you're from," said Rudolf. "And don't lie."

Sam blinked, but he still wasn't able to concentrate enough to slow his heartbeat. What could he do? How could he get Rudolf to spare his mother? Unless . . . He might have an argument that would appeal to Rudolf, one that Rudolf himself had used after kidnapping Alicia.

"I'm here to offer you a trade," said Sam, clearing his throat.

"A trade, eh? Is that so? What do you have in mind?"

"If you go away and leave my mother alone, I'll give you the Golden Circle."

A gleam of covetousness flashed in Rudolf's eyes.

"So you're the one who has it! You brought it from your time, right? What is that, four years in the future? Five?"

"About that."

"What Thoth stone do you use?"

"Barenboim's."

"The Barenboim stone, eh? You mean Martha let you in? I thought I was the only one."

"I . . . I was lucky," Sam said. "I snuck by when she wasn't looking."

239

"Lucky, eh? I worry about lucky people; they're dangerous. There isn't much you can do against luck, is there? Except when it starts to turn. . . . All right, what about the bracelet?"

"I'll tell you where it is as soon as I can phone for help," said Sam, improvising. "And you promise to leave."

Rudolf nodded and said, "I let you phone for help, and in exchange you tell me where the Golden Circle is. That certainly seems fair."

But his sarcastic smile undercut the friendly remarks.

"Let's think this through," he continued. "You pop up here while I'm . . . I'm working things out with your mother. You've obviously come from the future, judging by who you are, namely Allan's son, and the age you should be, but aren't. Not to mention that you're white as a sheet, probably from making the trip. So the question is, what made you decide to stick your nose in here today of all days?"

Sam struggled not to wince as another wave of pain engulfed his middle.

"How about this as a theory? Suppose my little chat with your mother didn't go well. Anything can happen, right? And sometime in the future, you get the idea that you could change that, provided of course that you go back into the past and bring me the Golden Circle, and do it this very afternoon. That would explain everything, wouldn't it? I don't know how you managed that, but the fact is, you're here. And by that logic, you should have the bracelet with you — on you, in fact.

"So if you don't want me to blow your brains out in a time where you aren't supposed to die, I suggest you pick up that end table and put the Golden Circle on it. Understand?"

Backing up his words, Rudolf now aimed the gun at Sam's eyes.

"Or I can count to three, if you prefer."

He was clearly prepared to shoot. There wasn't a shred of pity in his eyes, and after killing the son, he would get rid of the mother. Sam considered heaving the table at him, but he was so weak, he barely had the strength to hate him. The main thing was to stay alive so he could protect Elisa and wait for Rudolf to somehow slip up.

Sam bent over, holding his side and gritting his teeth so as to not cry out, and set the little black table upright. He then took out the Golden Circle — the original, which he'd gotten from Maggie Pye — and laid it on the tabletop. It looked like a horizontal sun setting into an ebony sea.

"It's glowing," Rudolf murmured. "It's really glowing. Only a traveler can make it shine, as I know well. That's my bracelet. Your father stole it from me about twenty years ago. In a way, you're making up for his mistake."

"So why don't you leave us alone?" said Sam. "Take the bracelet and go. I swear I won't tell."

"I doubt you would," agreed Rudolf, "but I have to be careful. How do I know you aren't armed? I don't want to walk out and have you shoot me in the back. Empty your other pocket. You've got something in there."

Sam had been pale before, but he now turned white. The Meriweserre bracelet! It hadn't occurred to him to hide it!

"What's the holdup?" asked Rudolf suspiciously. "Want some encouragement?"

He was now pointing the pistol at Elisa's face.

"If you don't want to do it for yourself, do it for her. You're so near your goal, it would be a shame to lose her, wouldn't it?"

Sam thought he was about to faint. If he gave up the Meriweserre bracelet as well, he would have no way to bring his mother back to his present, or even return himself. And he felt so exhausted. . . .

"Then it's too bad for you."

"Wait!" blurted Sam.

He put his hand in his pocket, took out Martha Calloway's key chain, and dropped it on the table.

"Keys," chuckled Rudolf. "Very impressive. What else?"

Moving like an automaton, Sam added the Meriweserre bracelet to the Golden Circle, the bracelet's six Re disks jingling in the silence. Rudolf watched him greedily.

"I can't believe it — the Meriweserre bracelet! Sammy, you're a real gold mine. But turn your pockets inside out, just to make sure there's nothing else. Go ahead!"

Sam obeyed again, and added the July 11 coin to the pile on the table. Rudolf gestured for him to move back and stepped closer. Keeping an eye on Sam, he first inspected the two Golden Circles, not trying to hide his glee at possessing them both. Then he turned to the July 11 coin and clicked his tongue in a disapproving way.

"Hey, wait a minute! This Re disk belongs to me! Where did you get it?"

Should he tell Rudolf the truth about the Church of the Seven Resurrections, giving him dangerous ideas that would occur to him soon enough? Sam decided against it.

"In my present," he said.

"Yes, but where in your present?"

"In Chicago," lied Sam. "At Arkeos headquarters."

"So you know about Arkeos too? Well, well. You may look like your loser daddy's little loser boy, but you're apparently more dangerous than he is." Rudolf looked at Sam intently, then went on. "Under other circumstances, we might have been able to work together. Who knows? Maybe you would have had more courage and foresight than your father. And maybe you wouldn't betray me."

Sam had heard this kind of speech before in the movies, and it usually ended badly.

"I'm sorry, boy, but life is made of choices, and I can't leave you behind, either you or your mother. So this is where we say good-bye."

Sam watched as the end of the silencer swung toward him, an empty steel eye aimed at his forehead. If he could only struggle, try something. . . . But his body was all exhaustion and suffering.

"Can I kiss my mom good-bye?" he heard himself say.

Rudolf paused and then shrugged. "Sure. I'm not a monster. But hurry; I hate these touching scenes."

Sam collapsed next to Elisa, ignoring the burning pain in his stomach. It wouldn't last much longer, anyway. He looked at his mother for the last time. She just seemed to be sleeping, with a red flower at her temple. Sam wished he could talk to her, tell her how sorry he was not to have measured up, ask her forgiveness. Tell her that she'd been a wonderful mom, and that if he had to die, he was glad to do it near her.

"Okay, that's enough," said Rudolf. "On your knees."

Sam squeezed his mother's hand. *All right*, he thought, *this is it*. He touched her gold wedding ring, the symbol of the love that Elisa and Allan had pledged each other. An eternal love of which he, Sam, was the fruit.

"Hurry up," snapped Rudolf, "or I'll start with her."

In a final gesture to his parents, Sam stroked the ring. Was love the only thing that was truly eternal in this world? He knelt on the carpet, preparing to die, when a brilliant idea suddenly occurred to him. The ring . . . *Why not the ring?*

Sam raised his head to his executioner.

"Before you shoot, I have one last proposition. If you spare our lives, I can give you something a lot more precious than the Golden Circle. I can give you the Eternity Ring."

CHAPTER TWENTY-SEVEN

In the Trunk

Rudolf looked at Sam thoughtfully, clearly weighing the pros and cons, then slowly lowered the gun. "I'm listening."

Sam took a deep breath. "I learned about the Eternity Ring after I was sent to Rome in 1527. . . ." He told him about *The Treatise on the Thirteen Virtues of Magic*, how it was full of clues about the location of the ring — which was true enough — and that he couldn't say which clues were useful and which weren't. But Sam swore that he had studied it at great length, and once they were at the right place, namely Setni's tomb, he would find his bearings and locate the ring.

"My first thought is that you're playing for time," Rudolf remarked. "But as it happens I've heard of this *Treatise* too, and it sounds like what you're describing. And you brought me both Golden Circles, so you deserve some credit, right? I'm going to give you and your mother a stay of execution. But it's just a stay, understand? If you break your promise, believe me, I'll keep mine."

He then marched Sam to the garage at gunpoint and forced him into the trunk of Elisa's Chevrolet. He shut the trunk. A few minutes later Sam heard a car door opening, and then a grunt of relief as Rudolf dropped something heavy onto the seat. He thumped on the trunk lid and said, "Your mother's in the back, so we can get going. If you behave yourself, everything will be fine."

The car started up at the exact moment when the surgeon's scalpel cut his alter ego's appendix back at the Sainte-Mary hospital, which caused Sam to curl up even tighter. In addition to the earlier burning sensation, and the car's none-too-gentle bumping and turning, he could now feel part of himself being amputated. Eventually this feeling passed, and he was sure he could feel a needle stitching up his belly. Add to that the cramped space, the heat, and the deafening noise of the engine . . . And what would happen when the Sam at the hospital came back to consciousness?

The trip was relatively short, confirming that their destination was indeed Barenboim Street. Between two distant sutures of his distant wound, Sam found himself wondering if he wasn't taking an incredibly stupid risk in promising Rudolf the Eternity Ring. If he ever actually got his hands on it, Sam could hardly imagine the catastrophes that might result. But beyond his desperate attempt to stay alive, he hoped that once in Setni's tomb, he might be able to put Rudolf out of action. That was the best he could come up with, at least.

The car stopped amid a storm of barking, and Sam had to wait more long minutes imprisoned in the trunk with the motor running, hearing only jumbled snatches of conversation. Then the engine shut off, and car doors opened and closed. Finally the trunk lid swung up, and he shaded his eyes so as not to be blinded by the light.

"Your mother's well guarded," warned Rudolf. "You make one false move, and Martha's doggies will eat her for dinner. But if you walk quietly into the house, nothing will happen."

Sam straightened up with great difficulty. The Chevrolet was parked in the yard between the rows of doghouses. Rudolf, who was holding his pistol along his leg, had taken the time to change clothes and was now wearing a linen outfit much like Sam's. He kept glancing around, but the neighbors didn't seem especially interested in the racket from old Calloway's place. They were probably used to it.

Sam walked awkwardly up the stoop, a pair of dogs yapping at his heels. The door closed behind him before he'd taken three steps into the living room.

"Is that him?" growled Martha Calloway.

"That's him," said Rudolf.

She stood in front of Sam and stuck her shotgun under his chin.

"How did you get by me and my babies without our seeing you?"

"I was lucky," said Sam, trying to meet her gaze.

She looked like an old dog herself, he thought. Growled like one too, with a yellow cigarette wedged in the corner of her mouth.

"Lucky, my butt," she grumbled, jamming the barrel into his neck.

"That's enough," said Rudolf, pushing the gun away. "I still need him for now. Go look after her."

He pointed to Elisa, who lay stretched out on a flea-bitten old sofa. She was still unconscious, and had been bound and gagged. Three pit bulls were lined up in front of her, drooling and whimpering from time to time.

"The keys are in the car," Rudolf continued. "You know what you have to do?"

"Of course; I'm not stupid," Calloway snapped. "If you aren't back at four thirty on the dot, I roll the nice lady and her car down Doomsday Hill. But you ought to know there'll be an extra charge for the taxi service, mister. A hell of an extra charge."

"That won't be a problem," said Rudolf. "And if she wakes up in the meantime, make sure she doesn't get away."

"The kid may have pulled that stunt once, but there's no way the mother's gonna double it up, believe me!" she spat. "And hey, while we're at it, when do I get back the keys this little thief ripped off?"

"I'll get them to you later," said Rudolf, annoyed. "We've got more important things to do. Come along, you."

He pushed Sam toward the basement stairs. Sam stumbled forward, glad that the basement lights were now on. The place was still in shambles, but at least he could walk through it without tripping.

"Go to the back," said Rudolf.

The space around the stone statue was clear, and the white cabinet next to it now stood open. It was apparently Rudolf's personal storage closet: His gray suit and other clothes were hanging in it, and a pile of traveler outfits lay on a shelf. A black Hathor sign was painted on the inside of the door.

"The setting is a bit sordid, but that's a point in its favor," said Rudolf. "Between this pigsty and the dogs, my little secret

248

has been kept pretty well — at least until you showed up. Here, put your arms behind your back."

He did so, and Rudolf took a pair of linen pants and tied his wrists with them. Sam groaned, not because the bonds were tight but because the new position put painful tension on his stomach.

"You'll have to be less of a wimp if you want to help your mother," chuckled Rudolf. "Are you suffering from Time lag? That would help me, in some ways."

From the closet he took a small black box, which he opened as Sam looked on. It was a travel alarm, and it read 4:16 p.m.

"Okay, let's cut to the chase. In fifteen minutes Martha Calloway is going to take your mother up Doomsday Hill. Sad to say, she's a terrible driver, and I'm afraid she may have an accident. You'll be motherless, poor boy. Unless you and I get back soon enough to persuade Martha not to climb behind the wheel, of course."

He folded the clock and put it away.

"As you may have noticed, time passes seven times faster in the past than in the present. In other words, once we leave, we'll have about seven times fifteen minutes to accomplish our task; nearly two hours. Is that long enough?"

Sam nodded, though he actually didn't have the slightest idea how to locate the Eternity Ring. What mattered was to change locations, and then to try to ditch Rudolf.

"Fine," Rudolf said, taking the Meriweserre bracelet and the six coins from his pocket. "Which Re disk are we going to use?"

"The . . . the glass one," stammered Sam. "It was part of a

jeweled scarab from Setni's time. But how can I be sure we'll get back here afterward?"

"No problem," said Rudolf. "We'll use the same coin that brought you here. When you use a Re disk to return to a place you've already visited, it sends you there *after* the last use of the stone. That way the traveler doesn't run into himself. Didn't you know that?"

Sam had to admit he didn't, which earned him a smug smile from Rudolf.

"You should have had a *real* teacher," he said grandly. "Allan was clearly pathetic, even with you."

"We're wasting time," Sam replied.

"You're right, my boy. We're wasting time! And what could be more precious than time, eh? Let's go."

Rudolf closed the closet, hefted his pistol, and stepped behind his prisoner as if to push him toward the stone. But before Sam could move, Rudolf slammed him on the head with the gun. Sam first had the impression that the ceiling had caved in on him, and then everything went black.

CHAPTER TWENTY-EIGHT

Two Suns Cannot Shine
at the Same Time

The first thing Sam realized was that his belly no longer hurt: no more burning pain, no more needle relentlessly jabbing into his skin. On the other hand, his neck was sore and he was lying on the cold, hard ground with his hands tied behind his back. Silence and darkness surrounded him. How long had he been lying there? And where had Rudolf gone?

Sam spat out the dust from his mouth, twisted around, and struggled to his feet by bracing himself against a rectangular block of stone. To the touch, it felt like the limestone plinth on which Setni's sarcophagus would eventually be laid. The coffin wasn't in place yet, which meant that he and Rudolf had probably landed in the right period — Egypt in 1180 B.C.

Sam took three steps to one side and ran into a wall. This would make the funerary chamber the right size, because he remembered it as being about twelve feet square, with the sarcophagus on the stone plinth in the center. Further investigation revealed a few funerary furnishings — an urn, a chest, a chair. But none of that explained what had happened to Rudolf. Had he been lost on the way, maybe swallowed up by some temporal crack? That would be excellent news, except that there was also no sign of the Golden Circle — either of the Golden Circles, for that matter — that Sam would need to leave. And for someone who theoretically had all of Time at his disposal, he was in a hurry.

Footsteps echoed somewhere above him, and Sam looked up. There was a large hole in the middle of the ceiling, with an orange light playing along its lip. The hole was the only access to the room, by way of a rope ladder, but someone must have pulled it up. And that someone . . .

"Well, it's about time you woke up!" Rudolf's head appeared over the edge of the hole. "I've been strolling around for a good ten minutes. I thought you were hibernating!" He was kneeling to look down at Sam, a flaming torch in one hand. "Shouldn't you be thinking about your mother? You aren't here to take a nap!"

"But you knocked me out!"

"Of course I knocked you out! Do you think I'm a rookie? I couldn't have survived this long without being a little cautious."

Rudolf passed the torch to his left hand, pulled out his pistol, and aimed it at Sam.

"I had two pleasant surprises when we landed here. The first is that I could transport the Golden Circle with the gun in the stone's cavity. You know that normally you can just bring one item from another time, but the Circle must be like the coins — part of the paths of Time or something. And then I found this torch lying on the ground, as if the last visitor had left it especially for us. And that last visitor was . . ."

He didn't need to finish. If Rudolf's theory was correct, a traveler using a Re disk to return to a place he'd already visited would be sent there moments after his last visit. So it was likely that the torch was the one Sam himself had left after his last visit to this time.

"What irony, eh?" jeered Rudolf. "As if you intended to illuminate the unique moment when I become immortal. And now, my boy," he added urgently, "it's time you finish the job. Where's the ring?"

Sam didn't answer, occupied as he was in searching among the funerary objects for something that would help him. Clay jugs, animal statues, a couple of chairs, a spear . . . *A spear?* If he could cut his bonds with it, maybe he could also use it as a weapon.

"You've dawdled long enough," said Rudolf. "The meter's running."

Sam closed his eyes and carefully concentrated on the twin pulses in his chest. The funerary chamber must have been alive with positive energy, because he was instantly able to align his heartbeat with the pulse of the Thoth stone. Brightening noticeably, the chamber took on a handsome, pale green color, and the air seemed to gather in long, flowing filaments. As easily as it seemed to happen, Sam didn't want to push the time-slowing effect too much; he'd just been in the hospital because of it, after all.

With his elbow, he knocked the spear to the ground and wedged it between his heels. Then he crouched over the metal end, and, after some fumbling, turned the blade upward so he could rub his cloth bonds against it. He could feel the fiber start to shred, but Rudolf had taken several turns around his wrists and tied multiple knots. This could take a long time.

As he worked to free his wrists, Sam studied the funerary chamber. The nearest wall was decorated with a huge picture of Thoth surrounded by a crowd of miniature figures. The torch created strange reflections, and turned Rudolf, who was holding it, into a shadowy creature frozen in an aggressive posture. And the sarcophagus base in the center of the room seemed translucent in places, revealing odd shapes hidden under its surface.

"No way!" exclaimed Sam.

He instantly remembered his experience in Emperor Qin's grotto — how the stone had seemed perfectly smooth and ordinary, but once he slowed Time, he could glimpse the outline for his carving hidden within it. In the same way, he could now make out the shape of a sun with long rays deep inside the sarcophagus plinth.

Sam squinted to better visualize the hidden design. He knew he had arrived by the sun on the opposite side of the plinth. But this other sun lay waiting to be carved by some future traveler. The mysterious sentence Emperor Qin had entrusted to him thus took on new meaning: "Two suns cannot shine at the same time." The two suns, of course! There wasn't *one* stone statue carved into the sarcophagus base, but *two* of them! And those two suns certainly couldn't "shine" at the same time, because they were visible only at different time periods.

That explained the feeling of unfamiliarity he'd experienced when he landed in the tomb at the time his father was excavating it. Then, he'd regained consciousness on this side with the Thoth mural, whereas before Setni's burial, the stone sculpture had been on the opposite side, on the part of the base facing the back of the room. That had struck him as odd, but he'd had plenty of other things to worry about that day. As for how this change could happen, Sam would put his money on Setni himself. Perhaps when he returned to his tomb to hide the ring, some day in the distant future, he would also erase the first stone statue and create the second, guaranteeing that only those who knew the secret of Time-slowing would ever have the chance to glimpse the ring.

Two large drops of sweat ran down his forehead, and Sam realized that he was starting to feel a familiar pain in his chest. He strained at his linen bonds, but in vain. He would never be able to free himself before he would be forced to release his hold on Time.

He redoubled his labors, sawing through another layer of cloth, and gaining the ability to move his hands a little. But the job was far from done, and the pain in his chest was getting sharper. He clearly wouldn't be able to free himself in time, so he thought it wiser not to tempt fate by risking another heart attack. Besides, the outline of a plan was starting to take shape in his mind.

Sam repositioned himself before the large Thoth figure in an attitude of surprise, as if he had accidentally knocked over the spear. He blinked to release Time, and a violent crack rang out, thunderingly echoing from one wall to the other in the confined space.

Just then, a clay pot next to him exploded, and Sam leaped back in genuine shock. Rudolf was shooting at him!

"What the hell did you just do?" screamed Rudolf.

"You're crazy! You could have killed me!"

"That's exactly what I'm going to do," Rudolf shouted in a fury. "Get up against the wall, and don't move!"

Rudolf unwound the rope ladder and dropped the torch to the ground a dozen feet below. Still pointing his gun at Sam, he climbed down, hanging on to the rope rungs with one hand. Once on the ground, he pushed Sam up against the Thoth figure and jammed the gun barrel into his left eye.

"You better explain the trick you just pulled," he shouted. "What was that thing that paralyzed me?"

"I don't know!" said Sam, improvising furiously. "I felt something strange too, as if I couldn't move! First this lance fell, and then . . ."

"A bullet in the head, that's what you'll get! I'm going to put a hole in your filthy little skull!"

"I had nothing to do with it!" said Sam, afraid his eyeball would burst under the pressure of the gun. "But I think I found something," he quickly added. "It's about the ring."

"About the ring, eh?" roared Rudolf, increasing the pressure.

"I think I know how to find it."

"You THINK, or you KNOW, you little jerk?"

"I . . . I think I can manage it."

Rudolf's hatred was now so intense, Sam could practically smell it, and for a moment, he was sure he was going to be shot. But Rudolf apparently thought better of it.

"I'm warning you," he growled. "This better be good."

"I'm sure there's a second stone statue," said Sam. "It's hidden inside this side of the base," he added, gesturing with his chin to the near end of the plinth.

"Another stone statue? Hidden?"

"Yes. We both know Setni hid the ring somewhere in his tomb, and we need both Golden Circles to find it. Why two Golden Circles, unless there are two stone statues? In the *Treatise*, the base is shown with a stone statue that you can see from the outside, and a second one hidden inside. And when you were digging here as a student, do you remember where the stone statue was on the sarcophagus?"

Rudolf stepped backward, releasing his hold on Sam in order to consider the question. "It was by the Thoth mural," he said reluctantly. "This side."

"Exactly!" Sam said, trying to keep the triumph — and his nervousness — out of his voice. "That stone statue is still hidden inside the plinth — it hasn't been carved yet. I think we have to use the two suns one after another to reach the ring."

"One after the other?" repeated Rudolf skeptically. "What kind of nonsense is that?"

"There's just one way," said Sam. "We have to come back to the tomb at another time, so we can use the second stone statue. Unless we've made a mistake, that should lead us to the ring."

"Oh? And just how are we going to get back here at another time?"

Sam tried not to look daunted before answering. It was time for his big lie.

"Among the seven coins you took from me, there's one with inscriptions in Arabic," he began. "It belonged to Garry Barenboim. You know him, right?"

Rudolf didn't even bother to nod.

"Chamberlain was Barenboim's grandson," continued Sam. "He inherited a ton of stuff from him, including some notebooks in which Barenboim writes that he once reached the tomb of the high priest of Amon, and it had no way out. Which means that he landed right here, sometime between the date Setni was buried and when Chamberlain first broke into the funerary chamber. That's the time we need to get to. And the coin he used was the Arab one, so it should lead us directly to the second stone."

Behind his back, Sam crossed his fingers, which he had just managed to work free. His story made sense, as long as Rudolf didn't examine it too carefully. The man was staring at him hard, perhaps sensing a trap.

"Since it now seems that our destinies are linked, there's something you should know," said Rudolf with a honeyed smile. "Whatever you may think, Martha will never let your mother free, so you'll never see her again without my help. Never. Is that clear?"

"That's exactly why I'm trying to help you," Sam said quietly.

"All right then!" exclaimed Rudolf. "At least you and I know where we stand. Now back up against the wall and don't move."

Sam did so as Rudolf set the almost consumed torch on the sarcophagus base. From his pocket, he took one of the bracelets with its Re disks and did something with the coins — Sam couldn't see what — then walked around to the stone statue that had brought them here. He must have put one of the Golden Circles on the sun, because the room was flooded in a warm glow.

"Face the wall."

Sam quickly gathered the shreds of cloth dangling behind his back and turned to the big Thoth figure, praying that

Rudolf wouldn't notice anything amiss. How would Rudolf knock him out this time — with a stone jug or with the butt of his gun again?

"Good," said Rudolf in a satisfied tone as he came over. "It's you and me now, Faulkner."

He jammed his gun in Sam's ribs, slipped his other arm around his neck, and started to choke him. Sam tried to struggle, but he couldn't breathe, and, as he had already discovered in the Sainte-Mary Museum, Rudolf was unusually strong. Sam started to pass out.

"Relax," Rudolf murmured. "I'm just taking you for a little spin."

CHAPTER TWENTY-NINE

The Guardian of the Stones

"Get up!"

Sam caught a nasty kick in the ribs, but with his mind still sluggish from the violence of the transfer, he only curled into a tighter ball on the ground.

"Get up!" Rudolf shouted louder.

His second kick caught him on the hip, and Sam rose painfully to his knees.

"What the hell have you been scheming?" yelled Rudolf. "There's no bracelet on the stone, and no coins!"

Sam blinked. Even in the faint light, he had no trouble making out the gun just two inches from his face. He thought he could even see Rudolf trembling.

"And why did you want to come to *this* time? When are we, anyway?"

Rudolf put the gun to Sam's temple and forced him to his feet. Sam looked around the funerary chamber. They had landed on the side of the plinth facing the tall Thoth figure, so he could see the second stone statue this time, but it was empty. Setni's sarcophagus lay on the plinth, and, on the other side of the room, Sam saw the tunnel that Chamberlain's excavation team had dug. It was the source of the faint light that allowed them to see their way around the tomb.

Under other circumstances, Sam would have exulted: He had won his bet! Thanks to Allan's Arabic coin, they had returned to Setni's tomb at the time of the archaeological dig, probably soon after he'd found Rudolf and his father fighting there. Sam had hidden Chamberlain's pistol among the funerary furnishings right after that; if he could just free his hands now . . .

"If you don't tell me how to get the ring right away," Rudolf said in an oddly hollow voice, "I'll shoot."

Even in the dim light, Rudolf was looking strange. He seemed very pale and was trembling violently.

"I'm really sorry," Sam said apologetically. "I never claimed to have exact directions to find the ring. All I know is that you have to use both stones and both bracelets. Are you sure the Golden Circle isn't on the other side with the coins?"

To his surprise, Rudolf neither screamed nor threatened to blow him away, but instead walked around the plinth to see for himself.

"Nothing!" he roared. "No Meriweserre bracelet, no coins!"

"What about the other Circle? Is it gone too?"

Rudolf reached in his pocket and withdrew the original Golden Circle, then said, "What doesn't make sense is that this Circle was in the cavity with the gun, but all the things that let us come here have disappeared!" He again aimed his pistol at Sam. "I suggest you tell me what you've gotten us into. Otherwise you'll never see your mother again, believe me."

Sam was desperately groping for a new strategy when they both heard a sound — the crunch of footsteps approaching through the tunnel. Rudolf spun around, his pistol aimed at the passageway.

"The tunnel!" he shouted. "Faulkner, you turd! That's why you brought me here! We're back at the dig, and you want your daddy to save you!"

They could make out a faint light in the tunnel, swinging back and forth, casting long shadows that danced on the tomb walls. The intruder must be carrying a lantern.

"Come on in!" Rudolph screamed at him, almost in a frenzy. "Come in here, or I'll shoot you before you even turn around!"

Sam suddenly had a terrible moment of doubt: What if this really was his father, coming back to the chamber after the two of them had talked? Rudolf would surely kill him this time.

"Two Faulkners for the price of one!" Rudolf exulted softly. "A good day's work."

At last, a man's silhouette appeared at the tunnel entrance, holding a lantern out in front of him.

"Put the light down, Allan," said Rudolf with a harsh laugh. "Don't be afraid. We're all old friends here."

The mysterious visitor seemed to hesitate, as if he didn't understand the order, then slowly brought the lantern up to his face.

Sam froze.

Rudolf shrieked, "No! It can't be!"

The young man emerging from the tunnel was Rudolf — the Rudolf Sam had knocked out when he'd been strangling his father, the one who was groggy when Sam left. *There were now two Rudolfs facing each other!*

Incredulous, Sam stared first at one, then the other. The young Rudolf seemed paralyzed to find himself facing an older doppelganger pointing a gun at him. The older Rudolf looked not just pale, but actually transparent. Powerful nervous spasms shook him from head to toe, as if an electric current was coursing through his body.

Half a minute passed in absolute silence, and then the older Rudolf raised his head. Legs bent, shaking all over, muscles tensed as if he was trying to hold something in, he turned to Sam.

"Think you got me, didn't you, Faulkner?" He seemed to be trying to snarl, but he couldn't muster the strength. "Think you can get rid of me and just take off, eh? Well, you're wrong. Whatever happens to me, my revenge is already happening! Good-bye, Sammy."

Frowning fiercely, he lifted the pistol and aimed it at Sam. He steadied his wrist with his other hand, cocked the trigger, and —

A brilliant flash lit up the room.

Rudolf's body suddenly glowed blindingly white. Sam thought he could almost see the particles of light moving within his outline, the atoms frantically careering about — his soul's energy trying to maintain itself in the presence of the same soul. The two Rudolfs stared at each other for a long moment. But then the gun clattered to the ground, and in another blinding flash, the atoms shot off in all directions, dissipating to nothingness.

For his contempt of people and time, Rudolf had paid with his life.

Rudolf's younger self dropped the lantern and ran back into the tunnel, screaming.

Sam walked over and picked up the lantern, which fortunately was still lit. Where the older Rudolf had stood, there was only a pile of linen clothes, the pistol, and a small, gleaming gold bracelet. Sam had won. But the most important thing still remained to be done.

Using a corner of the plinth, he sawed through the last layer of cloth and finally freed his hands. How much time had passed since they left Martha Calloway's house? Probably less than an hour, even counting the time he was unconscious. That meant he had a little more than an hour to work with. Sam raced to the other side of the room, kicked Rudolf's gun away, and snatched up the Golden Circle. Just as Rudolf had said, the coins had disappeared. Without any coins, it would be impossible to get back to Sainte-Mary. Or maybe he couldn't use them anymore. Maybe he was supposed to use the Circle itself.

"Two suns cannot shine at the same time." *All right, but why not one after the other?*

Sam brought the elegant bracelet over to the second stone statue — the one facing the Thoth mural. It fit the sun perfectly, without losing its brilliance, but also without causing any apparent reaction. Nothing changed with the stone or its transport cavity, or the plinth.

Suddenly Sam had an odd feeling that something was happening behind his back. He whirled around, fearing the worst, but what he saw on the gilded wall was unlike anything he could have imagined. The Thoth figure was moving.

Sam took a step toward the wall, wondering if he was hallucinating. The tall, ibis-headed god majestically bowed his neck and his long beak, handing a crown to some invisible pharaoh. The rite accomplished, Thoth slowly straightened up, then repeated his movement with the same solemnity.

On either side of the god's legs, little figures seemed to be doing a crazy dance, like scampering children. But on closer inspection, their movements weren't at all random. Each sequence introduced the same characters, who accomplished the same actions, in a repeating loop. It was like a comic strip come to life. Only one figure appeared in every scene: a small man wearing a tunic, with a shaved head and a bag slung over his shoulder.

Could it be Setni? The high priest certainly looked the way he had when Sam and Lily met him. There was no way to identify him for sure, of course; the figures carved into the wall were roughly sketched and had nearly identical eyes and expressions. But the little character seemed distinctive and somehow familiar. And after all, wasn't Sam in Setni's tomb, the very place where he was honored as the high priest of Amon?

Studying the images with that in mind, Sam realized that each sequence told a kind of short story about Setni. Next to Thoth's left knee, for example, a series of five animated vignettes showed him as a temple servant, prostrating himself before a colossal statue (Amon, Sam guessed); performing his ritual ablutions in a pool; finding a chest in the reeds from which he took several tablets, which might have explained how the stone statue worked; kneeling before a carved sun and touching it; and finally waking up next to a river near another stone.

The next story used five other vignettes to show Setni among a group of men in armor who seemed to be trying to enter a tower. The one after that was set on an island with luxuriant vegetation, its tall grasses swaying in the wind, where Setni tried to keep three excited men from destroying a half-buried Thoth stone. Judging from their funny triangular hats and their swords, Sam guessed they were pirates. From then on, Setni was always shown holding a tiny stone statue in his right hand, as if he had become the stones' representative or protector.

Sam crouched down to examine the rest of these bas-relief adventure stories. He didn't always grasp the meaning of certain scenes, such as one that showed the venerable time traveler in a sedan chair, playing an unknown game with a bejeweled princess, but others were much more evocative. In one in particular, Setni explored the center of a rounded mountain, found a pagoda-shaped palace, talked at length — over two "panels" — with a bearded old man with a cane, and eventually helped him into bed. That was Emperor Qin, of course. A little farther on, he could be seen carefully drawing a diagram covered with countries and continents — the famous map of the Thoth stones that Setni was so proud of! Some fifteen of these playlets served as the backdrop for the great figure of Thoth, who continued to bow gravely. They were the fifteen labors of Setni, in a way — the legend of the guardian of the stones.

Among all these stories, one in particular caught Sam's eye. It was the last series of images on the lower part of the wall, to the left. Maybe he wasn't being very objective, but he thought he recognized the high priest with two children: a boy and a girl. In the first of the five panels, Setni, with a stone in hand, was running after the two through a long tunnel — a train, Sam decided, like the one they took from Chicago. In the second, the high priest saved the same two children from a group of ruffians — Paxton's gang. In the third panel, the three were talking about the map of the stones. The fourth dealt with a stepped pyramid being built by an architect who was himself a time traveler — probably Imhotep, whose story Setni had told them. But in the fifth and final panel a strange ceremony was taking place. The high priest, standing, was holding out his stone to the boy, who was down on one knee. The boy received it with his eyes closed and his palms turned upward, as if he were being given an important mission.

Sam studied the vignette for a long time. The first four chapters of the cartoon story pretty much described his meeting with the high priest at Sainte-Mary, but the fifth incident had never happened. Was it merely symbolic, a kind of passing of a torch? Setni had said that Sam would make an excellent guardian of the stones, but Sam never agreed to take the job!

Or perhaps . . . Sam watched the old sage's repeated gestures, his dignified way of bowing to place the stone in his successor's hands over and over again. It was not unlike Thoth's action in the large picture above, except that the god wasn't holding a miniature stone, but a crown. A very ordinary crown, for that matter — a kind of headband, without decoration or ornament. Unless maybe it wasn't a crown at all, but a ring, greatly enlarged to show its importance. The Eternity Ring!

Sam hesitated, but he had nothing to lose by trying it. He knelt beneath the Thoth figure, at roughly the place where the god's bow reached its lowest point, and assumed the position of Setni's young companion in the vignette: hands outstretched and eyes closed.

After a few seconds, he heard a faint metallic jingle. Sam opened his eyes; Thoth now stood motionless above him.

Sam rushed over to the stone statue. The original Golden Circle was still in its place on the stone's sun, but the transport cavity now contained a handful of coins. Feverishly, Sam counted them: one, two, three, four . . . seven. He had seven coins, his own seven coins!

And that wasn't all: A rough stone ring lay stolidly among the glittering coins. The Eternity Ring.

Sam rolled the little ring around in his palm, feeling awed and impressed. There was no sign on it, no engraving; just a gray, unpolished stone ring. To look at it, who would suspect it had such immense power?

Sam turned around to express his gratitude to Thoth, but the fresco remained motionless. He bowed deeply nonetheless, grateful for the god's trust and, now, the chance to save his parents.

Then it was time to hurry home to Sainte-Mary. He took the Golden Circle and opened its delicate hook to string it with the necessary disks of Re. He first threaded the glass scarab disk, then Chamberlain's yellow coin, Qin's Chinese one, and his father's Arab one. He was about to add a fifth coin when something odd caught his eye.

The three remaining coins were ones that Rudolf had fabricated, and that Sam had taken from his office cabinet. They were very similar, cut from the same silvery metal and hand stamped with the date and hour. The first coin referred to Sam's birthday, June 5, in the present year. The second was the one he and Alicia had used to come back from the future. But the third was not dated July 11 three years earlier, as he had expected. Instead, it was stamped "July 23."

"The rat!" he exclaimed. "The dirty rat!"

Rudolf had surreptitiously swapped the coin that was supposed to allow them to return to Martha Calloway's! The July 23 coin probably corresponded to Rudolf's own present. So Rudolf never intended to save Elisa at all; he just planned to return to his own time once he had the ring. He was telling the truth when he told Sam that he would never see his mother again.

Sam felt such rage and despair, he almost sent all the Re disks flying. But he forced himself to be calm and examined the seven coins again. Only one offered any chance of success: the one for his birthday this year, June 5. At that point in Sam's life, his neighbor Max still had a couple of coins that Allan Faulkner had given him. They included the blue poker chip, which would allow Sam to travel to Rudolf's lair under the Church of the Seven Resurrections. Once there, he could get into the office cabinet and maybe find another July 11 coin. That meant making at least two extra trips before he reached his mother, and he would have to do it in an hour at most. It would be difficult, but not impossible.

The biggest danger was meeting himself on June 5. Wouldn't that kill him? *Rudolf survived for a few minutes before he saw his younger self,* Sam thought. *If I don't run into myself, maybe I'll be okay.*

Having made his choice, Sam strung the last two Re disks on the Golden Circle and was about to set it on the Thoth stone when he gave a cry of surprise. The bracelet had leaped from his hand and taken its place on the sun all by itself. It almost seemed alive, animated by its own willpower. A cascade of golden pearls erupted from the six slits and merged into a beautiful luminous bubble. Sam put the Eternity Ring in the transport cavity. Never before had he felt the pulse of Time in his chest or the movement of the ground underfoot so powerfully. He stretched out his hand and gazed at the stone as it irresistibly drew him to itself.

CHAPTER THIRTY

Presents

Sam awoke with a strange feeling: He was cold. Despite the
fiery blast that had shot him out of Setni's tomb, he now lay
shivering on a smooth stone floor. When he opened his eyes,
he found himself in an unfamiliar room, one that looked nothing like the basement of his father's bookstore. There was no
partition hiding the stone statue, no unicorn hanging, no yellow stool. And where was the stone statue?

He stood up shakily. As he looked around, he realized that
it actually *was* his father's basement, all right, but everything
about it was different. The partition and tapestry were gone;
the screen covering the window had been taken down, so warm
afternoon light streamed in. There were cardboard boxes everywhere, Styrofoam packing beans, string, a dolly, and a big
wooden table under the window. The place smelled of fresh
paint, like it was like moving day.

"The stone . . ." he muttered.

He found it in the far corner of the room under a plastic
tarp, with the Golden Circle and the coins in their proper

places, and gave a sigh of relief. But as he slipped the bracelet into his pocket, he noticed that he was shaking. He retrieved the Eternity Ring from the transport cavity and held it in his hand, hoping it would give him some warmth and comfort.

Then Sam noticed a big poster with green lettering lying on the table: JUNE 3 — GRAND OPENING OF FAULKNER'S ANTIQUE BOOKS!

He was stunned. How could the opening have been in June? His father had opened his bookstore in the winter, a few days before Christmas. What could this mean? Had the coin sent him back two days early? His legs buckled, and he grabbed at the wooden table for support, knocking over some Magic Markers in the process. He felt weak, partly because of the strangeness of the situation, but more because of a very peculiar sensation spreading through his body.

Bracing himself with both hands on the table, Sam tried to control his sense of fragmentation. There had to be an explanation for all this. The Re disk had brought him to the right time and place, but nothing was the way it used to be, and that could only mean one thing: The past had somehow been changed. Some other temporal sequence must have started in the weeks, months, and maybe years before the day he turned fourteen, leading to this improbable June 3 bookstore opening. And perhaps, in this new version of the past, Allan never disappeared, since he was launching his bookstore; and so his son didn't go to the basement looking for him, and find a strange stone statue. . . .

"I knew it," whispered someone behind him.

Still braced against the table, Sam turned around. A boy in jeans and a white shirt was standing at the bottom of the stairs with a package under his arm, looking at him intently. It was Sam Faulkner — *another Sam Faulkner!* About the same age, pretty good-looking, a hank of hair falling into his eyes, maybe a little less muscular. The boy didn't seem at all scared. He stepped forward, looking Sam over with a mix of kindness and intensity.

"This proves I'm not crazy," he said. "You really do exist."

Sam was incapable of answering, torn between astonishment and growing fear. His flesh and blood had begun to prickle under his skin, as if they were about to boil over.

"All those visions I've had for the last three years, since my operation and what happened to Mom," continued the other Sam. "I was pretty sure they weren't just dreams!" He took another step forward and stretched out his hand. "I've seen you plenty of times, you know. Here in Sainte-Mary, of course, but in lots of other strange places. Bruges, that snowy city where you were running inside a wooden wheel. The prehistoric cave where that huge bear threatened you. The island in the Middle Ages where the Viking boats landed. And the volcano that erupted and wiped out all those houses. I've always known it wasn't all in my head. They were real. *Those were my memories!*"

He spoke with a kind of distress, almost suffering, and Sam instinctively knew that he had caused it. When he'd made use of his appendicitis operation to visit Sainte-Mary three years earlier, he must have created a special link between the two of them, which would explain these eerie visions. After all, if the Sam of the future could experience the pain of the surgery, he could well have transmitted a part of himself to the Sam of the past.

"I'm so sorry," he said, barely able to speak.

"No need to apologize," said his double with a smile. "It's not your fault. Or it's both our faults, I guess. Because you and I are really the same person, aren't we? I finally understood that when Dad bought this house for his bookstore — I recognized the place, even though I'd never been here before! That's when I started searching, and — " He interrupted himself, looking concerned. "You look like you're shivering. Are you cold?"

In fact, Sam was on the verge of collapse. His muscles felt paralyzed, and he had the impression that the slightest move might split the thin membrane of skin that still held him together. He hadn't forgotten what had happened to Rudolf.

"I think I'm going to die," he whispered. "But that's all right. If you and Dad —"

He couldn't go on. Too many thoughts were filling his mind, which would soon be no more than a shower of sparks anyway.

"You aren't going to die," said the other Sam, stepping toward him. "You have the Eternity Ring, don't you? Just put it on your finger. It's all written in here."

He held up the paper bag he was holding, and took out a handsome old book with a red leather binding — the Book of Time!

"You look really pale," he added urgently. "Better hurry."

Sam sighed. It was already too late, he thought. His whole body was now nothing more than a bubble about to burst. With difficulty he unclenched his hand and clumsily slipped the ring onto his finger.

If it had any effect, Sam had no time to experience it. The world around him exploded in a blinding flash.

Sam lay sprawled on the ground. The idea that he might be dead occurred to him, but something was tickling his nose, and he opened one eye. He was still in this new, modern basement, and a piece of Styrofoam was stuck under his nostril. He wasn't shaking anymore, but his body felt oddly cramped. He was reassured to see the big red book a few feet away.

Leaning up on one elbow, he realized that he was wearing a white shirt and jeans.

"What the —" he swore softly.

He jumped to his feet, feeling a slight headache. He was alone.

"Sam?" he called.

Nobody answered. A pile of wrinkled clothes lay by the table. They looked like his time-travel clothes, as if he'd undressed in a hurry. Or disintegrated . . .

Feeling panicky now, he knelt to examine what remained of the linen clothes. It was certainly his time-travel outfit. The Golden Circle was even in the pants pocket, all six coins still attached, and he could see the Eternity Ring lying near one of the table legs.

Sam picked up the ring with some apprehension. It felt cool and rough to the touch. . . . This was no dream. He ran his hands over his arms, legs, and face. It was his body, all right. Not as filled out perhaps; a little less muscular, a little more clumsy.

You and I are really the same person, aren't we? The sentence still rang in his ears. He had woken up in a body that wasn't quite his, and he was alone. The only possible explanation was that Sam and his other self had somehow merged. He had survived certain death thanks to the Eternity Ring, but in another form . . . a new Sam, for a new sequence in Time.

Still in shock, Sam reached for the Book of Time. "It's all written in here," his double had assured him. He stroked the handsome crackled cover he knew so well. The book looked the way it had when he first saw it, as if the fire damage had been erased and Rudolf had never ripped out any of its pages. A new past, a new present . . .

He leafed through the book at random. All the spreads were identical, and each bore the same title on the upper left: "Seekers of the Ring." Before reading the text, Sam looked at the four nineteenth-century style illustrations. Each black-and-white engraving showed a different person, and he knew all but one of them: a bearded man with a hat pulled down over his face, whom the caption identified as Fouldr II. Sam had no trouble recognizing the other three: there was Klugg the Bruges alchemist, leaving an Oriental palace by the window. There was also Setni, opening a cabinet that looked like the ones in the Vatican library. The last one showed Sam himself down on one knee with his eyes closed, receiving the ring from Thoth. Sam had entered the Book of Time in dramatic style!

His curiosity aroused, he turned to the text.

"After centuries of uncertainty and speculation, the Eternity Ring was discovered and retrieved from the excavation site of the tomb of the high priest Setni (Illustration 1) at Thebes, in 4610 after Pharaoh Djoser, according to the Third Dynasty calendar. After a number of attempts, a young traveler by the name of Sem (or Sam, or Saum) reached the hiding place of the sacred ring, which the god Thoth, Heart of Re, Patron of Scribes, and Measurer of Time, personally gave him (Illustration 4). The Eternity Ring, also called Ring of Time or of Perpetuation, was fashioned to ensure that Re the Sun God, Great Judge and Master of All Things, would journey forever across the world on the Boat of Heaven. It is not known exactly how Re's ring fell into the hands of men, but it clearly excited the covetousness of many, who are sometimes referred to as the Seekers of the Ring. The first was certainly Nerferhotop in 885 after the Pharaoh Djoser according to the Third Dynasty calendar, who at the age of thirty-seven undertook to . . ."

A long account followed — Sam skipped several lines — describing Klugg and other ring seekers across the millennia. Sam's own adventures were described only at the very end, and somewhat succinctly, mentioning his trips to China and Rome without giving any details on how he succeeded in his quest. The Book of Time apparently knew how to keep Thoth's secrets.

The final paragraph described the powers attributed to the sacred ring, including "its capacity to preserve the life of its wearer no matter what the situation or the danger, until that person chooses to remove it." That passage must have given the other Sam, the one from the past, the idea that putting on the ring would save his older self's life.

Sam closed the Book of Time and put his head in his hands. He felt . . . odd. Not bad, not physically, just disoriented. And of course, if he wanted to save his mother, he was still racing against the clock. He had to run over to old Max's place, get the blue plastic chip, and leave again. And his father . . . His father must be around here somewhere. What should he do?

Just then, the upstairs door opened. He heard music, and then a very familiar voice.

"Sammy, you can come up now. It's all ready!"

It was Lily — his wonderful cousin Lily.

"Sammy, are you listening to me?"

He stood up, still feeling undecided. He would have to go upstairs in any case, if he wanted to see Max. He slipped the Book of Time back into the paper bag, tossed his travel clothes into an empty box, and put everything behind the tarp with the stone statue.

Lily was coming down the steps. She was wearing a pretty white dress and looking at him with amused reproach.

"Sammy, what are you doing down here in the basement again? You want your dad to set up a bed and a TV for you?"

Lily, at least, hadn't changed. She was as teasing and confident as ever.

"I . . . I was thinking," said Sam apologetically.

"Well, that's a change! Come on, everything's ready. We're waiting for you!"

He hesitated for a second before following her, which she immediately noticed.

"Hey, are you okay?" she asked. "You look a little out if it. Is it because of the idea of being a year older?"

"Yeah, it must be that."

"You'll feel better when you've had some cake! Come on!"

Sam followed her up, walking like an automaton. A year older . . . of course, it was still June 5, his birthday! His father must be right here in the house. He would be able to hug him, talk to him, just for a few minutes. Then he would go get the blue poker chip.

Upstairs, the delicious smell of chocolate replaced that of paint. An old Rolling Stones record was playing on his dad's ancient, beloved turntable. The door to the kitchen was closed but the one to the living room was open, and Grandpa was standing on the threshold.

"What are you doing, Sam, playing hard to get? I'm hungry!"

"He went down to the basement to *think*," said Lily sarcastically. "He's just turned fourteen, and he's worried about getting old!"

"So what should I say at my age?" said Grandpa, laughing.

Sam went over and took his arm. In his mind's eye, he could still see a haggard old man sitting on the edge of his bed, his gaze lost in the distance, shouting things that didn't make any sense.

"For a man your age," he said gently, "I'd say you're doing pretty well, Grandpa."

"I'll do even better when I've had a taste of that cake. Come on in!"

Sam stepped into the bookstore part of the house, which was furnished a little differently from what he had known. There were pastel walls, darker wood bookshelves, and the reading area had a more modern sofa and armchairs. It looked much nicer than the somewhat shabby furnishings that Sam had known, and it had been further decorated with streamers and bouquets of flowers for the occasion. Little signs hung here and there, reading: HAPPY BIRTHDAY, SAM! and WE LOVE SAMMY! and 14 YEARS OF HAPPINESS!

He had to make an effort not to be caught up by these messages of love. His feeling of disorientation was so strong that for a moment he was almost able to believe that this really was his house, and that he had physically helped set up this bookstore. He could have almost sworn, for example, that he had filed that collection of dictionaries along the left-hand wall, and pasted the RELIGION and ESOTERICA labels on the shelves to the right.

But he pulled himself up short. Whenever he may be feeling, he was still only in transit here.

"Is Dad around?" he asked.

"Over by the hi-fi with the presents," said his grandfather. "But no peeking, okay?"

Sam walked around a bookshelf marked: HISTORY: HIGH AND LOW MIDDLE AGES and saw his father, bent over a stack of records near a buffet table with two gift-wrapped boxes.

"Dad?" he called.

Mick Jagger was singing: "Time is on my side, yes it is!"

"Dad!" he called louder.

Allan turned around this time, smiling broadly.

"So they finally let you in! Your grandparents love this sort of thing, you know: locked doors, surprises, all that stuff."

Sam stared at him, hardly believing his eyes. It was his father all right, standing with a Rolling Stones record jacket in his hand, happy to be there, completely unaware of the drama that had unfolded and was still unfolding around him. Allan Faulkner, the original eccentric, a man with his head in the clouds, a lover of beautiful books and wonderful stories. Allan Faulkner, whose destiny had been linked since young adulthood to the stone sculpture, and who hadn't hesitated to face Dracula himself to save the woman he loved. Allan Faulkner. His dad.

Allan's face changed. "Hey, did I say something wrong? If it's about your grandparents, I was just kidding. You know I love surprises too!"

"Can I give you a hug?" Sam asked quietly.

"Of course! Since when do you need permission?"

Allan came over and they exchanged a big hug. "Actually you might want to hold off on the hugs until you open your presents," he said. "You're probably going to be disappointed."

That was his just like father. At every birthday, Allan swore that in spite of his best efforts, he simply hadn't been able to find the presents Sam asked for. And of course each time Sam unwrapped them, there they were. Today, Sam was prepared to bet serious money that he knew what was inside the two boxes. The small one would have a beautiful watch he'd seen at Victor's Jewelers, which displayed the time in several cities simultaneously. The bigger one was probably the encyclopedia on Egyptian civilization that he needed for a paper he was writing.

These thoughts came to Sam out of the blue, and he shook his head to drive them away. How could he possibly know about the presents? He'd never ordered an encyclopedia, much less chosen a watch at Victor's. And yet — and this was the strange part — he could clearly visualize both of them.

"All right, let's close the curtains. Turn off the music!"

Aunt Evelyn had burst into the room and was briskly ordering everybody around. When she saw Sam, she gave him a sly wink. In this version of the past, she got along with her nephew pretty well, apparently. She and Lily went around covering the windows, Allan turned off the record player, and Grandpa lit the candles.

Sam realized that if he didn't leave right away, this could all get terribly complicated. As casually as possible, he took a few steps toward the front door. He stopped in surprise when Grandma and another woman came in from the kitchen. The woman in question was Maggie Pye, squeezed into the most tacky-looking flowered dress on the planet. He watched as she went to lean against the back wall, seemingly avoiding his eye. Sam might have complained about her being there, or at least demanded an explanation, but he suddenly had a fleeting memory that suggested that Miss Pye had done something good for the Faulkners — something very good, in fact. Sam saw himself in her yard on a sunny morning, having brought her some of the chocolates she liked so much. She looked embarrassed, but accepted them anyway. But the vision vanished as quickly as it had come.

"I hope you're hungry, Sammy!" said Grandma, moving a pile of plates on the table aside to clear some space. She came over and brushed back some of the hair falling into his face. "You're going to love your cake. Maggie's recipe is simply scrumptious!"

She trotted off to the kitchen, leaving her grandson more perplexed than ever. Maggie Pye . . . a scrumptious recipe . . . Why was his family being so nice to that snippy old lady?

He had hardly asked himself the question when he suddenly remembered another scene. This also was an event he was sure he had never experienced, yet he remembered every detail of it. He was sitting on a chair down at the police station with his father. It must've been a few days after his appendicitis operation, because his stomach still hurt. The police officer was talking quietly to Sam about Maggie Pye.

"Your neighbor Miss Pye was the one who called us," he said. "She noticed strange things happening at your house. First a boy came by on a bike wearing these weird clothes, like he belonged to some sort of cult. Then an older man showed up on a motorcycle, and later he drove out of the garage at the wheel of your mother's car. Miss Pye had never seen him before, so she thought they must have robbed your house, and she called us. When we came, the house was open and there were signs of a struggle in one of the bedrooms. We were worried, of course, and then we found this near the bed."

The cop held up a plastic evidence bag containing a key chain with a name on the dog-shaped tag: MARTHA CALLOWAY, 27 BARENBOIM STREET, SAINTE-MARY.

"That's how we got the address," he said.

Sam wanted to hang on to this vital memory, but just then Grandpa turned out the lights and everybody started singing.

"Happy birthday to you! Happy birthday to you!"

Sam struggled desperately not to lose the thread of his vision, but without success. He was now positive that all the odd images popping into his head must be the memories of the other Sam. And they pointed to some big changes in the past — changes that had profoundly affected the course of the last three years.

"Happy birthday, dear Sammy! Happy birthday to you!"

The song ended in a burst of applause, soon replaced by a Faulkner chorus of cheers for the huge cake coming in from the kitchen, blazing with light in the semidarkness. To his surprise, Grandma wasn't the person carrying the cake, and it wasn't Miss Pye or Aunt Evelyn. Who, then? The shape . . .

The elegant hair . . . The regal posture . . . Was it an illusion? Another vision?

"Mom?" he whispered, his throat tight.

The sumptuous cake proceeded across the room amid laughter and cries of appreciation. Sam felt his eyes filling with tears.

"Mom, is that really you?" he said.

The light from the candles gave Elisa's face the shimmering glow of a goddess. It certainly was her. . . . Beautiful, radiant . . . Undeniably there . . . And so close! Sam felt something deep within him crack open. *His mother was alive!* She had survived! Thanks to Maggie Pye's information and Mrs. Calloway's key fob, the police had tracked Elisa to Barenboim Street and stopped Rudolf's murderous plan. Allan Faulkner didn't go into the past to save her; her son never wandered the paths of Time. It hadn't happened the way Sam thought it would, but he had saved his mother.

"Come on, Sammy," Elisa encouraged him. "Aren't you going to blow out the candles?"

Sam stepped away from the door and made his way to the table without taking his eyes off his mother. He noticed that Elisa had a small scar on her temple where Rudolf had hit her, but aside from that, she was as lovely as ever.

"The candles! The candles!" Grandma and Lily were chanting.

He turned to the meringue masterpiece with HAPPY BIRTH-DAY SAM! written in pink frosting. He took a deep breath and blew as hard as he could at the fourteen little flames, as if he was blowing away the memory of the dark years. But Sam hardly heard the clamor of compliments and cheers that followed. He was hugging his mother, his face buried in her shoulder, her hair brushing his cheek as he breathed in the heady perfume of his childhood and bit his lip so as not to cry.

"I love you, Mom," he murmured.

"I love you too, Sammy."

The clan greeted this display of affection with new roars of approval. As Lily switched the lights back on, Sam released his mother and went to thank everyone, including Miss Pye. Grandpa brandished two foil-wrapped boxes.

"And now, the presents!" he cried excitedly.

Sam untied the colorful ribbons, accompanied by an occasional "Oh" and "Ah!" But he kept glancing sideways at his father and mother, who were holding hands. As he had guessed, the smaller of the boxes contained a watch with an impressive chrome case, loaded with buttons and displays.

"The jeweler set it to the time zones for Bruges and Thebes in addition to our local time," said Elisa. "Just as you asked."

Bruges and Thebes: How far away that all seemed.

"What a pretty watch," Maggie Pye exclaimed. "It's so shiny!"

Sam then tore the wrapping from the second package, and took out a splendid *Encyclopedia of the Pharaohs*, which he had consulted — in another lifetime! — when he was researching the meaning of the Hathor sign. It was a particularly valuable nineteenth-century edition, and, coming from his father, a special sign of respect.

"If you continue to be interested in books, you can always help me in the bookstore a couple of afternoons a week," said Allan. "It's not that far from Bel View, and you'll be able to earn some pocket money."

"I'd really like that," said Sam. So in this new temporal sequence, the Faulkners hadn't sold their Bel View house — another excellent piece of news.

"So what about that cake?" thundered Grandpa. "Are we going to eat it, or is it just to look nice?"

"Donovan, you're worse than a child!" scolded Grandma.

"It's the only good thing about growing old, darling. The only thing!"

Elisa was about to cut the first slice when the front doorbell rang.

"Sam, would you see who that is?" she asked.

"It might be that neighbor Max," said Grandma. "He's hard of hearing, but so nice! I told him we were having a birthday party and that he should stop by."

Max! Sam thought. He was the only person missing from the picture. He ran to open the door — and his heart practically stopped.

Alicia was standing in front of him, looking more beautiful than ever. She had a carryall bag slung over her shoulder and a slim package wrapped in brown paper under her arm, and she was looking at Sam with wide, amused eyes.

"Surprise!" she exclaimed. At his confused expression, she added: "Mind if I come in?"

He stepped aside for her, and she was greeted by a salvo of "Alicia!" "At last!" "You're just in time."

"I'm sorry I'm late," she said, waving to everybody. "I would have come earlier, but I just got out of my photography class. I see I've gotten here after the presents!"

She dropped her bag near the door and turned to Elisa, who was serving Grandpa a slice of cake.

"Mrs. Faulkner, would you mind if I borrowed your son for a minute? It's personal."

"Of course, Alicia. But only if you promise to bring him back before Donovan eats all the cake!"

Alicia grabbed Sam by the arm, pulled him outside on the stoop, and closed the door behind them.

"Sorry to kidnap you like that, but I don't like it when Maggie Pye is around. She's the biggest gossip in town. Here, I've got a present for you too."

She handed him the big envelope, and Sam had to make an effort to stop staring at her. Alicia was looking incredibly lovely, her long blond hair caught in a big purple clip, beautiful tan skin, perfect features, ocean-blue eyes . . .

"Hey, are you dreaming, or what?" she teased him.

Sam opened the envelope to find a framed montage of photographs. On the left was an old Polaroid print of Alicia and him glaring at each other under the Faulkners' young tulip tree. A photograph on the right showed them the way they looked today: arms around each other's waists, standing under the same tree. Like them, it had grown a lot. The two snap-shots were surrounded by a bunch of pictures of Sam at different ages, some black and white, some in color, of different sizes and shapes. The result was both a striking mosaic of his existence and a real work of art.

"It's . . . it's beautiful, Alicia, thanks. Thanks so much."

"Do you recognize that Polaroid?" she asked. "It's the very first picture of us, right after I moved to Sainte-Mary. We didn't seem to get along in those days, did we?"

Sam looked at her, vividly aware that whatever might happen in the future, Alicia would always be his present.

"It's a good thing some time has passed since, don't you think? Happy birthday, Sam."

Alicia leaned back against the doorjamb and casually pulled him close. She slipped her arms around his neck and gently pressed her lips to his. To Sam, her kiss had the taste of eternity.

This book was edited by Cheryl Klein and designed by Phil Falco and Elizabeth B. Parisi. The text was set in Adobe Caslon Pro, a typeface designed by William Caslon I in 1734. The display type was set in Charlemagne, designed by Carol Twombly in 2000. The book was printed and bound at R. R. Donnelley in Crawfordsville, Indiana. The production was supervised by Susan Jeffers Casel. The manufacturing was supervised by Jess White.